The Gift of the Healing Stones

Healing Stones Series

This is a work of fiction. Names, characters, places, and incidents are either products of the author's imagination or are used fictitiously.

Copyright © 2025 Denise Marie Lupinacci
All rights reserved.

Print Edition ISBN: 979-8-9887014-9-1

Also by Denise Marie Lupinacci

The Highlander's Distraction

The Highlander's Bride Returns

The MacLeod's Destiny

Healing Stone Series

In the Falcon's Safety
Book One

The Gift of the Healing Stones
Book Two

CAST OF CHARACTERS

Alex Boswell—Anna's soulmate and her brother Robbie's best friend.

Robbie Duncan—Laird Duncan, Anna's older brother and Alex's best friend.

Anna Duncan—Robbie's sister and Alex's soulmate.

Mary Ellen MacKay Duncan—Robbie's wife.

Robbie and Mary Ellen's children, by age—Bryce, Alex, and Anna.

Willie—Robbie's younger brother.

Christy Robertson—Willie's wife.

Gavin Robertson—Christy's cousin and Alex's soul.

Alana Grant—Anna's soul.

Andrew Grant—Alana's brother.

Donald Grant—Anna's father, a drunkard.

Margaret—the Duncan housekeeper.

Brodie MacKay—Robbie and Alex's best friend.

Henry—Winner of Donald's contest to find the wolf and marry his daughter.

Michael MacIntosh—a lad who holds the curse over Alana and Gavin.

Cormac—a blacksmith in Grantown-on-Spey, who found Alana and claims to be betrothed to her.

Prologue

1727 Scotland

Alex briefly felt the tip of Robbie's sword upon his shoulder before it pulled away.

"For God's sake, man, pay attention!" Robbie yelled.

Alex snapped out of his thoughts of Anna and focused on his training, though it was hard.

Alex Boswell and Robbie Duncan were well-seasoned soldiers who had served the MacKay clan for several years. Both men were MacKays by birthright on their mothers' side.

Alex countered several of Robbie's attacks with his own before his mind drifted again. It was good that he was paired up with Robbie for the drills. A less experienced soldier may not have had as much control as Robbie, possibly sinking his blade into his flesh. A blow like that would have seriously injured him... and his pride as well.

Alex knew that Robbie understood where his mind was. Hell, Robbie was distracted from the time he was engaged to Mary Ellen until they wed. No doubt Robbie will be paying him back for all the teasing he gave him for daydreaming. Alex chuckled to himself. He did not mind much. Robbie knew the difficult challenges he faced to be with Anna, Robbie's sister.

Alex had his doubts that it would ever come to pass. He was surprised he survived his injuries, let alone finally being able to marry his soul mate. The fact that Anna would soon be his wife was constantly on his mind. His heart raced every time he thought of it, which seemed to be all the time.

God, how he loved her.

Alex proposed two days ago, the day before Anna and her father left to go home after visiting with Robbie. They agreed that the wedding would take place in two months in Dundee, Anna's homeland.

Alex focused back on the sparring match, taking the offense. "I remember before ye wed. Ye were useless for months," Alex said, grinning.

Robbie countered his attack with one of his own and replied, "And ye teased me about it every chance ye could."

"Aye," Alex agreed, driving Robbie back with his mighty swings as his concentration on the match returned.

Their swords clashed several more times when, all of a sudden, in mid-block, Alex felt a pain as if a charging horse had hit him. *Anna!* Alex's sword fell from his hand, and he doubled over, but Robbie's thrust was already in motion. When Alex bent over, it drove Robbie's sword into him.

"Alex!" Robbie yelled in horror at what he had done. He held the blade with one hand and wrapped his arm around Alex with the other.

Alex knew something had happened to Anna. Their connection was so strong, and they always felt each other's pains. It was part of their bond… their curse. He thought he had broken the curse with the death of Gregory MacDonald, but it was not to be.

A sorcerer cursed Anna and Alex centuries ago because

she had chosen another over the sorcerer. They would be soulmates but could never be together. Alex could not count the number of lifetimes he had been through. The pain of losing the one he loved time after time to the same wretched soul was more heart-wrenching each time. He thought after he survived his injuries several months ago after Gregory MacDonald, the man who held the curse over them, succumbed to his injuries that he had finally broken the curse.

He could not tell where his injury ended, and Anna's began. All he knew was he did not succeed in ending the curse. They would never be together.

Robbie lowered Alex to the ground, keeping the sword in him so he would not bleed out.

"Oh my God, Alex!"

Alex heard the desperation in his best friend's voice. He shook his head and whispered, "Anna… she's gone."

They felt the ground rumble as soon as the words came out of his mouth. A call from the castle wall called out, "Avalanche!"

Robbie turned. In the distance, about a day's ride out, he could see the freshly cut cliffside. The cliff was a drastic difference from the other part of the mountain, which was still white with the remnants of winter.

"Nae," Robbie's words were but a whisper. Anna and his dad were under that mountain.

Robbie turned back to Alex, his hands still applying pressure on either side of the blade.

"Alex, I'm so sorry," he said as the tears rolled down his face.

Alex smiled at his best friend. He was closer to Robbie than he was to his family. Robbie knew the circumstances between Anna and Alex. Though no one could carry their burdens for them, it was a comfort to have been able to share his secret with another person.

"It is better this way, my friend," Alex said to Robbie, "For I do not think my heart could live without Anna."

Robbie quickly glanced out toward the mountains.

An officer ordered men about for a search and rescue. Alex patted Robbie's hand as reassurance that there were no hard feelings. Robbie shook his head.

"Really. 'Tis better this way." If Alex survived Anna's death, he would be lost and forced to wait decades to find her again after she had grown up in her next life. Oh, they would find each other, no doubt about it, but it was a long time to wait. The only peace he ever had from the anguish of searching for her was before he remembered his destiny. His only hope was that he and his kindred spirit would grow up in happy homes.

Alex placed his hands over Robbie's with as much strength as he could muster and began to pull the sword out.

"I will call on ye one day, my friend," Alex whispered.

"I will be there for ye, Alex, I swear to ye," he replied as a tear rolled down his cheek. He helped Alex pull out the blade and watched the blood pour out.

Chapter 1

5 Years Later

Robbie, now Laird Duncan, sat in the front row of the small chapel with his wife, Mary Ellen, beside him, holding their daughter, Anna, who was six months old. His son, Bryce, sat beside him, trying to sit up straight. Like any five-year-old required to sit through a ceremony longer than five minutes, he fidgeted with the ceremonial Duncan tartan draped over his shoulder.

Robbie looked down at his oldest son and gave him a look indicating for him to be still before looking forward to the wedding of Robbie's brother, Willie, and soon-to-be sister-in-law, Christy Robertson.

Willie had grown up to be a fine man, and Robbie wished his father were here to see him. Willie had only been fifteen years old when their dad died. Robbie had been in the service of the Clan MacKay, his mother's family, and Willie was in his first year of training there.

Robbie's wife, Mary Ellen, was a MacKay, so Robbie stayed at her parents' estate. He had spent much time with his father-in-law, learning how to run a large estate. It was a big residence under Laird MacKay and gave Robbie good experience in running a large household, but it did not give him the experience of running a clan.

After marrying Mary Ellen, Robbie knew he would eventually return to Dundee to prepare for his role as Laird Duncan, which would ultimately be passed down to him as the oldest son. He never imagined it would be in his first year of marriage.

Thinking of his dad brought back memories of that fateful day when he became laird… and all he had lost. His sister, Anna, died with his father in the avalanche. Robbie fought the urge to shake his head as the guilt rose from the pit of his stomach. He could feel his eyes sting.

He looked back down at wee Bryce, who looked up at him with big eyes. Robbie smiled at him. His father and Anna were visiting for Bryce's birth. Had Robbie not invited them for a visit, would they still be alive? The question always plagued him.

He felt his chest tighten as he thought of Anna. She had been so happy during that visit. Anna and Alex, his best friend, had fought against such odds to be together and were convinced that they had prevailed.

But fate tore them away once more. The image of Alex at the end of his sword haunted him at night. He knew Alex collapsed at the same time the avalanche hit Anna. There had been a delay in hearing the rumble as it had been a distance away, but there was no doubt in Robbie's mind— Alex and Anna had a strong bond that allowed them to feel each other's pain.

Despite the fact that Alex doubled over as a result of Anna's accident and fell into Robbie's sword did not make the fact that he had killed him any easier. Alex said it was better that way but not for Robbie. He had not only lost his dad and sister but his best friend as well.

Alex believed he and Anna, or their souls, would return to find each other again. It was their destiny… their curse.

Robbie pushed that black day from his mind and focused on the wedding. *Ye'd be so proud of Willie.* Robbie talked to his dad in his thoughts, sure he was watching over them.

Robbie smiled as Willie leaned down to kiss his bride. They turned to face the people gathered. Willie wore his formal Duncan colors proudly. Robbie had never seen him so happy. Christy made a beautiful bride. Her long hair was piled on top of her head with wisps of soft curls on either side. Her light blue satin dress had an ivory stomacher with embroidered designs that matched the color of her skirts.

A happy occasion indeed.

The reception was outside. Robbie and Mary Ellen, who held wee Anna, followed behind the wedding party. Young Bryce followed behind his parents, holding his younger brother, Alex's, hand.

The streets were lined with friends and family of Christy's that could not fit into the small chapel. Robbie did not know any of the people, but they knew him. The Robertsons were distant relatives, and he had been there several times to discuss events. As a child, Robbie visited with his father when clan leaders gathered to discuss politics and again later regarding restoring King James III and VIII to the throne. Though familiar with the clan's leaders, he did not recognize any folk along the streets.

The townspeople smiled as Robbie and his wife walked by, but one boy was much more enthusiastic. He waved to Robbie with an excited smile, jumping up and down as his curly brown locks bounced around his face. His mother leaned down and whispered in his ear as she gently guided his hand down. The lad's enthusiasm toward Robbie lightened his heart. He remembered being noticed by Laird MacKay when he visited family during the Highland games. He had been so excited. Robbie smiled and winked at the boy before facing forward again.

Robbie and Mary Ellen had their hands full at the reception, as any young couple with three small children would. They had brought a servant girl to help with the children, but she had fallen ill. Though she was on the mend, Mary Ellen thought it best for her to rest since they would return home the next day, and she would be more helpful on the journey back.

Lady Robertson offered a servant girl, but the children were unfamiliar with her, so they decided to tend to the children themselves. Since they were not at home, they did not feel the need to put on a formal air.

Robbie smiled as he watched his wife lean down and say something to wee Alex, who grimaced but straightened and picked up his fork. She still made his heart skip a beat when he watched her. She looked up as if she felt him looking at her and smiled before turning back to help Alex.

Robbie's mother had died when he was thirteen. The thought of losing Mary Ellen scared the hell out of him. He pushed the thought away as Bryce tugged on his arm. Robbie bent down to hear what his son had to say.

It was a break for the family to be at an event where they could be casual. They would have another reception for the newlyweds on Duncan land, and things would be different.

The celebration lasted well past the bride and groom's departure, but Robbie and his family retired soon after Willie and Christy did. They would leave in the morn.

Chapter 2

Ten days after the wedding, Willie and Christy made their rounds, saying goodbye to her family. They would be living on Duncan land, not far from the keep.

Upon visiting Christy's cousin, her cousin's son, Gavin, came running into the house when he saw them. Christy knelt to hug him as he entered but was uninterested in returning her favors. He immediately turned to Willie.

"Where is Robbie?" he asked Willie.

"Gavin!" his mother snapped, appalled by the informal way he asked. "Laird Duncan," she corrected.

Willie smiled at the boy and crouched to be at eye level before answering. "He went back home the day after the wedding."

Gavin's eyebrows squeezed together as he frowned. "I thought he would visit me before he left. Robbie is my very bestest friend."

"Gavin!" his mother called to him again before turning to Willie. "He's been talking nonstop of Laird Duncan ever since he saw him in the wedding march. He was quite taken with him."

"He winked at me when I waved at him. I thought he remembered me," Gavin pouted.

"Well, my brother is a very busy man with a lot of responsibilities," Willie explained, seeing how disappointed the lad was. "But I will tell him how displeased ye were with him for nae stopping." Willie ruffled the lad's hair.

Gavin jerked his head, tightening one cheek as he considered whether or not he could trust the man. "Well, dinna forget," he said earnestly and left the house.

Willie straightened up and turned to Christy, a smirk on his face. She shrugged her shoulders and laughed.

***

Willie and Robbie finalized the reception details over dinner with the family. At one point, wee Bryce looked up and said something to his father, reminding Willie of the lad, Gavin. Willie chuckled, then changed the subject.

"I forgot to tell ye of my encounter with yer *bestest* friend," he said to Robbie.

Robbie looked at him, smiling at Willie's youthful choice of words. "Oh? Who's that?"

Robbie's mind wandered as Willie relayed the visit and how the boy had asked about him. *His best friend?* From the time he trained under the MacKay, his best friends had always been Alex and Brodie.

Willie laughed. "Ye made an impression on the lad. He was quite taken with ye." As an afterthought, he added, "But it was quite unusual that he called ye Robbie, naw Laird Duncan, Robert, or yer brother. He said Robbie."

Robbie's heart stopped for a second. *Could it be Alex in his new life?* His heartbeat heavily, and his eyes grew big. "How old is this lad?"

Willie's expression changed. Robbie knew his seriousness took Willie aback. By his laughter, it was clear Willie found it humorous. He shrugged his shoulders. "I dinna ken, perhaps wee Bryce's age." Willie stretched his arm toward the lad.

Robbie glanced at his oldest son. Alex had died a week after Bryce was born. That would mean Alex would be a little younger than Bryce. He recalled Alex's last words. *I will call on ye one day.* Alex truly believed that he and Anna would be back to find each other again. If Alex's comment were true, and he did seek him out, Robbie would help him end their curse.

Willie watched Robbie, who was lost in thought. "I dinna ken what the big deal is. Clearly, the wink ye gave him impressed him. It is not every day a common lad gets affection from someone with yer status."

Robbie immediately looked back at Willie as he recalled the walk to the reception. Gavin had been waving to him, trying to get his attention. The boy seemed so excited. Robbie had to acknowledge him. He did not want to wave and take the focus off Willie and Christy, so he winked at the child.

Perhaps Gavin was Alex returned. There would be no way for him to know, but the lad would remember Robbie if he was. His sister, Anna, had remembered where she hid a precious gemstone and that she was killed in her previous life. She was only six at the time, and nobody believed her.

"I want to meet this Gavin," Robbie declared.

"What for?" Willie asked. "The boy is fantasizing, nae more than wee Bryce pretends to fight a MacDonald warrior." He gestured to the lad again.

Robbie could not come out and say his true reasoning.

He realized his thoughts would seem irrational. "Have ye lost all touch with yer childhood memories that ye canna remember what it was like to look up to someone?" Robbie raised his eyes. "Do ye nae remember the day Lord Raey asked for ye to apprentice under him? That was all ye talked about for the rest of the games."

Willie smiled and nodded. "Aye, I remember. Da threatened to wait another year if I dinna stop talking about it."

That had been less than a year before their dad and Anna perished in the avalanche.

"I'm sure we can work out a visit from the lad," Willie said as he looked at his wife.

"Aye," she said, "I will write to my cousin."

They changed the topic back to the reception, but Robbie's thoughts kept returning to the lad.

Could Gavin really be Alex? Why else would he refer to me as his best friend? It has to be him. Oh, God, please let it be him.

Chapter 3
11 Years Later

Alana Grant made her way through the woods with as much stealth as the wolf beside her. She raised Thunder from a cub after her father had killed its mother two years ago. She found it one day after one of her father's drunken rages. She could not remember what he was angry about, but he hit her across the face, giving her a bruise on her cheek to match the ones on her arms from him shaking her two days earlier.

Once he passed out, she went into the woods. That was the place she always escaped to. It was where she cried and dreamed.

After her sobs seized, she heard an animal whining. She got up and followed the sound until she spotted the little grey and white wolf cub stuck in a thorn bush. She looked around, but there was no sign of its mother, no prints on the ground that had been softened by the rains the day before. No doubt, the mother was the wolf that her father killed two days earlier.

The mother had dug a hole under the fence around the chicken coop. Alana and her brother, Andrew, made the fence years earlier using long, sturdy sticks as posts and thin branches weaved around the posts.

Alana had been turning over the earth to prepare for the garden when her father came out and discovered the hole. He called to her, and she immediately came so as not to anger him. When she got there, she realized that the calmness in his voice was a ruse to get her to come because when he yelled for her in a rage, she would leave, sometimes to the woods or the village to pick up supplies or whisky if she had eggs or food to barter with. Sometimes, there was money that her brother had sent them left over from a previous trip to the village, and her father did not realize. She would save it for one of these trips.

Oh, how she missed Andrew. Her mother died when she was eight and her brother was the only person she was close to. Then, three years ago, her father enlisted him with the Black Watch so he could collect the money. Her father lied about Andrew's age, saying he was eighteen. Alana did not think her father had any loyalties to the crown to have sent his only son to be a soldier in the Watch. He just wanted the money to supply him with whisky.

When Andrew was home, he tried to protect Alana from her father's wrath, taking the brunt of his abuse, but after Andrew left, she was the only one there for him to take his anger out on.

Alana pushed memories of her brother away. She was halfway to her father's shack. She made her way to the edge of the woods at the top of the hill, so she had a good view, though the sight sickened her. She had left one year ago. It looked like he was fending for himself. He still had the goat, and the fence around the chicken coop was still intact. At least he would have eggs to eat.

A fallen tree lay on the porch. There were no trees that

were close to the house, so her father must have dragged it there. At least he was staying warm at night. If Andrew had made it home, the tree would have been cut up and stacked nicely on the porch.

She turned back toward the woods and headed down to the stream. She would wait until nightfall to stop by. Hopefully, he would be passed out.

Alana stopped by every few weeks to ensure he was alive and see if there was any sign that Andrew had returned. She would not see her father, only drop off jerky on the window frame. The glass in the window was gone. Her father busted it when he threw a wooden bowl at her, narrowly missing her head. He was so mad he punched her in the stomach before picking up a chair and bringing it down over her back. He tripped and fell, knocking himself out that time. That was the day she left home. She grabbed the sack she used when going to the village and stuffed some clothes in it. Then she took her dirk and bow and went to gather Thunder, where she had made a den for him under several trees that had fallen on each other. Once she grabbed him, she went deep into the woods, and there she stayed, all but for her several night trips to drop jerky off for her father.

Upon reaching the stream, she took a long drink, picked up a stick, and threw it into the water. Thunder splashed through the water to get it and carried it back to her. She took it from him laughing, fluffed the fur between its ears, and threw it again.

***

Alana walked to the edge of the woods by her father's house

before the sun was completely gone. She sat against a tree with Thunder lying beside her outstretched legs, his head laying across her ankles. She needed to be sure her father was asleep before she went to the house, so she stayed like that, watching for any sign indicating he was awake. There was no light in the small hut and no sound other than the crickets and the occasional hooting of an owl.

She glanced up at the sky. It was clear, and a million stars sparkled. The moon was three-quarters full. As she stared at it, she thought of her brother, Andrew, and wondered if he was looking at it at that moment.

An emptiness formed in the pit of her stomach. She took a deep breath. Thunder raised his head, turning towards her. He always sensed when she was sad.

Alana smiled as warmth spread through her at Thunder's concern. She leaned in and hugged the wolf. "I love ye, Thunder."

After a couple of hours, she picked up her sack and rose, placing a hand on Thunder. "Stay."

The wolf whined, so she bent down and cuddled against his face. "I'll be back in a wee bit."

Straightening, she left the woods. The moon lit the field enough for her to see. She walked past the fence enclosing the goat. Once close enough, it started to stir.

"Shh," she whispered, patting it before it made too much noise. Once she was sure the goat was content, she continued to the house, listening for any sound of her father. Everything was quiet.

Why does she bother with him? He certainly did not care about her. She thought… or hoped… that being on his own changed him. Even the townsfolk could not stand him.

She was sure he was grateful to have someone do something for him.

She rounded the tree, pulling out the jerky wrapped in animal hide from her sack. She still did not hear anything, not even the sound of him snoring. Was he dead? Maybe he received Andrew's pay and went to the tavern. There were many nights he did not come home after drinking. She would not go in to check in case he slept silently. She would not chance waking him up.

Very quietly, she placed the meat on the window frame and turned to leave as her father jumped out from the corner of the house, grabbing her, and throwing her against the house. She screamed as her head hit the wall, and she slid down, suddenly feeling dizzy.

He grabbed a log lying on the porch and raised it high. Before he could start his downward swing, Thunder lunged at him. Her father yelled, but the wolf hit him with such force that his head snapped back, and he slammed against the door frame. As soon as her father hit the ground, Thunder grabbed his arm in its jaw, trying to rip it off. Fear washed over Alana.

"Thunder, nae!" Alana called as she crawled over to the wolf, putting one hand on her father's arm and the other around Thunder's neck. "Leave him! He's out," she ordered, trying to pull the wolf away. The wolf stopped the tugging and loosened his grip but did not let go. "Let him go!"

The wolf slowly opened his jaw and backed away. It continued to growl, displaying his fangs.

She had to get out of there, but her head felt heavy, and her father's arm was bleeding badly. She needed to stop the bleeding.

She looked around franticly and grabbed the sack she had come with. She took her dirk and, with shaky hands, cut the strap she used to secure it to her shoulder and across her chest. Once separated from the pouch, she wrapped it around his arm and secured it tightly. Oh, God, what had she done? He would be furious when he awoke. She prayed he did not remember what happened, or else he would hunt her and Thunder down.

The wolf edged closer in a protective way as she administered to her father's arm. Once done, she folded her empty sack and placed it in one of her worn boots, putting the dirk in the other. As soon as she stood, the world seemed to spin. She moved her hand to her head and felt where it had hit the house. It pained her. She moved her hand to grip her forehead. Her head felt so heavy.

"Let's get out of here," she told the wolf. "Nae doubt he'll be looking for me when he wakes." *He will never change.*

It took her longer to make it to the edge of the woods. She propped herself up against a tree, wanting to lay down or at least sit, but she did not dare. She had to keep moving.

The budding trees let in little light from the moon. They seemed to come upon her quickly. She held her hands out, waving them in front of her so she would not walk into them.

She walked for what seemed like a few hours, but she was not sure how far she had gone or in what direction. Usually, she would stop by the stream and camp, but she must have missed it altogether.

She needed to rest, if just for a bit. "Stop, Thunder. Stop. I need to rest. My head hurts." It hurt so much that she was on the verge of tears.

She sat down against a tree, and the wolf walked over to her, whining, and licked her face. She pushed him away.

"I just need to rest. Lay beside me."

The wolf lay down and placed his head on her lap. She sighed and softly put her hand on the top of his head.

Chapter 4

Robbie, Bryce and Gavin headed back to Dundee. Robbie and several other clan leaders met with Clan Robertson to discuss the latest happenings in London concerning the Black Watch.

News had come that the Watch, who patrolled the Highlands for the crown, was ordered by King George II to march to London. Many of the Watch were not pleased as they were under the impression they would stay in the Highlands when they enlisted. Upon arrival in London, rumors spread they would be shipped to the West Indies. Many of the soldiers deserted but were captured and sentenced to death.

There had also been rumblings of another rising of the Stuart loyalists. The clan leaders discussed their views and concerns, if and when it would amount to anything.

Robbie, Bryce, and Gavin had stayed only three days, but they brought Willie, Christy, and their two bairns to visit with Christy's family, who would stay on for a few more days.

Though Gavin went to stay with his family, Bryce and Willie accompanied Robbie to the meeting. Robbie felt it essential for Willie to be informed firsthand and be recognized by the other clan leaders if something happened to him before Bryce came of age to take over the clan.

Gavin had come to work for the Duncans when he was twelve. His family were commoners who lived in the village. His father owned the general store, so Gavin and his four siblings worked there. Being offered a position at the Duncan residence was an exciting contrast to the routine village life.

Gavin remembered the first time Robbie invited him to visit as a lad. It was the first time he ever journeyed outside the village beyond a half-day's ride. He traveled with his cousin, Christy, and her husband, Willie, but he knew Robbie had invited him.

He received a message from Christy a couple of months after her nuptials saying that Laird Duncan was sincerely sorry that he had not stopped by for a visit and that he requested a visit from him. The next time Christy visited, about six months later, she brought Gavin back for a week.

The message had only encouraged his obsession with Robbie. He knew now that was Robbie's intent. Robbie did not want him to forget. Had Robbie not requested a visit, perhaps his memories would have faded as a childhood fantasy. That is how it usually happened. Only years later would he correlate his fantasies to reality… his reality.

Once Gavin arrived at Duncan Castle, everything started to come back. He commented to Willie and Christy that it was just as he remembered, which was received with unusual looks.

When Robbie came out to greet them, Willie laughed and told his brother about Gavin's comment. Gavin could tell from Willie's laugh that he thought he was talking nonsense, but Robbie just nodded and smiled as he looked at the lad. Once alone, Robbie explained that he should not speak of his memories to anyone else because they would not understand. And so it was, and the strange looks ended.

He did not remember everything at once, and Robbie did not offer any memories. The memories came gradually. Perhaps a smell, sound, or place would trigger them. Most did not come on that first visit or even the next several. It was the year Robbie had taken him in when he began to spend a lot of time with him. Gavin smiled as he reminisced about his relationship with him.

Each new memory with Robbie poured in through other memories that he had—more lifetimes than he could count.

Robbie, Bryce, and Gavin traveled most of the day, and by the look of the sky, it appeared they would not be home until late the following morning. At least they made it to Duncan land. It would be a short ride in the morn.

Robbie looked at the sky as the clouds rolled in. "We'd better set up camp before we get soaked."

They did not always set up a tent when camping, but with the approaching rain, which was not unusual for May, they would. They branched out, looking for a small clearing.

"How about here?" Bryce called out. It was a small clearing, just enough to pitch their tent and room to sit outside if the rain held off a bit.

"Aye, this looks like a fine spot," his father replied.

They set up their tent swiftly as they made casual talk. Once it was done, Gavin and Bryce went to gather firewood. They did not go far. Bryce asked Gavin about Laird Robertson's middle daughter as they collected the wood. He was smitten with her.

All of a sudden, Gavin had a strange feeling that they

were not alone. He stood up and looked around.

"What is it?" Bryce asked, straightening up and listening.

"I dinna ken," Gavin replied. He felt an inward pull. Placing the wood down, Gavin walked deeper into the woods. He did not get far before seeing a man's stretched-out legs as he sat against a large oak tree. Gavin put his hand on the hilt of his sword and quietly walked around the giant tree, giving it a wide berth.

The man was dirty and injured. His sword was on his lap, and when Gavin rounded the tree to face him, the man immediately held it up with unsteady hands. Gavin looked around for anyone else, but the man was alone.

"Master Bryce!" he called.

Bryce dropped his wood and hurried over, putting his hand on his sword when he saw Gavin on guard. He came to stand beside Gavin.

"A soldier," he said. He could only have been a couple of years older than them. The man's dark straggly hair was dirty, and his face was smeared with blood. The left side of his kilt was caked in blood. "Perhaps one of the Watch who deserted."

"Go get yer father," Gavin said. There was something about this man that drew Gavin to him. The man did not appear to be a threat as he was having enough trouble holding his sword with two hands. It was unlikely that he had the strength to use it.

***

Bryce returned immediately with his father. "What should we do with him, Milord?" Gavin asked. Despite their special relationship, Gavin always referred to him formally in front of others.

"I think he is a desert of the Watch," Bryce said. "Should we kill him?" The Watch was looked down upon by many, and the crown would consider him a deserter.

Robbie shook his head, suddenly glad he had involved Willie in as much of the clan business as he had. If something were to happen to him, his son would be too sporadic in his decisions, not thinking them through. It would be good for him to have an older and wiser person to guide him.

Robbie walked over to the man with his outstretched arm. "Give me yer sword."

The young man narrowed his eyes at him and then the others, who immediately drew their swords and closed in on him. He looked back at Robbie, motioning with his hand to give it up.

Slowly and very unsteadily, he handed the sword over to Robbie.

"Help him over to the campsite," Robbie ordered as he walked away.

Bryce and Gavin helped the man, putting his arms around their shoulders. The soldier groaned as they stood and walked over to the campsite. When they sat him on a log, he crouched over, gripping his left side.

"What's yer name?" Robbie asked.

"Andrew," the man replied. He looked up at Robbie cautiously and saw that he was expecting more. "Grant," he whispered. "Andrew Grant."

"What is yer business then, Andrew? Are ye with the Watch?"

Andrew looked at him. Robbie kept his expression

blank as Andrew studied him. The boy did not look old enough to be in the Watch.

"Aye. I am."

"Ye're a bit young to be with the Watch," Robbie commented.

As if offended, Andrew countered, "I'm nineteen."

Seeing the lad there, only a few years older than Bryce, made Robbie's gut ache. The thought of Bryce, or any of his children, being injured and alone somewhere gave him chills.

"Let me take a look at yer wound," he said.

The end of the man's plaid, which generally would drape over his shoulder, was tied around his chest. The man grimaced as he slowly raised his arms, and Robbie unwrapped the cloth.

The laceration was a sword wound in his side. It had stopped bleeding but was infected. Robbie could feel the heat from Andrew's body and could tell he had a fever as well.

"When did this happen?" Robbie asked as he wrapped the plaid back around, securing it tightly.

"Two days ago, sir. We were on our way to London. Many of us turned around when we heard they were sending us to the West Indies." He paused. Robbie suspected Andrew tried to determine his thoughts, but he had mastered keeping his expression neutral. "The Redcoats ambushed us."

Robbie knew the boy would not survive. He had seen men with more severe wounds survive, but they were healthy, and their wounds tended to immediately. This lad looked like he had not eaten in weeks. Robbie grabbed his flask of whisky and handed it to him. Andrew took a swig, and when he handed it back, Robbie gave him some jerky and bread.

"So, yer headed back home now?" Robbie asked.

"Aye."

"The Grants on Loch Ness?" Robbie asked.

"Nae. Grantown-on-Spey."

Robbie nodded. He planned on eating what little food they brought, but he had not counted on another person, and after looking at him, Robbie thought it might be his last meal. He grabbed his bow and ordered the boys to get a fire started. He looked up at the sky and hoped the rain would hold off.

In less than half an hour, Robbie returned with a hare and was pleased to see a nice fire going. He sat down and started to gut and skin the animal. Usually, he would have given it to one of the lads to do, but he felt pressured as the clouds looked more ominous. He cut it into small pieces to cook faster and skewered it.

"Take him into the tent," Robbie ordered as the thunder rumbled.

A few minutes after they got Andrew into the tent, the sky opened up to torrential rains. Robbie grabbed the skewers and entered the tent, drenched. It was going to be a long, cramped night.

***

The rain kept a steady flow for the next several hours. Robbie knew the lads were asleep, as he could hear them snoring, but he could not sleep in the cramped tent. And worse, the water was coming in through a small hole and rolling down to drip on his head.

He contemplated what to do with Andrew. Had the lad

been well, he would have had to decide on handing him over or letting him go, which would have been harder. The lad only had a week left at the most, and Robbie doubted he would last that long.

The boy may be nineteen but was too young to die away from his mother and father. God forbid if something happened to one of his own children, Robbie thought. If so, he would hope that someone would deliver him home to die in the loving care of his family.

But Robbie had to get home. He had responsibilities that needed tending to. He decided he could bring the boy with him and make him more comfortable in his final days. It was much closer. That would be better than letting him go on his own. Andrew would not make it but a day on his own.

"Ah!" Gavin yelped as he raised his hand to the back of his head. It was not unusual for Gavin to experience sudden spurt of pain. Robbie knew that Gavin felt the pain of his kindred spirit, Anna, Robbie's sister...or at least Anna's soul, which was now someone else.

The onslaughts of pain were much more frequent a few years ago, but the random pains had seized over the last year. Robbie knew this girl must have had a rough life and knowing that this lass was someone he had once held dear, even if she did not know them, made him sick to his stomach.

When the occasional pains seemed to stop, Robbie wondered if she had not survived, though he never shared his thoughts with Gavin.

Thinking about it now, Robbie realized that Gavin had not always had these occurrences. They started about three years ago... unless Gavin never mentioned them. Or perhaps they had just gotten worse with time.

Once they became more frequent, Robbie stopped training Gavin to swordfight. He could not chance it happening when he was sparing with someone, not after what happened to Alex.

"Gavin, are ye hurt?" Robbie asked as Gavin continued to moan.

He sat up and Robbie heard him take long, deep breaths. He had seen him do this many times. Gavin once told him that it helped ease the pain. After a minute, Gavin replied, "Aye, I'm fine. I'm sorry I woke ye."

"I was already awake, lad," he said. "I thought yer pains had stopped." He did not say more in the event Bryce or Andrew were listening.

"They had," he replied, and as if to confirm that he shared the same thoughts as Robbie, he added, "It's a promising sign."

Gavin would see it that way. It was an indication that his kindred spirit was still alive. Robbie nodded, though Gavin could not see him in the dark.

"Can ye nae sleep, Milord?"

"Nae. I was thinking about what to do with Andrew. He willna last but a few days. His wound is too bad. It would take two or three days to take him to Grantown-on-Spey and another three back. I can take him to Dundee. If I leave him to travel alone, he willna make it far on foot. I predict he willna last a day on his own."

"I can take him," Gavin said.

"Ye canna take him on yer own. If anything happened to ye, yer parents would have me drawn and quartered."

Gavin got quiet for a moment. "There's something about this whole event, but I really feel I need to do this. I dinna just stumble upon him. I was drawn to him. I kenned he was there and looked for him. Do ye ken what I mean?"

Robbie knew all right. Alex had been the same way. He could sense things, especially when it had something to do with Anna or their adversary. Alex did not know he was Anna's brother when they first met, but they bonded like brothers. Robbie figured it was this feeling that drew Alex to him. He suspected Andrew was somehow related to Gavin's kindred spirit.

What were his options? There was no way he would let Gavin go on his own. His soulmate was clearly in trouble since Gavin had felt her pain so much. Robbie had promised Gavin that he would help him find her, and he would not go back on his promise. He considered his choices.

"Alright. But ye canna go alone. We are on Duncan land. I will send Bryce home, and I will go with you."

"Thank ye, Milord." Robbie heard the relief in Gavin's voice. "Ye have nae idea how grateful I am to have ye."

But Robbie did know. Alex had once confided in him that he was the first soul they had ever told in all the centuries they carried the curse. The fact that Robbie knew had sped up the memories in Gavin. If he had not, Gavin and his kindred spirit may not find each other until one or both were married. Both would long for the other for the rest of their lives.

Robbie had to help him.

Chapter 5

Alana woke in the morning to Thunder licking her face. Her head still hurt. She pushed the wolf's face away but did not open her eyes yet. The wolf gently took her hand in his mouth and tugged on it as he whined. She slowly opened her eyes and everything began to spin. She squinted to get the wolf in focus.

"I'm so dizzy," she said to him.

Thunder dropped her hand and started licking her face in acknowledgment.

"Stop." She pushed him away again. She knew he was worried about her, but his nudging her in the face only made it worse. She was not sure she could get up but knew she needed to keep moving. Her father would no doubt be looking for them.

She slowly looked around and found a sturdy stick. Just leaning to reach for it made her head feel heavy.

Once she retrieved it, she used it to aid her in standing. She gave herself time to adjust and look around. Everything was blurry. She could not tell what direction she needed to go.

Thunder walked up to her, stood against her side, and gave a small whimper. She dropped one arm and petted him softly. "I canna see that well, Thunder. Ye need to get me home, to the cave, boy. Lead me to the cave."

Thunder turned around and started walking. Alana had to squint to see Thunder; still, it was just a blur. She followed the wolf slowly, causing Thunder to stop frequently and walk back to her.

"I'm coming," she said, petting the top of his head, which came up high enough that she did not have to bend over.

After a few hours, she called to him as she leaned against a tree and closed her eyes. "Hold up, Thunder." She was so tired, but she did not dare sit down for fear she would not be able to get up.

The wolf walked over to her and sat, rubbing his head against her leg until she finally put her hand down and scratched his head. "I just need to rest a bit. I'm so dizzy."

By evening, she reached a spot by the stream she frequently visited. Getting to her cave from there usually took her under two hours.

"We'll have to stay here the night," she said, kneeling by the stream to drink. Bending over made her head pound and spin. "I'm hungry. Can ye get me something to eat?" The wolf tipped its head at her. "Go get a hare, Thunder. Can ye get me a hare?"

The wolf sniffed around to find the trail. Once found, he took off.

Alana grabbed a few sticks and scooted to a tree to sit against. She grabbed her dagger from her boot and the sack, which she cut into strips and placed on the ground. She was sure there was something better to use as kindling, but with her head feeling like it would split open and her vision blurry, she thought she might be unable to find her way back. She laid the sticks on the scraps of material.

Reaching into her pocket, she pulled out a piece of flint and struck it against her blade, creating sparks until the material finally caught. She bent down to blow the flames, and her head felt as if it would explode. She squeezed her eyes shut against the pain but continued blowing. She needed a fire.

Once the cloth caught, she leaned her head back against the tree and occasionally fed the fire with small sticks in her reach.

Thunder returned in less time than she would have hunting with perfect vision.

"Good boy." She patted him on the head as she grabbed the hare. "Now get me some sticks," she ordered. When he did not immediately move, she repeated herself. "Go get a stick. Fetch me a stick."

He left and immediately came back with a stick. She took it from his mouth and repeated the command. "Get me another one. Go fetch a stick."

She played that game for several minutes until her fire was large enough that it would not die out. She grabbed the dirk but had to squint to get the hare in focus enough to prepare it. Her knife slipped, and she cut herself.

"Ouch!" she yelled, placing her thumb in her mouth. She could taste the blood and knew it was a deep cut.

The wolf looked up at her and whined, nudging her with his nose. Alana ripped another piece of the material from the sack and wrapped it around her thumb. She grabbed the hare, bunched up the fur, and carefully broke the skin before pulling it from its body.

As soon as she placed the meat on the fire, she started the stick game again. "Go fetch me another stick." She continued until she had a nice stack beside her to keep her warm through the night.

By the time she and Thunder had finished their meal, the sun was completely gone. She threw some more wood on the fire and leaned her head back against the tree. Just the thought of laying down made her head throb and the bile rise in her stomach.

She patted the ground as she closed her eyes. "Come here, Thunder. Lay down beside me."

The wolf got up and circled close to her a couple of times before lying down against her legs and putting his chin on her lap.

***

Halfway through the night, it started to rain.

"Great!" Alana exclaimed. She opened her eyes and watched the glow of the hot coals sizzle away.

Figuring she would be warmer snuggling against Thunder, she lay down, and immediately, her head felt as if someone had smashed it with a log. She was in excruciating pain and debated which was worse, the cold and wet or her throbbing head. Thunder adjusted himself by settling the length of her, but her head hurt too much. She pushed herself back up and cried as the cold rain soaked her.

Chapter 6

Robbie did not sleep much. Once the birds started chirping, he called the others to get up as he left the tent.

"Get up. It's time to get moving. Help Andrew out of the tent."

The rain had stopped, and it looked like the sky was clearing up. Bryce and Gavin helped Andrew out of the tent and sat him on the log. Robbie walked over to him and offered him his flask. "How are ye feeling?" he asked.

Andrew sipped and replied, "A bit better than yesterday."

Robbie detected a bit of hope in the lad's voice. He felt his assistance and a full belly had given Andrew a false hope that he may get better. "I will take ye home, Andrew," Robbie stated, accepting the flask back and turning to ready the horses.

Bryce and Gavin quickly tore down the tent. "Help me secure the tent, Bryce," Robbie said to his son. Bryce brought it over to Gavin's horse, where his dad stood.

While securing the tent, Robbie explained his plan. "Gavin and I are going to take Andrew back to his home. We are on Duncan land. Ye ken we are but two hours from home?"

Bryce nodded.

"I will be passing back through the Robertson's lands and will send Uncle Willie back to aid ye with some business that needs tending to. I need ye to stand in my stead."

Robbie went down the list of business that needed to be taken care of. All the while, Bryce nodded his understanding and stood a little taller. Robbie's chest swelled. Maybe he should have let him handle more things on his own. He hugged him. "Ye will do fine, son. I ken it."

Andrew stared at the interaction between the two. When Robbie faced him, he looked close to tears. Robbie suspected he was missing his family, and there was a good chance he might not see them again.

They all mounted and left.

As they rode on, Robbie questioned Andrew about where he lived, his parents' names, and anything that would help him find his house if Andrew did not survive. Andrew answered all his questions but did not offer up anymore.

Robbie was mindful that the Redcoats would be patrolling the area for deserters. He ordered Gavin to take the lead a distance ahead. By early afternoon, Gavin signaled that riders were approaching. Robbie immediately stopped his horse and helped Andrew down so he could hide in the woods.

Gavin dismounted ahead of them and picked up one of his horse's legs, inspecting its hoof. He started cleaning it out.

"Ach. Is yer horse still giving ye trouble?" Robbie asked as he approached from behind as the two Redcoats neared.

"I think he'll be fine once I clean the muck out of his hoof," Gavin replied as mud dropped from the hoof he cleaned.

"Is there a problem?" one of the soldiers asked as they approached.

"Nae, sir. This horse seems overly sensitive to the wet ground, is all," Robbie replied.

"Who are ye, and what is yer business?" the soldier asked.

"I'm Laird Duncan, sir, from Dundee, and this is my man, Gavin Robertson. We are headed to the Robertson land to fetch my brother and his family. They are having a holiday with his sister-in-law's family."

The soldier scratched the whiskers on his chin as he watched Gavin.

"He'll make it, sir," Robbie reassured the Redcoat. "We are only a couple of hours away."

The Redcoat nodded before asking, "Have ye seen any of the Watch on the road? Some men have deserted and perhaps traveled back to the Highlands."

Robbie shook his head. "Nae, we havena encountered a soul, sir," he lied, praying to God for forgiveness, as Gavin finished cleaning the last hoof.

"That should do it, Milord," Gavin said, dropping the last leg and walking the horse around in a circle, guiding him with the reins.

"I think that did the job," Robbie declared, nodding to Gavin.

"Well," the soldier said as Gavin mounted, "Safe travels."

"Thank ye, sir." Robbie remounted and continued slowly.

The Redcoats kicked their horses into a gallop and took off the other way.

Robbie fought the urge to turn around, praying they would not see evidence of where he and Andrew entered the woods.

After several minutes, Robbie reined in his horse. "We're naw far from yer home. I want ye to ride there and tell Willie the situation… and be discrete. Get his cart and tell Willie I need him to return to Dundee as Bryce's advisor. We will pick Christy and the children up in a few days."

Gavin nodded his understanding.

"Ye need to get a different tartan and shirt for Andrew, fresh bandages, and food."

"Aye."

"And try to be back before dark," he said as an afterthought. "I will be in the woods just past where the two paths come together. Signal for me."

"Aye, Milord,"

Robbie turned his horse back around as he repeated, "Be discrete. Tell naebuddy but Willie."

"Aye," Gavin said, urging his horse into a gallop.

Robbie trotted off toward Andrew. He found the spot quickly enough since the ground was still damp, leaving prints. Any good tracker would have found him, but the Redcoats took off like a blazing fire… to match their red tunics. Robbie chuckled at the thought.

He followed the trail through the woods on horseback. He would not take the road anymore. Once he found Andrew, he dismounted, grabbed his flask with the last of his whisky, and handed it to Andrew. "Drink."

They continued through the woods slowly, only close

enough to the road to keep it in sight. Once they were close to where the road intersected the way to the Robertson's, they dismounted.

Robbie estimated they had an hour until Gavin returned with the cart. He picked up a fallen branch and walked to the road, leaving it partway in the path.

***

The sun was halfway set when Robbie heard the cart. It stopped, and Gavin signaled with a bird call. Robbie rose and signaled back as he leaned down to help Andrew up. He put Andrew's arm around his shoulder and grabbed his horse's reins. Once at the cart, he grabbed the spare plaid and bandages Gavin held out.

"How did it go?" he asked.

"Good," Gavin replied, "Willie will leave in the morn, and I got the supplies and a casket of whisky."

Robbie smiled and nodded. Turning to Andrew, he said, "I want to redress yer wound."

Robbie untied the makeshift bandage. It was hard to see in the fading light, but the wound appeared to have stayed closed. He rolled the new bandage around his chest, tying it tight before helping him put on the clean shirt.

Gavin had already pleated and laid the Robertson plaid out on the ground. As soon as Andrew dropped his old plaid, Robbie picked it up and walked into the woods. He found a hollow tree and rolled it up, shoving the evidence of the Watch into the hole. Once back, Andrew was dressed.

Gavin and Robbie assisted him into the back of the cart. Gavin grimaced at one point, yanking his hand, and gripping his thumb. Robbie glanced over at him, watching him wiggle his thumb around. Robbie knew it was another injury of his soulmate.

By the time Andrew was settled with food, drink, and a blanket, the night was upon them, and they were on their way.

They rode on through most of the night, stopping only to rest themselves and the horses for a couple of hours.

Chapter 7

Alana's head began to nod as she slept, sitting against a tree. She jerked it back, hitting the trunk.

"Ah," she cried out, keeping her eyes shut tight. Her hand went to the back of her head to explore the knot. Thunder sat up immediately and started licking her face.

"Stop it," she pushed his face away and hugged him, wiping her tears in his fur. Thunder sat and let her cry for several minutes.

Finally, she sniffled and pulled away. "Ye're a good boy. I love ye," she said as she pat his head.

She could tell it was morning. The birds were chirping. She cracked her eyes open, trying to get everything in focus. It did not happen. She was not sure if it was better or worse than the previous day.

She grabbed her walking stick and slowly got up. Her clothes were still damp, and she was cold. All she wanted was to get home to her little cave.

"Let's get going," she said to Thunder. He quickly got up, wagging his tail. "Lead the way," she motioned with her hand. "Let's go. Take me home, to our cave."

The wolf started walking, and she followed him, his long coat looking like only a blur.

***

Gavin rested in the back of the cart with Andrew.

"Ah," he moaned, rubbing the back of his head.

Robbie turned a bit in the coachman's seat to look at him. "Are ye hurt?"

Gavin grumbled and sat up.

When he did not respond, Robbie asked, "How's Andrew?"

Gavin gently shook Andrew. He received a groan in response, but Andrew did not open his eyes. Gavin looked at Robbie and nodded.

Robbie pulled on the reins, bringing the cart to a stop. Gavin placed his blanket over the one already covering Andrew and jumped down. They stretched for a bit, feeding the horses.

"How far do ye think we are from Grantown?" Gavin asked.

"Well, at the pace we are going, perhaps we could get there by evening," Robbie replied.

"I'm naw sure Andrew will last that long," Gavin whispered as he looked at Andrew.

Robbie tipped his head and tightened one side of his mouth. "He made it this far. People often hold on at the end… for closure."

***

By late morning, Alana made it to her cave. She was drenched, cold and hungry. She moved most of the branches from the cave's opening when she went in, but with the overcast sky, not much light made its way inside.

She quickly got out of her wet clothes and wrapped a blanket around her, gathering items to build a fire. She had a place for everything: a pile of kindling, a pile for small sticks, and one for logs.

She fingered for them all in the decreased light and then, for her fire pit.

"Thunder," she called. The wolf walked over and put his nose under her armpit from behind as she fumbled to stack her sticks in the pit.

"Go get something to eat," she said. "Get a hare or a squirrel."

The wolf put his nose out further under her arm.

"Go get a hare," she repeated.

The wolf ran out as she got her fire going and put her dry dress on.

The first time she had built a fire there, the cave filled with smoke. She spent weeks digging a hole in the side of the cave near the fire pit. It did not eliminate the smoke, but most of it went out.

Once Thunder returned with his kill, she cooked and ate before lying on her deer skin bed mat. It was early, but she was tired, and she quickly fell asleep.

***

They could see the village ahead.

"We made it, Andrew," Robbie turned in his seat as he called back. "Ye hear me? Ye're home."

Gavin turned around and leaned over the seat to rouse him. He poked at him and was rewarded with a small moan.

"Well, at least we still have a couple of hours of light

left to find his house," Gavin commented.

"Aye," Robbie said as he pulled on the reins to stop in front of a tavern.

"Stay here," Robbie ordered as he jumped from the coachman's seat, tossing the reins to Gavin. He walked into the tavern, and everyone quieted to look at the stranger. One burly man at a table with three others looked him up and down and whispered something, gaining a laugh from the others.

Robbie approached the counter.

A man behind it was drying off a mug. He looked up. "Can I get ye something?"

"I'm looking for a man: Donald Grant."

"Are ye a wolf hunter, then? Come to claim the prize?" a man at a table asked with raised eyebrows.

"Nae," Robbie replied. "I've come to bring his son, Andrew, home. He's injured. Why do ye ask about a wolf?"

"Ach, Donald came in here yesterday saying a fierce wolf attacked him," the man behind the counter replied.

The man at the table chided in, "Aye. He had his arm all bandaged up." The other men at his table nodded in agreement. Their expressions gave Robbie the impression that they did not believe the man.

Robbie turned back to the man behind the counter, now shaking his head and with a smirk on his face. "Can ye tell me where he lives?"

"Aye, it's about a half-hour ride from here at the most." The man continued to give Robbie the directions.

"Thank ye," Robbie said as he laid a coin on the counter.

As he opened the door, the man at the table yelled, "Make sure ye announce yer presence as ye come up his path. He's likely to be trigger-happy with a wild beastie running around." Several men laughed.

Robbie closed the door and walked back to the cart.

"Did ye find where he lives?" Gavin asked as Robbie climbed up onto the seat.

"Aye. 'Tis a half hour away."

***

Halfway there, Gavin began to get anxious. He raked his fingers through his hair. The closer they got to the house, the more uncomfortable he was.

"I dinna like the way I feel right now," he said quietly. He could not describe it, but a sense of dread lingered in the pit of his stomach.

Robbie snapped his head toward him. "What is it?"

"I dinna ken, but I have a bad feeling."

"Should we turn around?"

"Nae. I think I need to be here."

Robbie nodded his acknowledgment and faced forward again. He felt to make sure his pistol was under his belt.

As they approached the house at the end of the path, they could see a man sitting in a chair on the porch with a rifle. He got up as they approached.

"Ho!" Robbie called to him as he raised his hand in greeting. "Are ye Donald Grant?"

"Who asks?" the man yelled.

Robbie brought the cart to a halt in front of the house. "I'm Laird Duncan, from Dundee. I've brought yer son. He's severely injured." He prayed Andrew had not died yet.

The man just looked at him.

"Andrew Grant, sir. Is that yer son?"

"Aye," the man mumbled.

Robbie and Gavin hopped down and went to the back of the cart. Donald stood where he was.

Gavin's unease continued. He was not sure if the man stood there because he did not want to see his son injured or if it was something else. Gavin suspected it was the later of the two. He jumped into the cart and put his arm around Andrew, lifting him to a sitting position.

"Andrew, Andrew, ye're home."

Andrew moaned and opened his eyes slowly, looking around.

"Come on, let's get ye out of this cart," Gavin said.

Robbie jumped into the cart, and the two helped him down to the ground, supporting him so he could at least try to walk.

His father looked him up and down, frowning.

"Can we put him inside?" Robbie asked.

The man said nothing but turned around and led them into the house. The house was a mess, and it smelled like a privy. There was an overturned chair by a table, a small puddle in the corner where the roof leaked, and a bed that looked like it had never been made.

Robbie and Gavin sat Andrew on the bed.

"Father," he said. His father did not even acknowledge him, only scowled at his son. "Where's Alana?" Andrew asked.

As soon as the name came out of Andrew's mouth, Gavin's heart tightened. *Alana. She's the one I'm looking for!* There was no doubt in his mind.

"Ach!" the man yelled. "She left me... the damn wench!"

Andrew's eyes went wide. "Left? What did ye do to

her?"

Do to her? It felt like someone kicked Gavin in the stomach.

"I dinna do a damn thing. She's out there, in the woods with some evil wolf beast," he spat as he flung his arm toward the door.

"A wolf?" Robbie asked.

"Aye!" he yelled even louder, holding up his bandaged arm. "It tried to kill me two nights ago. As we speak, a team of men is searching for the wild beast."

Gavin stood frozen. Was Alana in danger? He needed to know more.

"But, Alana," Andrew repeated.

His father repulsively looked him over. By now, Andrew's back rested against the wall, and he was slipping sideways.

"Ye canna even hold yerself up," Donald spat. "Did ye desert?" He got closer.

Andrew did not answer. His father grabbed him by his shirt and started shaking him, so his head bashed against the wall. "Ye damn fool! Ye deserted!"

Panic shot through Gavin. He propelled himself toward Andrew, trying to push Donald away. Robbie grabbed him from behind. He smelled of whisky. Donald turned, pushed Gavin against the wall, and crossed the room as he swept his arm across the table, throwing the contents across the room.

"The Devil! I willna get me money now!" He reached for the rifle he had propped against the wall and pointed it at his son. Robbie's arm came up from under the gun and knocked it up as a shot went off into the roof. The kickback of its firing pushed the man off balance, and he stumbled over the turned-over chair, knocking himself out.

Now lying, Andrew grabbed Gavin, standing next to the bed.

"Ye have to find Alana and take her away from here." Gavin did not need to be told to find her. He knew he had to. It was his destiny.

"Aye," Gavin said as he knelt beside the bed and laid his hand on Andrew's. "I will find her and take her away from here. I swear."

With that, Andrew closed his eyes and nodded. He took a strained breath, then another, and then his breathing ceased.

Robbie walked over and put his hand on Gavin's shoulder. Gavin took a deep breath and stood. He turned to Robbie and said, "I need to find Alana."

Robbie nodded. "I ken, Gavin."

They both looked around the one-room house. It was amazing that one room could display so much destruction. With all of the broken things and what they had just witnessed, there was no denying what life Alana had lived… and what life Anna had gone to.

Gavin's insides trembled. *God, please help me find her.*

"Let's get out of here," Robbie said as he stepped over the man's passed-out body. "We'll get a room at the tavern tonight and see what we can find out about Alana… and this wolf."

Chapter 8

It was a somber ride back to the tavern. Neither said a word. No words could describe the scene that they had just witnessed.

Though Gavin had not met his kindred spirit, he finally had a name for her—Alana. The rampage her father displayed toward Andrew spoke volumes about the life she had.

Each new life had unique circumstances. Sometimes, they would live happy lives; sometimes, not. One lifetime, he would be a poor peasant; the next, perhaps a wealthy man. On one occasion, he was born into slavery.

They were both fortunate to have had loving families in their last lives as Alex and Anna. It killed Gavin to know his sweet Anna was now in an abusive home. He would give anything to have Alex's special abilities. No doubt, it would be easier to find her. But he wasn't Alex. His unique gift was a birthright of the Boswell family, which he was no longer a part of.

Finally, they made it back to the tavern. As Gavin waited with the cart, Robbie entered. The room quieted instantly.

"Did ye find him?" the man behind the counter asked.

"Aye. He wasna verra happy to see his son," Robbie said gravely.

"I wouldna think so," the man said. "After he left his father to join the Watch, Donald had to tend the lands himself. Andrew was sixteen but lied, saying he was older."

"Hmm," is all Robbie managed. Donald's words contradicted this man's story. "I need a room for the night. Do ye have one available?"

"Aye."

"I also have a cart and an extra horse. I'd like to keep it here for a couple of days extra. Is that possible?"

The man put down the cup and bottle he was pouring, rested his hands on the counter, and leaned closer. "It'll cost ye."

After negotiating the price, Robbie returned to the cart and brought it to the stables. He and Gavin carried their necessities to their room before returning to the tavern to eat.

The owner brought them each a bowl of stew and some bread. Robbie thanked him and asked, "Where are folks looking for this wolf?"

"Ah, ye're going to hunt for the wolf, aye?" the man asked.

"Aye, I think we may."

"Are ye doing it for the sport or the prize?"

"The prize?" Robbie asked.

A man from another table turned around and said, "Ye dinna ken the prize?" Robbie shook his head. Gavin's stomach knotted. "Well, it's his daughter. What's her name?" he asked as he nudged the man beside him.

Gavin's jaw tightened.

"Alana," the man replied.

"Aye, that's right, Alana. She comes with all that land once he dies. It's a nice piece of property. His father had it before him."

"What of Andrew?" Robbie asked, not mentioning that he had passed shortly after their arrival.

Gavin's eyes darted between Robbie's and the men at the other table.

"Ach, he disowned him. Donald wasna happy when he left, but Alana seemed to have taken over the slack nicely. Well, until she disappeared."

"Disappeared?" Robbie asked.

"What's she like, this Alana?" Gavin hardly recognized his own voice. It was strained. He had not meant to talk but needed to hear about her.

"Quiet, submissive. A good worker. I havena seen her for quite a while. She was always disheveled but pleasant. She'll clean up nicely, though."

"I wouldna mind seeing how submissive she is," the guy beside him said as he smirked and took a gulp of his ale.

A rage inside of Gavin was about to explode. His palms began to sweat, and his insides shook. Robbie locked eyes with him as if to order him to calm down.

"Neil is out hunting the wolf. He doesna have a use for her. He's already married. The same with Johnie," another man said.

"Aye, I ken, but they'd take her anyway. She comes with all that land. Neil says he'll just give her to Mistress Molly."

Gavin fisted his hand holding his spoon and his face turned bright red. Robbie stepped on Gavin's foot under the table to stress that he needed to stay calm. His eyes warned

Gavin to say nothing more. Gavin was not sure he could keep his mouth shut. He swallowed the bile in his throat.

The men all laughed at the recent comment.

"Ah, that'd be good. We can all have a piece of her."

Gavin clenched his teeth as hard as he could to keep from saying anything.

Robbie quickly changed the subject. "Where are most folks looking for this wolf?"

"Well, most got a head start on ye, ye ken. They started on Donald's land. It stretches out to the river about thirty acres to the west. I'd start further west if I were ye."

"Aye," a couple of men nodded their agreement, then began taking bets on who would find the wolf first. There seemed to be several people searching for it.

Robbie and Gavin wasted no more time in the tavern than needed to finish their food.

Chapter 9

Alana slept most of the afternoon, evening, and night, only waking once to add more sticks and wood to the hot coals.

When she woke in the morning, she lay with her eyes closed, contemplating how she felt. Her head still hurt a lot. *Please let it be clearer when I open my eyes,* she prayed.

She slowly opened her eyes. They were still out of focus, but she could see the soft glow of the hot coals. She squinted, and the hot coals became clearer but far from normal. She felt the tears of disappointment threaten. She would not cry. She would get better. She only needed time.

She sat up slowly, but her head immediately began to throb more. Thunder stood and began licking her face.

She pushed him away. "Ye're making it worse!"

Thunder whined and nudged his nose under her hand.

"I'm sorry, Thunder," she said as she pet his head.

Everything was still spinning, but not as much as the day before. That gave her hope. Maybe the dizziness would be gone with one more day of rest.

She added more sticks to the hot coals and walked toward the front of the cave, stretching out her arm to guide her along the stone wall. She went outside to relieve herself.

Thunder followed her closely.

"Go on," she gestured for him to go. "I'm going back in to sleep." He looked at her, tilting his head to one side. "Go on, I said."

The wolf took off, and she returned to her cave, leaving the entrance partly open for him to come and go as he pleased. Seeing that the fire had finally caught, she added another log and went back to sleep.

***

Gavin was anxious to get started. He hardly slept; his mind full of fears of what might happen if someone else found Alana first.

After grabbing a quick bite to eat, he and Robbie set off, deciding to search further west than Donald's house, as suggested.

They entered the woods a few miles outside of town. All morning, they traveled with no signs of a wolf anywhere. There was evidence found of other wild animals, but not a wolf. By midday, they reached a stream and stopped to drink and water the horses. As Gavin cupped the water, he stopped and looked across the stream.

"Look at that!" He rose, grabbed his horse's reins, and went to the other side.

Robbie crossed behind Gavin. The rains had washed away any evidence of a person or wolf except the small pile of half-chard sticks.

"Perhaps we can find some tracks in the woods," Robbie suggested.

They each guided their horses and entered the woods a short distance from each other. *Please let me find her*.

Gavin only made it a few steps into the woods before pausing with the urge to go a different direction. He walked back around to be on the other side of Robbie.

After a few minutes, he called out, "Over here!" His heart raced as he looked at the tracks he found.

Robbie walked over to where Gavin stood and knelt to study the tracks. "Aye, those are wolf tracks, alright," he agreed. The ground had softened from the rains, leaving perfect paw prints, but sadly, none from a human.

Gavin took the lead, following the tracks. Something pulled him in that direction. It was more powerful than anything he could imagine. He was definitely on her trail.

Robbie followed behind. They both remained quiet, focused on the path ahead and the sounds of the forest. Suddenly Gavin stopped and pointed to a print in the ground made by a small man or a young woman.

"Look!" he exclaimed.

Beside it was the wolf prints. Gavin's heart pounded so hard he thought it would explode. They were close.

They continued for another hour into the evening. Though they still had a few hours of sunlight, it was shaded by the branches of the dense forest, making the air cooler. Gavin tightened his cloak around him as he continued.

They crested a hill and immediately had a view of the landscape. A small stream of smoke rose beyond the next hilltop. Gavin pointed.

"Do ye see that? It's a campfire." It could be a hunter, but Gavin knew it was Alana's.

"Aye," Robbie agreed.

Gavin nudged his horse to start his descent down the hill. Robbie immediately grabbed his reins, shaking his head.

Quietly, he said, "Remember, if it's her, she has a wolf with her."

In his eagerness to find her, Gavin forgot about the wolf. Robbie checked the pistol in his belt and the rifle in the sling secured to his saddle. Gavin also checked his rifle but would not shoot it unless he had to. This wolf was Alana's protector.

They continued their descent and headed toward the billowing smoke. The closer they got, the more it appeared that the smoke was coming out of the hillside.

Robbie shook his head and pointed to go around. It was coming from inside the hills. There had to be a cave on the other side.

Gavin put his hand on Robbie's arm to stop him. "The wolf is her protector. If ye kill it…" He did not finish. He understood that it may be necessary. They had discussed it earlier, but he was concerned about how she would feel if they did.

Robbie nodded. "Perhaps we should wait until morn," he said.

He knew Robbie was right and they should wait to approach her and the wolf in broad daylight. If they were attacked by the wolf that evening, they would not be able to travel at night for help. Gavin did not care. He could not wait until morning.

Gavin looked up toward the cave and then around to the surrounding woods. He shook his head. "Nae. What if someone else finds her?"

Robbie sighed, then nodded.

They rode the horses around, finding the other side was much taller. It looked like a hill, but they then realized they were halfway up a mountain.

Robbie pointed to the partly covered entrance to the cave. Gavin looked up, and as soon as he spotted it, he felt a jolt in his chest. She was in there. He knew it. They dismounted away from the cave and walked the rest of the way.

***

Alana woke to a slight rumble in Thunder's chest as he lay beside her. He propped his head up and continued to growl. Alana sat up, ignoring the pain in her head.

"What is it, boy?" She stroked his head.

Her body tensed as fear rose from deep within. She knew her father would be looking for them. She thought she was deep enough in the woods not to be found. If her vision had not been blurry, she would have left the cave and gone deeper into the woods, at least for a couple of weeks.

Now, it was too late. Her father would kill Thunder and most likely beat her close to death. Why in the world would she have thought he would change? She never should have gone back.

The wolf stood, ears straight up as the rumble in his chest surfaced to a deep growl. Alana stood up and moved back against the wall. She had put wood on the fire not long ago, so there was a slight glow, and the last of the daylight could be seen from where she had left the branches off the entrance.

She groped for her bow and quiver, which she swung over her shoulder before pulling out an arrow, her eyes never leaving the opening. She squinted in hopes of seeing clearer.

"Alana?" she heard a call from the outside. Thunder's

growl got louder.

The voice soothed her, no doubt a ploy to get her to come out.

It was not her father's voice, but he would not have come himself. He would have hired someone. Her chest was tight with fear. Her hands shook as she placed the arrow in her bow.

"Alana, please come out. We just want to talk to ye."

It was the voice of a young man. It seemed to calm her immediately, but she could not trust anyone now. She knew she was trapped. There was no escape.

A blurred figure blocked the light in the opening. Alana pulled her bow tight.

Gavin slowly entered the cave with his hands in the air. "I willna harm ye, lass. I'm here to help."

Help? She did not believe him. He just wanted to get her guard down.

Robbie entered behind him, one hand up and the other one on the pistol, but she could only see that a second person had entered.

"Who are ye?" she asked loudly so they could hear her over the growling.

It was hard to see anything in the cave. The dying fire only gave a slight glow, and Robbie stood in the opening, blocking the last of the fading light.

"I'm a friend of yer brother, Andrew," Gavin replied.

"Andrew." A tinge of hope made her chest thump. She wanted to believe him. Oh, how she wanted to, but her thoughts kept returning to her father. He would use every piece of trickery he knew to get her.

"Nae. My father sent ye."

"I swear to ye, he dinna," Gavin declared.

With her back against the wall, she moved around the cave wall to put more distance between them. She stepped on something sharp, and when she jerked, the arrow released. Immediately, the wolf attacked.

The arrow brushed by Gavin's arm. The wolf threw himself at Gavin and grabbed his arm in his massive jaw.

Alana saw Thunder spring on the form, but when the pain seared through her, she cried out in unison with Gavin. Alana did not know what happened, but the instant the wolf's teeth sank into the man's arm, she felt it as if it bit her, yet she knew she had not been bitten. She fell to a sitting position and doubled over, clenching her arm in the crease of her stomach, and let out a cry.

Robbie instinctively pulled out his pistol and aimed it at the wolf as it thrashed its head back and forth with its teeth sunk into Gavin's arm.

"Nae!" Gavin yelled. "Dinna shoot it, Robbie! Alana, call the wolf off!"

His voice made her feel something inside, contrary to how she felt. She was so confused. She did not know what to do. The pain in her arm and head made it hard for her to think. Certainly, if they were sent by her father, they would have shot Thunder and carried her off.

Robbie called to her with the pistol still pointed at the wolf with Gavin's arm in its mouth. "Alana. Call it off now, or I'll shoot it!" he ordered.

His voice jolted something in her. It yelled, which frightened her, but it was also familiar.

"Now!" he ordered.

"Thunder. Nae! Let him go!" she cried. "Let him be!"

The wolf loosened its jaw and stopped thrashing but did not release.

"Thunder, come here, boy! Leave him be! Come here," she called, still doubled over, but the pain seemed to ease as the wolf stopped thrashing around and loosened its grip.

The wolf let go and ran over to Alana, turned around, and continued to growl from her side. The pain in Alana's arm lessened considerably once the wolf let go of Gavin. She had never experienced anything like it before. Her insides shook. She rocked herself back and forth, rubbing her arm.

Robbie immediately put his pistol in his belt and knelt beside Gavin. "Are ye alright?" he asked, quickly removing his neckerchief.

Robbie's voice was more familiar now that he was not yelling. Alana was so confused. Where had she heard it before?

***

Gavin crouched down, holding his arm at his stomach, but his eyes were on Alana's silhouette as she rocked back and forth. He knew she felt the pain of the wolf biting him just as he had felt every one of her injuries. He also knew she had no idea why she had just experienced it.

"Give me yer arm," Robbie ordered.

Gavin slowly held out his arm. It was too dark to see the damage, but he could feel the warm blood dripping down.

"Put some wood on the fire so I can see," Robbie called over his shoulder to Alana as he wrapped his neckerchief around Gavin's arm, not bothering to pull up his shirt sleeve. He pulled it tight to stop the bleeding.

Alana did not move from her spot crouched on the

ground other than to swing one arm over the wolf, the other still in the folds of her stomach.

Robbie got up and looked around. There was enough light to see a stack of wood. He stepped slowly toward the wood. The wolf's growl intensified.

He stopped. "Please, Alana. Put some wood on the fire." He did not dare pick up an object that might threaten the wolf more than it already was.

Alana talked to the wolf. "Stay," she said, petting its head and getting up. "Stay."

Thunder looked at her, then at Robbie, again growling. Robbie backed away as Alana moved closer to the wood pile.

She turned her back to them and picked up her dirk with one hand and small sticks with the other. Her arm eased to a dull pain as she concentrated on her task.

She walked back to the pit, placed the sticks on the fire, and knelt, blowing on the flame. Her head pounded, but she ignored it. The wolf moved protectively toward her, never taking its eyes off Robbie.

Once the sticks caught, she stroked the wolf's head. "Get me another stick," she said. She did not want them to see her groping around, letting on that she could not see well. Though they had not killed Thunder, she did not trust them.

"Go get a log, Thunder."

Gavin's eyes lit up when he heard her wolf's name. Thunder was his horse's name in their previous life.

The wolf walked over to the pile, continuously looking at Robbie and growling. He got a stick and brought it back to Alana. She took it and placed it on the small fire.

"Another one. Go get me another stick." She blew

again on the flames until the wood caught. It warmed the cave immediately and illuminated the room...but everything was still a blur to her.

She grabbed the wood Thunder dropped in front of her and placed it on the fire as well. The wolf stood guard over Alana, facing Robbie and Gavin while she attended the blaze. His growl had softened, but he did not let down his guard. Alana scooted back to sit with her back against the wall. The wolf turned and followed before turning around to face the others, standing protectively over her, watching Robbie back up to sit beside Gavin.

"Sit down," Alana softly ordered the wolf, pushing on its backside as if she could force it down. "Sit." The wolf finally sat but did not relax.

"Give me yer arm," Robbie ordered Gavin. His eyes bounced between the wolf and Gavin.

Gavin slowly held out his arm, and Robbie unwrapped it. He pulled back the torn sleeve to reveal the deep gashes in his arm. They were bleeding freely but not sputtering blood.

"Ye're lucky." Robbie said, shaking his head and wiping away the blood, just to be replaced by more. He wrapped it again and tied it tight. "How do ye feel?"

***

She knew that voice, but from where? She squinted her eyes to see better but could not get him in focus. She raked her mind, trying to remember where she heard it. Friends of Andrew, they had said. She thought back. He had no friends that came over as a youth. They had not dared bring anyone over for fear of her father's reaction.

Perhaps it was someone in the Watch. He visited once with another soldier, but she did not remember his voice. This man's voice was more familiar than someone she had known for two days. He was not one of the soldiers.

"I'll be fine," Gavin said as he slowly fisted and unfisted his hand on his injured arm.

She could see enough to make out him fisting his hand. As he did, she felt the dull pain in her arm pulsating. She massaged her arm until the pain went away. Why did she feel the pain he was feeling?

"Ye're friends of Andrew?" she asked softly, stroking the wolf's back. "Are ye in the Watch with him?"

"Nae. My name is Robbie Duncan. I am Laird of the Duncan clan, and this here is Gavin Robertson."

Robbie Duncan. Not only did his voice sound familiar, but the name as well. How did she know him?

"We came across yer brother a few days ago." Robbie continued. "He was injured, lass."

"Injured? Is he all right?" Immediately, she dreaded the answer. If he died, she had no one. She stroked the wolf. *Please, God, let him be okay.*

"Several of the Watch deserted when rumors spread that they were being shipped to the West Indies. Most were captured during an ambush, but yer brother escaped, though injured. His injuries were," he paused. She immediately shook her head at the pause. "Serious," Robbie finished.

She stared at him. *Nae!* A knot formed in her stomach, and she thought she might throw up.

"He passed away yester-eve at yer home."

She had missed him by a couple of days. Her chest filled with heartache. She turned her head away, trying to keep the tears at bay, but it was useless. They rolled down her face. She hugged Thunder, turning her face into his fur. Thunder turned his head to her, sniffing her hair. He was in tune with her feelings.

"I am sorry, lass," Robbie said sincerely.

"We want to help ye," Gavin said.

She sniffled, wiped her eyes, and raised her head. Gavin sounded younger than the other. She did not recognize his voice, but something about him, his voice, or his tone, comforted her. She did not understand why but assumed the words had given her hope. She knew better than to trust them.

Once, when she was much younger, she went to the village to trade some eggs for flour for her mother. She had a bruise on her cheek from where her father had slapped her the day before. The storekeeper asked what happened to her face. When she said her father had slapped her, the man looked down sternly at her and said she should not anger her father. She left, embarrassed that the man had thought she was a disobedient child. From that point on, if anyone asked her about any injury, she lied and said she tripped and fell.

"I dinna need any help," she spat as her arm pulled the wolf in closer again. She put her face into the animal's side to wipe her tears.

"Alana," Robbie started, "Yer father has a search out for the wolf. He has offered a reward to the person who can return it to him."

She froze as the words sunk in. "A reward," she repeated. She knew that her father would hunt for the wolf or hire someone. She figured he would have to decide between the wolf or the whisky when his coin dwindled low. A reward meant several people were looking and would not stop until Thunder was dead. "What is the reward?"

"Yer inheritance, lass."

She grunted a laugh. "I dinna care about my inheritance. I willna leave him." She continued to stroke the wolf.

"Alana," Gavin said softly. "It's more than yer inheritance. He plans on marrying ye to the person who kills the wolf."

She stopped stoking the wolf and shook her head but ceased when the pain and dizziness increased. "Nae!"

"Ye cannot stay here," Gavin pleaded. "I swore on yer brother's deathbed that I would take ye away from here."

She stared at him even though she could not make him out. She did not trust this man. Thunder was all she had left. She could not leave him. "I willna leave Thunder."

Gavin smirked, hearing the name again. "Thunder," he repeated. Gavin's kindred spirit had a habit of naming her pets with names from previous lifetimes. As Anna, she named her horse Butterfly, her pet name in a previous life.

She could not see his smirk, but she heard the humor in his voice. She glared at him, "Is something funny about his name?"

"Nae, lass. I once had a horse named Thunder, is all."

She nodded and turned her head toward the fire, repeating, "Well, I willna leave him."

"Perhaps we can take him with us," Gavin said hopefully as he turned to look at Robbie.

"Are ye out of yer mind, Gavin? That's a wild animal. He just tried taking off yer arm!" Robbie reminded him and shook his head.

"Only because it saw us as a threat," he argued.

Alana could not believe he dared to talk back to the man, a laird at that.

"I have kids," Robbie declared.

"Ye've woods a plenty for it to roam." Gavin's tone was hopeful. Was he really trying to help her?

Robbie shook his head. He slowly started to get up and said with finality, "Nae. We need to go back and check on the horses. We will make camp down there."

Gavin looked at him, then to Alana and back. "But…"

Alana held her breath, ready for Robbie to backhand Gavin for impudence.

"We cannot leave the horses alone, and ye willna be staying in a cave with a wolf." Robbie's voice was stern.

Alana stiffened and Thunder felt her tense and gave a deep but quiet growl.

Gavin glanced over at the wolf and then back to Robbie, who looked at him with a *see what I mean* look.

Gavin took a deep breath and slowly stood. "Aye."

Alana looked at him, then at Robbie, still waiting for Robbie to teach Gavin a lesson for his lip. She held her breath in anticipation, but it never came. Instead, Robbie casually put his arm around Gavin's shoulder and said, "We'll be able to see anyone who would approach the cave, aye?"

"Aye," Gavin agreed before turning to Alana, fear written all over her face.

It was a show; she knew that. The man would take the lad out and beat him for his cheek, but she did not dare say anything. She just watched, frozen.

"We willna let anything happen to ye or Thunder. I promise ye," Gavin assured her.

How can he be so calm? Didn't he know he would be

taught a lesson for his backtalk?

They walked out of the cave opening, covering it up as they left.

Chapter 10

Gavin was anxious to see Alana again. He made his way up the path toward her cave. The sun had barely come out, but they wanted to leave quickly.

I finally found her. He wanted to take her away from this place and keep her safe.

Well, that was not *all* he wanted to do. He loved her. He had loved her without ever meeting her, but now he finally had a name and face to go along with this person that made him whole. He knew she did not recognize him, but it would come. He was sure the loss of her brother and the fear of someone killing her wolf was at the forefront of her mind.

Also, the cave had been dark; otherwise, he was sure she would have recognized Robbie, as he had not changed much in sixteen years, only matured.

He smiled as he climbed up to the cave. Alana would be happy that he had convinced Robbie to take the wolf. He would, however, have to travel on foot once they got to the road that would take them to the Robertson's lands. Until then, they would put the tent up in the cart where, hopefully, the wolf would ride with Alana.

Gavin removed some branches from the cave opening

and paused, expecting a growl.

"Alana," he called.

There was no response. Gavin immediately knew she was not there. He removed another branch and called again. He raked his fingers through his hair as he looked inside. It was dark, not even a glow from hot coals.

He slowly crept in, moving around the cave wall, though he knew she was not there. The happiness he felt moments earlier was now fear that she would be caught and returned to her father. He bumped into a stack of wood, then a pile of sticks. The fire pit was next. He put his hand to it. It was not even warm. He continued the rest of the way and left the cave, replacing the branches.

Gavin hurried back to camp. "She's gone!" Gavin exclaimed in a panic. Robbie had just finished readying the horses.

"Gone?"

"Aye. She must have left shortly after we made camp. The fire has been out for a while."

Robbie looked around, frowning. "Let's find her before the others do," he said, mounting his horse.

By midday, they heard a shot ring out. Though it was a distance away, Gavin immediately felt Alana's anguish, and he realized that her precious Thunder had been shot. They stopped. Robbie pointed in the direction of the shot, "Over there."

They changed directions just as another shot was fired.

***

Alana was tired, and her head spun. She walked most of the night and half the day, only stopping for an hour to rest, if you could call it rest. She snuggled up against Thunder, holding him tight, and cried. Her head pained her more when she lay down, but with her eyes closed, the dizziness went away. The crying made her head worse, which made her cry more.

She could not believe Andrew was dead. He was the only person who was ever nice to her other than her mother. She always dreamed Andrew would return a strong warrior who would save her from her father's wrath. Her father would raise his hand to strike her, and Andrew would step between them, catching his arm and telling her father he could not hit her anymore. Oh, she knew her father would be infuriated. He would punch Andrew with his free hand, but it would not phase Andrew, being so strong. She knew her dad would not be deterred that quickly, forcing her brother to punch her father, putting him in his place. From then on, her father would realize he had to be kind to her.

Alana always knew it was a fanciful dream, but she wanted the abuse to end. She missed Andrew, and now she would never see him again. No one would rescue her.

She thought of the two men who found her and her cave. Gavin said he wanted to help her, but could she trust him? He said he promised Andrew to take her away from there. He did not say he swore to protect her, though. What good would taking her from there do her if they mistreated her elsewhere?

She knew Laird Duncan would never allow Thunder to go with them. And what was it about that name... Duncan? Why was it so familiar? And his voice! The familiarity of his name and voice made her ponder half the night, but not as much as she thought about the feeling she had when Gavin spoke. His words washed over her like her mother's kisses on the top of her head as she stroked her back. Thinking about being in her mother's arms was always what comforted her when she was in her worst despair.

That was not the strangest thing about Gavin, though. The pain that seared through her arm when Thunder bit him was. The pain was almost too much for her. And then he ordered Laird Duncan not to shoot Thunder. It did not seem possible. The whole scene scared her more than she had ever been in her entire life. That is why she had to leave. Besides, Laird Duncan would never let her take Thunder, and she would not leave him.

Gavin tried to convince him. She could not believe Laird Duncan did not slap Gavin for his backtalk. Perhaps he was afraid of Thunder, and it was no more than that.

She had the impression Gavin truly wanted to help her. The feeling she had when he talked pulled at her, making her want to believe him, but he was careless in his words with the laird. How could he protect her if his words got him beat for contradicting authority?

It was for the best that she left. She would go further into the woods, somewhere nobody would find her. That was why she left shortly after Gavin and Laird Duncan left her cave.

Unfortunately, her travels were sluggish through the night. Her poor vision hampered her progress. As unclear as it was during the daylight, at least she could still make out objects, allowing her to move between the trees faster.

Her head still hurt where it hit the side of the house, but she trudged on. At least she was getting used to the blurriness. If something were close, she could get it into focus by squinting.

She stopped at a stream to drink but did not linger. As

she got up to move on, she was startled by a gunshot, and Thunder let out a yelp and collapsed.

Her heart jolted. She fell to the ground, groping for the wolf, using its whine to guide her. No! Not Thunder. God, no! Thunder tried to get up but stopped when she reached him.

"Nae!" she screamed, running her hand down the length of its body as she buried her face in its neck. Tears streamed down her face. Her hand brushed across his back thigh, and she felt his thick fur laced with warm blood. "Oh, Thunder." This could not be happening!

A hand grabbed her from behind and pulled her off of the wolf as she screamed. The wolf bared its teeth, trying to rise as she was yanked away. Her hands lashed out, and she swung around, trying to claw at the man.

The man behind her extended his other hand from around her, aimed his pistol, and shot the wolf in his head.

"Nae!" she screamed, pulling out of the man's grip. She fell to her knees. No! Not Thunder. God, this cannot be happening. "Nae, nae, nae!" She wrapped her arms around Thunder, pulling his limp body into her arms.

"Well, well. What do we have here?" another man said as he approached them.

"Ha, ha!" a third man chuckled. "Donald dinna say ye would receive yer reward as soon as ye killed the wolf."

It was the tanner's son. She had recognized his voice. He was a couple of years older than Andrew.

The man who shot the wolf grabbed her, pulling her to her feet.

"Aye," he said. "It's Alana." Alana recognized his voice, too. He was often in the tavern when she would fetch whisky for her father. He carried the barrel out several times and put it in the small cart she pulled. He was always the loudest one in the tavern, constantly arguing with someone.

She struggled to get loose.

"Cease yer thrashing, wench!" he yelled as he shook her. Her head snapped back, making the pain almost too much to bear.

"A feisty one," the first man laughed. "Do ye think ye'll need help with that one?"

She stopped struggling, only to stop him from shaking her. She wiped her eyes before glaring at the man. Not that she could see him clearly, but he did not know that. Everything was spinning, and she thought she might be sick.

"That's a good lass," the man holding her said as he walked her over to a large stone and sat her down. "Now sit here nicely while I tend to my kill. Yer dad will be mighty pleased."

A panic tore through her with the mention of her father. He would beat her to a pulp.

As soon as he turned and headed for Thunder's limp body, she got up and ran into the woods, grabbing her dirk from beneath her belt. She had to get away. She could not face her father.

"Ah!" the two men laughed, not bothering to give chase. "There goes yer reward, Henry," yelled the tanner's son.

Henry looked up and saw her running away. "Damn ye, lass!" Henry yelled, stomping toward her, his long strides closing the distance quickly. He came up beside her, grabbing her by the arm. As he turned her around, she slashed the knife toward him.

He grabbed her other arm by the wrist, but not before

the blade sliced him in the side. It was not deep, but she felt it hit flesh.

"Ye bitch!" he yelled. His grip tightened to the point that it pained her, and she dropped the knife. He bent down to pick it up, keeping his other hand on her arm. He placed the blade in his belt and then pulled her along.

The other two men had not moved but laughed at the display.

He threw them a look. "Get me a piece of rope to tie this bitch's hands together," he ordered as he plopped her back down on the same large stone as before, not easing his grip.

The tanner's son brought over a piece of rope.

"Tie her," Henry ordered.

She was trapped. They were taking her back to her father.

The man chuckled as he bound her hands.

"Can ye manage her while I tend to my kill, or do I have to tie her to a tree?" Henry asked.

The third man called, "Ye better learn how to control her sooner rather than later!"

Henry glared at the man, grabbing her arm, half dragging her to a tree. "I see I canna depend on ye." He loosened his belt and strapped her to the tree. "I'll have the last laugh when I'm sitting pretty on that nice piece of property and yer still living at home with yer folks," Henry continued.

The other two men joked about the different methods of taming Alana as Henry tied Thunder up and secured him to his horse.

She closed her eyes, trying to shut out the sound of their words. She couldn't believe he killed Thunder. She wanted to rip Henry's heart out. She wished she was dead.

***

They traveled until dusk and set up camp. The ride had made Alana nauseous. She could not decide if it was riding on a horse with her blurred vision or the fact that the man behind her killed her precious Thunder. She could not go back to her father. Twice, Alana tried to fling herself off the horse, but Henry gripped her tighter. She no longer cared to escape but hoped the horse would trample her to death.

Henry again tied her in a sitting position against a tree but away from the campfire. The night was cold, and she was chilled to the bone, but that was nothing compared to the pain in her heart. She hoped it would turn colder, and she would freeze to death.

Their boisterous voices as they ate rang through the night. She tried to concentrate on breaking loose but had little success. The thought of Thunder made the bile rise to her throat. She could not stop crying, which made her head worse.

After a couple of hours, Henry got up. "Well, men, I think I'll go sample me reward." The other two laughed, calling out a few suggestions.

She had given up trying to get loose but began again with renewed interest. She pulled at her hands, but the ropes dug into her already raw wrists.

He pulled out a dirk and cut the rope holding her to the tree before tossing the knife and pulling her to the ground. Her head hit the ground, and excruciating pain shot through it. Her hands were still bound, but she jerked one way and then the other, trying to kick him as he forced her legs apart.

He bent his leg, laying his knee on one of her legs, and grabbed her shoulders, forcing her down. She screamed. Letting go with one hand, he reached down to pull up her dress and his kilt.

She screamed again. Henry grabbed her jaw with one hand and bent to cover her mouth with his, silencing her cries. All of a sudden, he dropped onto her as dead weight.

Robbie grabbed the now knocked-out man and rolled him off of her as Gavin picked her up.

"Alana," Galvin whispered as he quickly scurried off to where they had hid their horses.

Confusion muffled her brain. What happened? Gavin put her down. She just sank to the ground, putting her face in her tied hands, and cried. Her whole body shook. She did not understand; it had happened so fast. Had she been knocked out and just came to? Was it all a bad dream?

Pulling out his dirk, he knelt, reached for her hands, and cut the binding. "It'll be all right, Alana. We're getting ye out of here," he whispered as he brushed a stray hair from her face.

She shook her head as a moan escaped her lips.

She could not believe this man came for her. He said he promised he would take her away, but to where? Why should she think that place would be any better? His voice washed over her like a cool breeze on a hot day. It made her feel safe, but she could not believe he would keep her safe, could she? No. She needed to get up and run, but her head ached too much, besides the fact that she could hardly see. They would catch her. She knew she could not outrun them.

Robbie swept her up before she had time to act and jerked his head to Gavin's horse. Gavin immediately mounted. He held his hands down as Robbie helped the girl up. Gavin cradled her in his arms and put his horse in motion, not waiting for Robbie.

Chapter 11

They rode through the night without stopping. Alana's whole body shook as the tears rolled down her face. Gavin whispered soothing words to her the entire time they rode. She heard them, but they were distant. Her heart ached. She wanted to give in to the reassuring words he whispered, but she could not. Her brother and Thunder were dead.

"Shh, Alana. Ye're safe now," Gavin whispered.

They stopped at a steam shortly after the sun rose. Robbie dismounted and held his arms up to grab her so Gavin could dismount. All comfort was gone as soon as Gavin relinquished her to Laird Duncan. Robbie walked her over to the stream, bent down to one side, and placed her feet on the ground. She was so weary she could not stand. She slipped down to the ground to sit.

Robbie squatted before her, softly putting her chin between his index finger and thumb. Gavin came to stand beside him as he turned her head one way and then the other to look her over. She stared at his chest in a stupor.

One side of her face had bruises from Henry's fingers and the other from his thumb. There were streaks down her face from tears mixed with dirt and blood. Her hand and dress had dried blood on it.

She was completely numb. She looked at this man as he studied her but did not see him. She could have squinted and seen his features more clearly, but she no longer cared. Her brother and Thunder were the only two things in the world she had trusted. They were gone, and she did not want to live anymore.

"Leave me be," she whispered.

Gavin knelt beside Robbie and gently touched her hand. His hands were warm on her icy fingers. "Alana, come to the stream and drink," he urged, gently tugging her hand.

She shook her head and turned her face away, jerking her hand out of his.

Robbie got up and nudged Gavin. They walked to the stream where the horses were now drinking. Robbie grabbed his flask and began to fill it.

"I kenned I should have stayed in the cave," Gavin whispered, but she heard.

"I wasna going to leave ye in a cave with a wolf," Robbie snapped quietly.

"Aye, but –"

"Nae!" Robbie said louder as he swiped his finger in the air and pointed behind them. "Ye canna believe ye would have actually been safe there."

The louder Robbie's voice raised, the tenser Alana got. She was sure Robbie would teach Gavin a lesson. She was so worried about him. She did not know why. She supposed it was because of his soothing words throughout the ride. She feared Robbie would beat him. Her eyes grew big, and terror washed over her. She tried to scoot back but could not move.

Gavin's head snapped her way.

"Ye'll naw make me –"

Gavin looked back at Robbie and raised his hand to signal him to stop. "Robbie!" Gavin only ever called him by his given name when something was important. His eyes were big, and he tipped his head toward Alana.

Robbie looked at Alana. All the color drained from her face. They walked over, and Robbie laid the flask against her leg. She tried to move away from them again, but she was shaking too badly.

"Drink," Robbie ordered, then gently grabbed Gavin's arm so he would walk with him back to the stream.

"Nae!" she yelled, her eyes focused on the hand he had placed on Gavin's arm. *What was he going to do to him? How bad would he beat him? Would he beat me after?*

"Robbie, let go," Gavin whispered.

Robbie immediately let him go. They stood momentarily looking at her, but she was lost in a daze. Robbie flicked his head toward the stream, and they both walked away to distance themselves.

She was sure she saw Robbie grab him. It had been blurry, but he definitely raised his arm. She sat there and watched them walk. She looked around, debating if she should run, but there was something about Gavin. As leery as she was of others, something about his touch comforted her. She did not know why.

"Are ye sure she is the one ye seek?" Robbie asked quietly. "She doesna recognize me and doesna seem to be comforted by ye either."

"Aye," Gavin said. "It's her. She's been mistreated, Milord. She's scared."

Robbie looked back at the girl. She was staring at them

in horror. He turned to Gavin and said, "Let's move on."

***

They arrived at the road by late afternoon. Robbie turned to Gavin and said, "Ye stay hidden. I'll go back and get the cart."

He dismounted, holding his hands out to take Alana, who slept in Gavin's arms. The sudden shift in handing her over woke her. She started to squirm to get loose.

"Be still, lass, less I drop ye," Robbie said.

He placed her down on the ground, not bothering to place her on her feet again, as each time they stopped, she let herself drop to the ground. He was starting to wonder if her legs pained her.

"Stay hidden," he ordered Gavin as he grabbed the reins of his horse and walked down the road a bit. He dragged out a fallen branch part of the way, but not so far that it would block a cart's path.

He mounted and kicked his horse into a canter.

***

Robbie walked into the tavern, and the room got quiet.

He nodded to the men at the table, then approached the man behind the counter. "Good evening," he said.

"Any luck finding the wolf?" the man asked.

"Nae. I heard shots, though, so I'm thinking someone got it," Robbie replied.

"What can I get for ye?" the man asked.

"I'll have a whisky." As the man poured him a glass, Robbie asked. "How much do I owe ye for storing my cart and horse?"

"Yer naw staying the night?"

"Nae," Robbie replied. "I've been gone longer than I had expected already."

The man rambled off an amount as he handed Robbie his whisky. "Where's yer man?" he asked.

"His horse was starting to limp, so I left him by the road to rest it," Robbie lied.

The man nodded. Robbie dug into his purse and laid some coins on the counter for his horse and cart's keep, the whisky, and provisions.

"Thank ye, sir," he said before making his way to the stables.

***

Gavin tried to talk to Alana, but she mainly shrugged or gave short-clipped answers. Eventually, she rolled over and feigned sleep.

Gavin sat beside her, so his legs lay against her back. He rubbed his hand up and down her arm. The feeling of Gavin trying to soothe her made Alana think of her brother, which made her cry. Andrew was the only person since her mother's death who ever tried to comfort her.

It felt so good to have Gavin comforting her, but she was scared to trust him. He may be gentle now, but he would change. Why should he care about her anyhow? Perhaps he just wanted her father's land? She did not care about it. She did not care about anything. If she had her dagger, she would end her life now.

***

It was nearly dark when Robbie came to his marked spot. He signaled Gavin with a bird call and immediately received one back.

Gavin came out, holding the reins with Alana atop the horse. He brought the horse to the cart and hopped into it before stretching his arms to Alana. "Come on into the cart," he told her.

She could not see a thing, but Gavin softly tugged her hand before putting his hands in her armpits, lifting her. She did not make an effort to help, letting him place her in the cart.

As soon as her feet touched the flat of the cart, she went limp, but Gavin held her firmly and guided her to a lying position.

Robbie tossed them a loaf of bread and some cheese that he had acquired, and said to Gavin, "Rest for a bit after ye've eaten." He tethered the horse to the back of the cart. "I'll wake ye in a few hours, and ye can take over."

"Aye," Gavin said as he ripped off a piece of bread and placed it into Alana's hand.

She did not want to eat. She wanted him to go away. She knew he was only being kind to her because he promised Andrew. She didn't care about his promise. He couldn't replace him.

"Eat something," Gavin said.

She took a bite just to shut him up.

Chapter 12

Alana pretended to sleep for most of the ride.

They traveled through the night and most of the next day, taking turns resting. Robbie had told Gavin he was anxious to get off the road in case someone came looking for Alana. The fact that he had left at such an odd hour for traveling would point them to him as the person who took her.

Her father would look for her. She had no doubt. What would happen if he found her? She did not want to think about it, but it kept going around in her mind.

The jostling of the cart made her head bang around, making it feel like it would split open. She sat up a few times, hoping it would ease the pain, but watching the blurry landscape going by made her dizzy. She would lie down and cry in hopes that sleep would finally come. Would her head and vision ever get better?

Gavin rode his horse. At one point, he pulled up next to her when she was sitting up. "How are ye feeling, Alana?"

She looked at him as she brushed a stray hair away from her face but said nothing. Why was he being so kind to her? What did he want from her?

"Everything will work out, ye'll see,"

She turned her head and continued to look behind them. His reassurance gave her a dash of hope, but she disregarded it just as quickly. What did he know anyhow? She had lost everything she had ever loved. The only comfort was that they had traveled farther than she had ever been. Perhaps her father and Henry would not find her. But she did not dare to hope for that either. No doubt, her father would revoke the giving of his land if she disappeared. Perhaps he would say it was the wrong wolf.

And what if they did not find her? What then? A woman's lot was a hard one. She had seen her mother beaten enough during her father's rages. No, she was better off alone in the woods but could not even see enough to find her own food. She had lost her bow and dirk with her struggle with Henry. She did not care. She would rather starve to death than be forced into a marriage.

She laid back down and fell asleep.

***

Alana woke as they stopped in the middle of a town. She peeked out from under the blanket wrapped around her. What were they going to do with her?

"James," Gavin called.

Alana clenched the blanket in fear. Who was James?

"Christy told us ye'd be back," James said as he locked the store door. Alana stayed hidden with the plaid covering her. She did not dare move. "I'll tell Mom that ye'll be eating with us," he continued as he walked toward the house behind the store.

"Set an extra plate. There'll be two of us," Gavin called out.

James turned to look at Robbie, who was not paying him heed. Robbie never ate with them because he always stayed with Christy's family. They had a much larger house and a barn big enough to store the horses.

"Alright," James said as he turned back toward the house.

Gavin walked to the side of the cart. "Alana, come on. It's time to get down," he said as he slowly peeled back the plaid that covered her head. He smiled down at her. "It'll be all right. It's just my family."

His family! She sat up as she contemplated her options. She could run once she got down. Nae, she would stumble on a cobblestone. She could refuse, but she would most likely get beaten for that. She surrendered to the only option she felt she had. Scooting to the side of the cart, she placed a hand firmly on the edge and got up enough to swing her leg over the edge, but she lost her balance and fell over. Gavin caught her, placing her securely on her feet.

She looked around, not noticing that he had put his arm out for her to hold. When she did not take it, he turned to her, gently took her hand, and placed it on his arm.

"'Tis only my family," he repeated.

He walked her across the cobblestone road. Her legs were unsteady. As he brought her onto the porch, she completely missed the single step up and tripped up onto the porch. He caught her again.

"Easy, Alana," he said. "Are ye alright?"

Her heart was beating so hard, and she was on the verge of tears. She nodded her head in answer.

Gavin's mother came out the door, "Gavin!" she said in a honeyed voice as she hugged and kissed him.

With Alana's blurred vision, she could not make her

out other than she stood the same height as Gavin and her hair appeared to be dark as it bounced.

"Hi, Mom."

She turned to Alana and asked, "And who do we have here?"

Alana wanted to turn and hide. She knew she looked terrible. She had the same dress she had worn for two years, alternating it with only one other. It was dirty, bloody, torn, and too small. Her hair had not been combed since she left home. It flowed past her waist. She knew she had scars on her cheeks, and that was just the beginning.

"This is Alana, Mom. We found her in…er…some distress."

Alana felt the heat rise to her cheek. She looked down at the ground.

"Well, welcome, Alana," Gavin's mother said. "Won't ye come in?"

"Thank ye," she mumbled quietly.

Gavin walked through the door with Alana's hand still on his arm. She tripped as she crossed the threshold and bumped into the door frame before Gavin caught her.

"Watch yer step," he said.

Her hand started shaking. She nodded, still looking down. They stopped once inside, and Gavin introduced her to his family.

"Please have a seat, dear," his mother said.

Gavin walked her to a chair, which she fingered before firmly grabbing it and sat down.

"Thank ye," she said again shyly.

"What happened to yer arm?" Gavin's mother asked.

Alana tensed.

"Ugh, I got bit by a dog. 'Tisna bad," he replied.

Alana looked down at her hands, half embarrassed, half trying not to cry at the thought of Thunder dead.

Gavin put his hand on her arm from behind and stroked it.

Was he trying to comfort her after her wolf almost ripped his arm off? She could not believe it, though she had to admit that his touch did calm her.

"Supper will be a while," his mother said. "It looks like ye've had a long journey. I will have the boys prepare a nice warm bath for Alana, and then I will tend to yer arm." She turned toward the others and said, "Gideon, John, go get more wood for the fire. Katherine, see if ye have something clean for Alana to wear."

Alana was embarrassed. She knew she was blushing. The tears stung her eyes as Katherine went upstairs and the boys outside.

"Now, dear, it's nothing to worry yerself with. We'll see to whatever ye need."

Alana was grateful when Gavin made casual conversation. She felt he purposefully did it to take the attention off her. Why was he so kind to her?

"I hadna planned on seeing ye until Gideon's wedding. How goes the plans for it?" he asked his mother.

She answered as the two boys pushed open the door, letting it slam against the wall. Alana jumped out of her seat and turned toward the door, half expecting her father to storm in.

"Ye should've been a girl," Gideon teased John. "Little Mary can carry more wood than ye."

John dropped the wood at the hearth, making her jolt again. John shoved Gideon, who was much larger than him. Alana's eyes got huge over the confrontation. She was sure the older one would whack him a good one. Gideon laughed at his younger brother.

"Enough!" their father yelled. Alana immediately fell back into the chair, raising her arm above her head expecting something to come flying across the room like her father did when he yelled. They all looked at her, but she did not see it. Lowering his voice, their father said, "We have a guest. Mind yer manners."

They looked at their father, but their eyes wandered back to look at Alana before settling back on him. "Aye, sir," they replied.

"John put this pot of water on the fire, and Gideon, carry this one up to yer sisters' room to heat. Then bring the tub into their room as well," their mother ordered, trying to get everyone's focus off Alana.

Gavin sat beside Alana, so their arms touched. She knew it was him. There was something about his touch. It warmed her. He continued his small talk with his parents.

She lowered her arm but still shook as she looked around the room. She could make out one area as a kitchen, and they sat in a dining area the size of her father's entire one-room house. Opposite from the kitchen appeared to be a couple of chairs by a hearth.

The bedrooms, she supposed, were all upstairs. She had never been in a house so big. There were two-story houses in Grantown, but she had never been inside them.

"I've placed the tub in the girl's room," Gideon announced, slowly descending the stairs.

"I'll take the water upstairs," Gavin said as he gently patted Alana on the shoulder. "I'll show ye the room."

Worried she might misstep, she followed directly behind him to the hearth, then to the stairs. As he started up the stairs, she bumped into the banister before grabbing it and ascending the steps, tripping at the top.

"Careful," he said, turning just long enough to see she did not fall.

She held her hand out, touching the wall as she walked along the hallway, allowing her to find the doorway as she followed Gavin in.

A large bed sat in the corner with a chest on both sides of the room.

"I put two dresses on the bed," Katherine said. "I wasna sure which one will fit ye."

"Thank ye," Alana replied shyly.

Gavin poured the water from his bucket into the round wooden tub then did the same with the one heating in the room. "Come downstairs when ye are done."

She nodded as Kathrine and Gavin left, closing the door behind.

She could not remember the last time she had a warm bath, perhaps several years ago. It was before her mother died. She did not have any privacy after that to do so. Her father eventually put the barrel outside and had her fill it with water for the horse and goat.

She placed one hand on the tub and ran her fingers along the edge as she dipped her other hand in the warm water. She could not stop the tears from coming.

She quickly removed her clothes, letting them drop to the floor, and stepped into the tub, firmly gripping the edge. She let out a deep sigh and sat. The warm water felt like heaven. She splashed some on her face, wiping the tears away.

She glanced over the tub in hopes of finding soap. There was what appeared to be a cup. She reached for it and bought it up. The soap inside slid on the bottom, clicking against the wooden cup. She grabbed the soap with her wet hand, and it slipped through it, splashing into the water.

She dropped the cup into the water and searched for the soap with her hands. Once caught, she brought it up to her nose and smelled it. Flowers! She rubbed it in her hands, closed her eyes, and lathered her face before rinsing it.

Grabbing the cup, she poured water on her long hair before searching again for the soap and lathering her hair up. She could not remember the last time she felt so clean.

Once the water started to chill, she stood, holding the tub firmly and stepping out. She looked around in hopes of finding a towel. There were two piles: the towel, and her dirty clothes, but she could not make out which was which. She squinted to see them better. Certainly, if her sight were going to get better, it would have been by now. The tears started to flow again as she looked between the two piles.

A soft knock came on the door, and it opened a crack. "Alana," Gavin's mother said as she peeked in, seeing Alana bent over, squinting at the two piles, trying to bring them in focus. Gavin's mother caught sight of Alana's back, which had several scar marks across it. Gavin had told his parents how they had found her.

She walked in, closed the door behind her, and picked up the towel as Alana reached for the dirty dress. She opened it and laid it on her back, wrapping it around so she could grab the front of it.

Alana took it in her hands and wiped the tears rolling down her cheeks with the end of the towel before crossing it over the front of her.

"Come. Sit on the bed, and I will help ye with yer dress," Gavin's mother said, putting one hand on Alana's shoulder and moving the two dresses with the other.

Once Alana was seated, Gavin's mother picked up one of the dresses and silently helped her put it on. She gently pulled Alana's light brown hair outside the dress. "Would ye like me to brush yer hair, or would ye like to do it?" she asked.

Silent tears ran down her cheeks as she put her hand out and whispered, "I'll do it."

She placed the brush in Alana's hand and turned to leave. "I will come up when supper is ready."

Alana only nodded to her. Once the door was closed, she buried her face in her hands and wept freely. She was so humiliated. She could not even dress herself.

She did not cry for long. She did not want her to return, and her hair not be combed. She did her best to comb the knots out, then braided her hair to hide any remaining.

As she put her hands on the bed to scoot herself back to rest against the wall, her hand brushed against something. She grabbed it, bringing it in front of her face. It was a mirror. Her mother once had a looking glass, smaller than the one she held, but it had been broken when her father had thrown it across the room.

She moved the mirror to her face and squinted her eyes to bring herself in focus. She could not see her whole face at once, but she could partly see her features. Her green eyes were swollen and red from crying. She had an old scar beside her right eye, one above her left eye, and another left of her mouth. There were bruises on her cheek and jaw from when Henry grabbed her, but they were fading.

She watched as the tears rolled down her cheeks.

***

Gavin's mother came down the stairs, white as a ghost. She gestured to Gavin to join her in the kitchen. She shooed the girls out and quietly asked him, "Do ye ken she has trouble seeing?"

He shook his head. No wonder she never came to him when he offered his stretched-out arm to help. He thought she was just distraught since every time he placed her on the ground, she went limp. The only time he saw her walk was from the cart to the house and she did trip several times.

"Aye. I peeked in, and she was squinting, trying to see the towel from her discarded dress," she said. She swallowed hard before continuing, "She has marks on her back as if she had been beaten with a belt."

It did not surprise him. He felt every lash she received, but his mother would think he was crazy if he said so.

"I left her brushing her hair. I'll get her in a couple of minutes."

"No," Gavin said. "I'll get her."

***

Gavin opened the door a crack and looked in. He saw Alana looking into the mirror so close one would not be able to see their whole face in it. Her fingers brushed over a scar, then the bruises on her face. Tears rolled down her cheeks. She had braided her hair, but several strands were astray.

No wonder she did not recognize Robbie.

Gavin wanted to run up to her, fold her in his embrace, and tell her everything would be all right, but he knew it would frighten her. He needed to give her time, time to remember.

Secondly, he could not be sure everything would be all right. They had never managed to stay together before. They thought they had succeeded in overcoming their fate in their last lifetime, but they had been mistaken. He needed to find a way to end this curse.

He knocked on the door. "Alana, I've come to see ye down to dinner," he called to her softly.

She quickly placed the mirror down and used her sleeves to wipe away the tears. "Come in," she replied and stood.

He walked over to her and placed her hand in the nook of his arm. "I'm sure ye're as hungry as I."

"Aye," she mumbled, letting him lead her out the door.

***

She was starving, but the fear of eating with so many people made her prefer to forgo dinner. She was shaking because of it.

Gavin paused at the top of the steps, placing his hand on the one that held his arm. "Are ye ready to go downstairs?"

She looked at him, but it was blurred. "Aye," she said, putting her arm out to the wall but finding the rail instead. They descended the stairs slowly.

When they came to the floor, he pulled back slightly and paused. "Ah, here we are," he said softly.

The whiff of fresh bread hit her and made her mouth water. She had not had fresh bread in a very long time.

He walked her over to the table and pulled out a chair for her. She held onto the table and felt for the chair before sitting. Gavin took the chair beside her. They all waited quietly until their father took a loaf of bread and ripped a piece off.

Gavin grabbed the bowl in front of Alana and put in a spoonful of what would have been stew had it been later in the season. It was more meat covered with thick brown sauce than hearty vegetables. He placed it in front of her and started asking Gideon questions about his upcoming nuptials and details about where they would live.

They casually talked but all the time glancing toward Alana, who studied her food carefully as she squinted before stabbing the meat with her fork and letting her breath out when she succeeded. It was the best meal she ever had. She ignored the conversation around her. At one point, she realized she had finished her meal and set her fork down.

Gavin ripped off a piece of bread and moved it to touch the back of her hand that rested on the table. "Would ye like some bread to slop up yer sauce?" he asked. He would have given her more stew, but they all had tiny portions with the two extra mouths to feed. His mother had made two extra loaves of bread to fill them all up.

"Aye." She took the piece and wiped the bowl with the bread before bringing it to her mouth. She continued to do it past the point that the bowl was cleaned, unable to see the difference between the brown sauce and the wooden bowl.

Gavin's youngest sister, Mary, who was only five, came to sit on Gavin's lap. "Will ye take me fishing tomorrow?" she asked, glancing between Gavin and Alana.

"Ah, lass, but I am only staying one night this time," he replied, giving her his last piece of bread. She smiled and popped it into her mouth.

She glanced once again at Alana, who was using the last of her bread to slop up the gravy that was not there.

Mary turned to Gavin and asked, "Can I come with ye?"

Gavin laughed as he poured some wine into a cup. "Ye would make fine company, Mary, but I daresay that I am verra busy and wouldna be able to tend to ye."

Mary frowned with a heavy sigh and leaned back to place her cheek on Gavin's chest. Gavin placed the glass so it touched the back of Alana's hand, "Something to drink?"

Alana took the cup and gulped it down. She became frantic when she realized it was wine, coughing as it went down her throat. They used to drink wine when her mother was alive, but her father never stopped. By night's end, he would have downed several days' worth of wine in one sitting. He would start getting mean after a couple of glasses. Everyone stole a look at her. She went from calm to scared in a matter of seconds.

"Perhaps ye would prefer water?" Gavin's mother asked as she got up.

"Aye," Alana replied, placing the glass on the table and sliding it as far away as possible.

His mother returned with a glass of water and placed it in her hand.

"Thank ye," she replied shyly, taking a small sip to ensure it was water. Her shoulders relaxed as she exhaled and drank the glass down.

"Katherine and Mary, go up and get yer things for bed and bring them down here," Gavin's mother ordered.

"Aye," they both replied. Mary hopped off Gavin's lap, startling Alana before she realized it was the girl.

"We'll be leaving first thing in the morn," Gavin said. "Christy and the wee ones will be with us, and we hope to make it to Dundee by eve."

There it was again… Dundee. It sounded so familiar.

She did not know where she had heard it before. Perhaps Andrew had talked about it when he visited.

The girls returned with their sleeping gear, and Gavin's mother escorted her to their room.

Alana's mind wandered as she lay in the bed. She missed her brother and Thunder. She cried. She did not know what would become of her. Had her eyesight been fine, she would have run, but now she was at the mercy of Gavin and Robbie.

Her pain eased a bit as she thought of Gavin. He had been kind to her these past few days, but what would happen when they got to Dundee? What if she angered one of them? Would they beat her?

She tossed in the bed. It was too soft. She did not even have a bed at her father's house. Bringing the blankets with her, she chose to sleep on the floor instead.

Chapter 13

Gavin's mother woke Alana. "Gavin said ye will be leaving soon."

Alana opened her eyes and yawned. It did not appear that the sun had come out yet. "Aye," she replied. She had refused aid, changing into a sleeping gown the night before. She did not even bother with it and slept in her dress. Now, it was wrinkled, and her hair was halfway undone since she had not tied it with a ribbon.

"Come sit on the bed, and I will braid yer hair again," the woman said.

Alana dreaded sitting up, but she did so she would not upset Gavin's mother. As soon as she did, the room immediately spun.

Alana hesitated, then, using the bed to aid her, she sat down, thankful she did not topple over.

The woman loosened her hair and brushed it out, humming softly. "Yer hair is so long. It is a beautiful, soft brown color," she said, then continued humming.

Alana's mother used to braid her hair. She felt a pang in her chest when she thought of her mother, but she would not cry.

Alana sat still, afraid to move as the woman did her

hair, tying the end with a ribbon. "There ye go, it will stay nice and neat all day as ye travel," she exclaimed. "Shall we go downstairs and eat something?" She took her hand and gently tugged. Once Alana stood, she put Alana's hand on her arm and patted it as a mother would with her own child. Alana swallowed down the tears.

They walked down the stairs, and she took her to the table where Gavin was eating. Most of the household was still asleep, but little Mary sat on her brother's lap as he ate.

"Robbie will be here soon, so eat up," Gavin said as he put some porridge in a bowl for her.

They heard the cart pull up just as they finished eating. Gavin set Mary down, kissed her on the top of her head, and stood up.

"Are ye ready?" Gavin asked as he gently took Alana's hand, helping her up.

They followed his mother and Mary out the door. Robbie hopped down from the coachman's seat and greeted them.

As Robbie chatted with Gavin's mother, Alana felt a slight tug on her sleeve. She looked down at the wee girl. "I brought ye a flower for yer hair," Mary said.

Alana looked but could not see the tiny flower the lass held. Her eyes began to well up. She did not know if she wanted to cry because of the lass's kind act or because she could not see the beauty of the flower. She tried to force a smile.

"I will put it in yer hair for ye," Mary said quietly.

Alana knelt as Mary put the flower in her hair. She reached up to feel it as she straightened. "Thank ye," she whispered as a lone tear rolled down one cheek.

"Let me help ye in," Gavin said. As he lifted her, his

tone changed as if talking to a child, "Move over, wee Billy." The child was not in the way, but he wanted her to be aware that others were in the wagon.

Once settled in the cart, he introduced her to Robbie's kin. "This is Christy, Laird Duncan's sister-in-law with her bairn Sophie. And this one," he ruffled the lad's hair, "is wee Billy."

"It's nice to meet ye," Christy said.

Alana responded shyly.

Gavin untied his horse and waved Robbie out of Alana's listening distance.

"She canna see well," Gavin said. They both turned toward the cart, casting a look at her as she sat stiff as a board, looking out the side she was facing.

Robbie nodded his acknowledgment and walked toward the front of the cart. "Are ye ready?" he asked.

"Aye," Christy replied.

Billy stood up. "Aye, Uncle Wobbie!" he exclaimed.

Christy tugged on the lad's sleeve as Robbie said, "Then sit down, Billy, and we will go."

Robbie climbed onto the coachman's seat as Gavin mounted his horse and waved to his mother and sister.

Robbie set a much quicker pace than usual with the cart and young ones in the back, but he had already told Christy that he wanted to return that day. If it started to look like rain, he would stop and put the tent on the cart instead of camping. She did not question him.

They did not want to chance Henry or Alana's father catching up to them on the road. Since they had traveled through the first night, they had a head start, but they lost a day's ride to pick up Christy and the wee ones. Henry would not have left immediately from the woods. He would have taken the wolf back to claim his prize and tell Douglas news of his daughter. That would delay him a day.

Alana turned her head a bit to watch the trees receding. She could not tell if her sight was getting better or if she was just getting used to the blurriness. At least she did not feel as nauseous anymore watching the trees. It was part of the reason she had slept most of the ride.

Gavin rode behind them. She bounced between watching him and the trees. She wondered what their plans for her were. They seemed true to their word that no harm would come to her, but she did not trust that everything would be okay once they got to this *Dundee*. What if she did something to displease one of them? The more she thought about it, the more scared she got. Her panic would get so bad sometimes that she contemplated getting up and jumping out of the moving cart in hopes of getting trampled on. Each time she felt that bad, Gavin would ride up to the side of the cart where she sat and ask how she faired. An instant calmness would ease through her despair. Did he know what she was thinking?

At one point, she felt the wee lad come to rest on her lap as his mother nursed the bairn she held. Alana became very still as Billy sat on her lap and grabbed her long braid. He giggled as he stretched it across his eyes and pulled it down.

"Boo!" he exclaimed.

Alana twitched at the exclamation.

Seeing Alana's apprehension, Christy said to her son, "Billy, let go of her braid and get off her lap."

Billy slid off of Alana's lap, and she resumed looking at the trees as her thoughts bounced between worrying about what would become of her then to the deaths of her brother, which made her think of her father. Andrew would still be alive today if her father had not sent him to soldier with the Watch.

Then she thought of the wolf hunt. Thunder's death was his fault as well. She should have stayed away. Why did she ever think he would change? She felt sick to her stomach, and the tears began to build up. She closed her eyes and tipped her head back, but it banged on the side of the cart as they bounced along the uneven path, causing the pain in her head to increase.

She slumped to the side, resting her head against the rolled-up tent and curling her legs into the folds of her skirt. She let the rhythm of the horse's hooves lull her to sleep.

She woke a couple of hours later to the cart coming to a halt. Billy was sitting against her stomach with her legs curled around him. He had the end of her braid and pretended to sweep her legs.

"Hello, sirs," Robbie said as a couple of horses stopped by the cart.

She closed her eyes, pretending to be asleep, but her heart sped up. She willed the tears away, praying they would not look at her.

"Have ye seen any of the Watch during yer travels?" a Redcoat asked.

Dread washed over her. They were looking for her brother. She could feel her insides trembling.

Christy softly bounced her baby as she quietly hummed a lullaby.

"Nae, sir," Robbie said. "We only left a couple of hours ago. Ye are the first folk we've seen."

Alana could hear the horses' hooves as the men walked on either side of the cart. Billy stopped his sweeping with her braid and waved with a pudgy hand.

"Hi," he giggled as the man continued their inspection of the cart.

"Carry on," the solder said, kicking his horse into a canter. Robbie shook the reins to get the horses back in motion.

Once moving, Alana let go of the trembling she held in, and her tears spilled out. She did not open her eyes for fear she would see the pity on Christy's face, not that she could see her expression. Certainly, Robbie had told her about her brother. She knew they were looking for the Watch that had deserted. She did not want to think about it.

She finally got her tears under control. Opening her eyes, she watched as wee Billy stuffed the end of her braid in a wooden cup and pulled it out.

"Clean," he said as he showed it to his mother.

"Is it all clean?" Christy asked.

The lad nodded.

Alana squinted her eyes to see the lad better. Both of his chubby hands grabbed the cup again, and he placed it between his legs. He grabbed the end of her braid and stuffed it in the cup before pulling it out and tossing it aside.

He grabbed the wooden cup again, bringing it up to get a better look inside.

"Clean," he proclaimed again to his mother.

Alana started to feel at ease as she watched the lad. At one point, she even found herself smiling.

***

They rode nonstop, except for brief stops to water the horses and tend to their private needs. They ate their meals in the cart.

By evening, they had arrived at Christy's house. Willie came out at the sound of the wagon, which stopped at the steps of the big house.

"Dada!" the lad called out as he got up, holding on to the edge of the cart.

"Willie," Robbie called to his brother. The name said in Robbie's voice gave Alana a strange feeling, as if she had heard it that way often.

"How'd everything go in my absence?" Robbie asked.

"Good," Willie replied, picking Billy out of the cart, and kissing him. "How was yer visit, wife?" he asked Christy as Robbie and Gavin came over to help her get down. Robbie took the bairn from Christy's arms as she stood and walked over to the edge.

He put his son down and held his hands up to Christy. She put her hands on his shoulders and swung her legs over. He twirled her around once and planted a kiss on her lips as she laughed.

Billy laughed and put his hands up to his father. "Me, me!" he yelled.

Christy said goodbye to Alana and Gavin, then thanked Robbie before gathering the bairn and lad and bringing them into the house.

Robbie quickly introduced Willie to Alana but immediately started questioning him about clan affairs as the men unloaded half of the cart.

"I will come over tomorrow to discuss matters," Willie said. "Oh, and Brodie stopped by on his way to London."

"Brodie?" Robbie asked. Brodie was his best friend. When Alex was alive, the three of them did everything together. They had met when Alex and Robbie went to train under the MacKay. They soldiered together for several years.

Alana was only half listening, but when Robbie said Brodie, it was reminiscent of something. She was not sure of what. It was not necessarily the name but Robbie's voice saying the name.

"Aye," Willie replied. "He said he would stop by on his way back in hopes of seeing ye."

"It will be good to see him. Well, I'll see ye tomorrow, then. Thanks for yer help," Robbie replied, then turned toward the cart and held his hand out to Alana. "Would ye like to ride up front, Alana?"

She looked at his extended arm and paused. She was unsure how long it would be until they got to wherever they were heading, but she was still unsure of Robbie. He had not raised his voice at Gavin since the first day they found her. Could she trust him? Sitting in a seat did appeal to her after being in the cart for as long as she had been. She slowly stretched out her arm and let him help her out of the back and into the coachman's seat.

***

About an hour of light was left when the dirt path through the woods opened up to a path flanked by fields leading up to the castle. A strange feeling washed over her as the manor house came into sight. It was as if she had been here before. She squinted her eyes to get a better view but had little luck.

A dog barked in the distance before running up to the cart.

"Hello, Orion," Robbie called out as he looked down at

the dog. "Did ye keep all predators away while I was gone?"

The dog answered with two barks and ran in front as if to lead the cart to the keep.

The cart stopped in front of the house. If she thought Gavin's parents' house was large, this house was enormous.

Two children came out of the house. "Da, da! Angel is having puppies!" a wee lass called as she ran down the steps, her golden braids bounding behind her.

Robbie jumped down from the cart and crouched, bringing them both in for a hug.

Alana looked at the steps, following up to the door. She could not shake the feeling that she had been there before. She turned her attention to Robbie and the children, and sadness washed over her. She never remembered running into her father's arms. The only person she was excited to see after her mother died was Andrew. Any other comfort she had found was with Thunder, and now both were gone. She felt a lump form in her throat.

"Alana," Gavin called, turning her attention away from Robbie and his children. Gavin's arms were outstretched to help her down. She reached out to him, letting him place her firmly on the ground.

Immediately, the dog barked and ran around the cart to where she stood. She backed up until she was against the cart with her palm held out as if to tell the dog to stop.

"That's Orion," Gavin said as he bent down to scratch the dog's head, but it wanted nothing to do with him. It sniffed at her palm, but she snatched it away, putting it on her chest. The dog continued to sniff at her for a bit more before running to the other side to get attention from Robbie, who had just gotten up.

The Gift of the Healing Stones

A man came over and helped Gavin unload the cart while Robbie went up the stairs, holding his daughter's hand. The lad walked with him on the other side, and the dog squeezed between them and took the lead. They stopped at the top of the stairs to talk to someone waiting.

"Leslie, this is Alana," Gavin said before turning to Alana. "Alana, this is Leslie. He is the stable master here."

"Nice to meet ye, lass."

She timidly greeted him as he tied Gavin's horse to the cart and climbed up to the coachman's chair to bring the horses and cart to the barn.

Gavin picked up a sack and flung it over his shoulder. He offered his arm to her. When she did not notice, he took her hand and tucked it into the nook of his arm. Grabbing a basket from the ground, he brought it over, so it touched her empty hand. "Will ye carry this?"

She looked down and wrapped her hand around the handle as he bent to pick up another sack.

"Let's go inside," he said as he led her to the front steps. He paused at the bottom.

She stared at the door at the top of the steps. It was so familiar, but she had never been here. Perhaps she had dreamed of this place?

"Are ye ready to go up?"

She nodded and looked down at the steps. Gavin went slowly, and she concentrated on each one. Once at the top, he said, "Here we are." He placed the object he held on the top step and opened the door for her, guiding her in.

She stepped in and froze. Had she been there before? She was sure she recognized it. She wished she could see it clearly.

The stairs were straight ahead of her, and there were

two large doors to the left that she knew led to the great hall. How can that be? Where had she ever heard the term great hall before? She moved back toward her left and sat on a bench without looking but knew it was there... or did Gavin guide her. She shook her head.

Gavin took the basket from her hand and opened one of the big doors to the left, and a whiff of... of... fresh rushes hit her. She had never been anywhere with fresh rushes. How could she recognize the smell? The scent of herbs mixed in with the rushes... lavender. She did not know where her thoughts came from. Her heart raced. She put her hand to her head, massaging her temple. The pain in her head, which she had finally gotten used to, intensified and throbbed. She could feel the tension building inside.

Gavin came back out, closing the door into the hall.

"Are ye alright?" he asked worriedly. The color had drained from her face.

She shook her head.

"Come along. Let us go to the kitchen and grab a bite to eat," he said, grabbing her hand and pulling her up.

The kitchen! She almost knew the formal dining area was to the right, and just beyond was the kitchen.

Gavin guided her to the doors to the right and pushed them open. As she looked at the room, it started spinning just before everything went black.

Chapter 14

Alana woke to a woman calling to her. The sun had not yet come out.

"Time to get up," the woman said as she stood by the bed holding a candle to see her. "I'm sorry I dinna properly greet you last night, but I was up to my ears with puppies."

Alana sat up and swung her legs off the bed. She couldn't make out the features of the stocky woman before her, but she swore she had heard the woman's voice before. She squinted her eyes to get a better look, but the woman took a step back.

"My name is Margaret. Laird Duncan said ye are here to help me. I start early every…"

Margaret! Alana did not hear anything past her name. It was so familiar. She did not even have to see her clearly to know what she looked like. Was she going crazy?

"Well, don't just stare! Let's get moving! We've got things to do," Margaret ordered from the doorway.

Though the woman sounded familiar, the tone of her voice was nothing like Alana expected. Perhaps she sounded like someone else… another Margaret. But Alana did not know any other Margarets. She rubbed her head. She still wore her dress, so she got up and followed the woman. She tried to recall the night before. She remembered Gavin placing her on the bed and telling her to rest.

He returned later, waking her up for dinner. She refused, and not because she was not hungry, but because she did not want to eat with others and… and…

She tried remembering as she followed the woman down the hallway and into the kitchen.

The kitchen! She had been here before, or had it been a dream? A long table stretched the length of the enormous kitchen. There was a big fireplace along one side of the wall. It was so big that a whole pig or deer could be roasted in it. A fire blazed inside, illuminating the room.

Pot, pans, and utensils lined another wall. The outside wall had a stone oven where bread was made. She could see the glow from a fire in it.

The entire room was a big blur, yet she knew exactly what it looked like. That was the reason she did not get up last night. She feared she would recognize something… or someone, without understanding.

"Did ye hear me?" Margaret snapped, pulling Alana out of her daze.

Alana turned to Margaret. "I'm sorry, what did ye say?"

Margaret exhaled sharply. "Do ye have any experience in the kitchens?"

"Nae, ma'am," she replied. Margaret's tone did not seem right for her voice. The confusion of it overrode Alana's concern that she was ornery.

"Verra, well then. I'll have to show ye. Get the sack of oats against that wall on the third shelf from the bottom." She pointed. "Bring it here."

Alana walked over to the wall where she knew it would be. There were other sacks, but she grabbed the bag of oats... as if by memory. Nae! She had never been there before. She hoped she had chosen the correct one.

She resisted shaking her head as she brought the sack to the middle of the long table.

"Good, good," Margaret said as she began giving Alana directions on how to make the porridge and biscuits and set the table.

Alana followed her directions as if spellbound, moving to get items with as much ease as if she'd put them there herself or as if she could see clearly. Being ordered around did not give her time to contemplate why everything seemed second nature. It also kept her mind off of her throbbing head.

Once the laird and his family were seated in the formal dining area, Margaret handed Alana a platter of biscuits before picking up a large bowl of porridge.

"I daresay ye dinna have time to meet Laird Duncan's family last night. Come along, and ye can meet them now."

Alana froze. The idea of serving the laird's family scared her. What if she tripped and dropped her plate on the ground? Or worse, what if it dropped on one of them? Would he beat her for her carelessness? She could feel her hands getting sweaty.

Margaret saw her hesitation. "They willna bite ye. Come along now," she ordered, waiting for Alana to go through the door before her.

The family quieted as she walked in. Margaret curtsied quickly, and noticing that Alana did not, she leaned toward Alana, so their shoulders touched and whispered, "Curtsy."

Alana curtsied quickly with the biscuits in her hand, then straightened and froze again.

Margaret placed the porridge beside Laird Duncan and

waited for Alana to put the biscuits on the table. "The biscuits," Margaret said to her when she did not move, snapping her out of her stare.

Alana quickly looked around for a spot to place the platter but could not judge where one person's shoulder ended and where the next person was.

"Here, lass," Robbie held his hand out at the end of the table once he saw her squinting.

She walked around and handed the plate to Robbie with an unsteady hand and clumsily curtsied. One of the younger children snickered, and Alana could feel the heat rise to her face. Robbie quickly glanced at the child, stopping the snickering instantly.

"I'm afraid ye havena been properly introduced to my family," Laird Duncan began. "As I told ye before, I am laird here. My name is Robbie Duncan." His wife gave him a quizzical glance. "And this is my wife, Mary Ellen… Lady Duncan."

Mary Ellen? Alana was starting to get overheated. She turned to Mary Ellen because she knew the lady would sit on the opposite side of the table from the laird.

"Milady," she whispered in a shaky voice.

"It's nice to meet ye, Alana," Mary Ellen replied.

By now, Alana could feel her heart pounding hard in her chest. She was sure they could all hear it. She nodded to Mary Ellen since she did not think she could curtsy another time without falling over.

"My eldest, Bryce," Robbie said. Knowing she had trouble seeing, he placed his hand on Bryce's shoulder, so she knew which child he was referring to. "And beside Bryce is Alex, then Anna."

Alex and Anna! All color drained from her face. Her

chest tightened at the names, and she could not breathe. The dull pain in her head throbbed again, and the room started to spin. She felt herself beginning to sway. She shook her head and, unknowingly, backed up until she hit the sideboard. Who were these people? It was as if they were from a dream she could not remember.

Margaret opened her mouth to say something, but Robbie immediately raised his hand and shook his head. Everyone at the table stared at her, the younger ones gapping openly.

"Alana," Robbie said as he rose from his seat. He gently touched her arm, and she jerked it away as if he burnt her.

"Margaret, has she eaten today?" he called over his shoulder.

"Nae, sir," Margaret replied.

"Please take her to the kitchen and give the lass a bit to eat. I daresay she dinna have much yesterday on her journey."

"Aye, Milord," Margaret curtsied and escorted Alana to the kitchens.

***

Once gone, Robbie's second youngest, Kyle, let out the laugh he had been holding in.

"Now listen," Robbie began sternly, looking from one child to the next, "Alana's brother died less than a week ago. She has had a hard life," he paused, debating whether to say more. "A violent life, and she is frightened very easily. It will take time for her to feel comfortable around us, so give her some space. Do ye understand?"

"Aye," the children all acknowledged with serious

faces.

Robbie understood why she reacted to their names, but there had been no way to predict her response or to avoid it. He was sure now that she was the one. It ached him to know who she was and not to confront her about it. Clearly, it was coming to her, but slowly.

He had confided in his sister, Anna, that he knew about the curse between her and Alex, his best friend. Alex had told him. Alana would approach him once she remembered.

After Alex and Anna died, Robbie told Mary Ellen. He did not think she believed him, but he could not blame her. He suspected he would have difficulty accepting the idea if the roles were reversed.

But he knew Alana and Anna were the same people.

He had promised Alex that he would help him end the curse. He had been fortunate to find him… Gavin… at such an early age, but the realization that his happy, carefree sister had become an abused child made his stomach turn.

He looked at his bowl of porridge in disgust as he continually folded it over with his spoon. His thoughts clouded his head and finally, he just pushed the bowl away and looked up to find his wife studying him carefully.

Perhaps she would believe it now if he told her. He told her everything else in his life. She was his confidant, and it was tearing him up inside, not being able to confide in her.

***

Gavin rose early and started the fire in the big kitchen hearth before doing his morning chores.

It was not long before he started feeling his chest tighten, and he knew Alana was up, but it seemed to ease as the morning moved on.

He had just started collecting eggs in the chicken coop when a jolt of anxiety shot through him.

Alana! He dropped his basket and ran to the kitchen.

Alana was seated on a stool at the long table as Margaret put a spoonful of porridge in a bowl and pushed it in front of her.

"Ye heard what Laird Duncan said. Ye need to eat, lass. Ye're as white as snow!" she ordered sharply.

"What happened?" Gavin asked as he tried to catch his breath from running.

"Ach," Margaret exclaimed, wiping her hands on her apron and turning to Gavin. "Milord was making introductions, and she stood there looking as if the devil himself walked in the room." She gestured by waving her hand toward Alana.

Gavin turned his head to look at Alana. She sat on the stool with her hands under the table and her head bowed as she stared at the bowl of porridge. He could see her shaking.

"Milord said she hadna eaten much yesterday, but she doesna seem hungry."

"I can watch her so ye can tend to the family."

Margaret took a deep breath as she looked at Alana, then turned to grab the kettle and made tea for the laird and his wife.

Once Margaret left the room, Gavin grabbed a bowl and spooned some porridge in before placing it across the table from her.

"Do ye mind if I join ye?" he asked, pulling a stool from underneath the table.

***

Alana raised her eyes to Gavin. His presence eased her apprehension for some reason, and she was grateful. She took a deep breath and looked at him. She could not see him clearly, but he was close enough that his features stood out. His eyes were like dark clouds that faded toward the outside. His eyebrows were more defined as they outlined the top of the dark clouds. His nose was harder to see but had a light fuzzy outline. His lips had a reddish tint, so they stood out a bit more.

She shook her head and turned her eyes back to her bowl.

Margaret returned to the kitchen to grab a few more items, then left.

"Would ye like some honey in yer porridge? I ken where she hides it," Gavin whispered to her. He got up, found the honey jar, and sat back down just as Margaret stormed back in. He put it under the table between his legs, picked up his spoon, and smiled at Alana.

She could see the smile, but she frantically looked at Margaret as she moved about the kitchen, sure she would see him, and they would both be in trouble. Margaret quickly found what she was looking for and left. Once gone, Alana let out the breath she had been holding.

He brought out the pot from under the table and poured some into her bowl before doing the same to his.

"Ye'll get in trouble," she whispered as she glanced between his face, the door, and back again.

He chuckled and quickly put the pot back in its secret spot. Her heart raced as she eyed the door until he finally sat back down.

He picked up her spoon and held it out to her. "Try it."

She never had honey before but knew it was something savory. Would Margaret know he poured some in their bowls? She did not want to disappoint him after taking such a chance to get it for her. She looked at the door and then at the spoon he held.

Gavin picked up his spoon in his other hand and put it in his mouth. "Mmm, it's good."

She watched him take another bite, then looked down at the spoon he held out. Finally, she took the spoon, dipped it into the porridge, and put it into her mouth.

The minute her lips closed around the spoon, her lips curled up, and her eyes got big. The sweet honey had made the plain porridge a treat. She had had fruit before in her porridge, which improved it considerably, but this topped that by far. She slowly removed the spoon.

"See? It's much better with honey. Aye?" Gavin whispered as he leaned toward her.

She nodded and took another spoonful but froze with the spoon in her mouth as Margaret returned. She followed her with her eyes as Margaret grabbed something off the shelf and left again. Alana looked across the table at Gavin and pulled the spoon out of her mouth.

Gavin laughed. She was not sure if he laughed at her or the idea that they had not gotten caught, but her tension lessened even more.

They ate their porridge in silence. Once done, Gavin got up and grabbed a biscuit.

"How about a biscuit?" he asked, handing one to her and taking a bite out of his.

Margaret came in and looked at both of them from behind Gavin. "Well, I see ye got her to eat. And it looks like ye helped yerself as well. I doubt that yer chores are done."

"Well," Gavin said as he shrugged his shoulders. "Since I was already here." He smiled at Alana and appeared to have winked at her. Alana jerked her head to Margaret's face. She could see the woman's lips drawn together as one arm rested on her hip.

"And ye are here with nae eggs," she said as she lightly swatted Gavin across the back of his head, but it startled Alana.

"Milord said I could show Alana around today," Gavin announced. "I thought I would be finished with my morning work before she got up. Perhaps she can help me?" He looked up at Margaret and gave her his most persuasive smile.

"Well," she hesitated.

"Just for a wee bit," he added. "We'll collect the eggs, and I'll bring her right back."

Maragret exhaled sharply. "Alright, but dinna be long," she ordered, leaving the room.

Alana stared at the door as it closed behind Margaret.

"Are ye ready to go?" Gavin asked as he stood up.

She looked at him and nodded before standing and moving along the other side of the table as he did.

He opened the door and grasped her arm. "Watch. There's a step here," he said as he guided her down, letting go of her arm when she got to the bottom.

They took a few steps in silence before he asked, "Are ye feeling any better now?"

She shrugged her shoulders before replying quietly, "A bit."

They walked along in silence before he spoke again. "Ye have trouble seeing," he commented. Alana did not reply. "Has it always been that way?"

She stopped walking as a lump came to her throat. She shook her head, and her eyes immediately teared up as she thought of that night. She should never have gone back. She had hoped that her distorted vision was temporary, but if that were the case, certainly, it would have come back by now.

"I'm sorry," Gavin said as he faced her and gently touched her arm. "Ye dinna have to answer that. I dinna mean to pry, lass. I dinna want to upset ye." He gently tugged her arm to start her walking again in silence.

After a few steps, she whispered, "It happened about a week ago."

Gavin's head snapped to look at her, but she was staring at the ground. Once at the chicken coop, she paused and studied the building. She would have sworn she had been here before but knew it was impossible. She tried to place what it reminded her of, but she could not. If she could only get a clearer view, perhaps she could remember.

She looked back at the keep. Everything about this place seemed familiar. She could feel the tension building inside.

"What is it?" Gavin asked as he patiently waited at the door, his voice calm and curious, not harsh as if she was wasting his time.

"It's just…" she paused, unsure if she should say something. Perhaps he would think she was crazy, but there was something about him, something urging her to trust him. She took a deep breath and said, "It is as if… as if… I've been here before."

"I ken what ye mean," he replied, his voice light as if smiling, though she could not see from that far away.

"When I first came here, everything looked familiar to me, as if I was in a dream."

Her eyes got wide as he said it. She could not believe it. He understood!

"It was almost… magical."

Alana took two more steps, so she was right in front of him and whispered, "Are we in the land of the faeries?"

He silently chuckled. He opened the door. "Nae, lass, we're just on Duncan land."

She walked into the chicken coop, and he continued. "I wouldna mention yer feelings to anyone, though. I dinna think most would understand." He picked up the basket he dropped and looked inside to make sure the eggs had not broken before handing it to her. "Except Robbie," he added. "He would understand."

"Ye are familiar with Laird Duncan," she asked as he put an egg in her basket.

"Well… aye," he said. "But naebuddy else kens, ye see?"

She got quiet again, following him with the basket as he filled it. He trusted her with his secret. The only person who ever shared anything with her was Andrew.

Gavin seemed kind, and she felt peaceful when she was with him, but she was apprehensive about getting too close.

"How long have ye been with… Laird Duncan?"

"Well, I first saw him at Willie and Christy's wedding when I was five or six. Christy is my cousin, ye see," he explained. He put the last egg in the basket and took it from her. Walking her out the door, he continued, "Since I was so intrigued with the laird, he invited me for a visit several times. Once I turned twelve, he invited me to apprentice under him."

They made it back to the main house at the kitchen door. Alana's tension had eased considerably. Listening to Gavin talk made her feel better than she had since losing her sight.

He opened the door for her and followed her in, placing the basket of eggs on the table.

"Milord would like to see ye in his study," Margaret said to Gavin.

"Aye," Gavin replied. He turned to Alana and gave her a bow. "I bid ye good day."

Margaret gave him a look. Gavin smiled at her with a shrug and left the room.

Chapter 15

Gavin knocked and opened the study door. "Ye called for me, Milord?"

"Aye," Robbie said as he gestured for him to enter.

Gavin stood in the corner of the room as Robbie finished his discussion with Bryce. He did not pay attention to what they were saying. His mind kept going to Alana. She lost her sight a week ago! That was a couple of days before they found her. He wanted to ask how it happened but did not want to upset her more.

Once Bryce left, Robbie turned to Gavin and gestured for him to sit. "How does she fair?"

Gavin sat down and replied, "She seems a bit better than when I first entered the kitchen. She's trying to figure out why things seem so familiar. I think remembering will be harder for her because she is having difficulty seeing." Gavin smiled and added, "Though she did confide in me that things look familiar." That was a big step. Telling him meant she trusted him.

"She told ye she recognized things?"

Gavin nodded happily.

"Well, that's good. She looked so scared when I introduced her to Alex and Anna that I thought she would die of fright. I'll have to think of something to help make her more comfortable here."

They were quiet for a minute when Gavin remembered Alana's comment. He laughed and said, "She asked if this was the land of the faeries."

Robbie chuckled and asked, "How bad is her sight?"

"I dinna ken." Gavin's mood instantly sombered. "She dinna seem to want to talk about it when I asked, but she seemed to see objects. Perhaps they are only blurry." His eyebrows turned in, and he looked down at the floor, wrestling with the fact that it had happened only a couple of days before they found her.

"What is it?" Robbie asked.

Gavin took a deep breath and raked his fingers through his hair. "I asked her if she'd always had bad eyesight. I dinna think she would answer at first, but she finally did."

"And?"

"She said it happened a week ago. That's just a couple of days before we found her!"

"Did she say how it happened?"

Gavin shook his head, but he remembered the onslaught of pain he had felt the night when they found Andrew. Her father said he was attacked by her wolf two days before the arrived.

"Well, there is nothing we can do about that now. We have other things to worry about. For one, we need to be on the lookout for her father and the man who killed her wolf. It is only a matter of time before they come here, being that I quit the hunt, picked up my cart, and left."

Gavin nodded.

"Also," Robbie continued, "Once she remembers, we need to figure out how to end this." He waved his hand.

Gavin nodded, knowing he referred to the curse.

"I've been thinking about that," Gavin said. "There is rumored to be a seer at yer northeastern border, along the coast. I'd heard of her a couple of years ago in the village. It was after my pains went away, and I dinna want to go before because I was afraid to hear news that Alana dinna make it. I ken she had a hard life."

Robbie nodded.

"But now that I ken she is safe, perhaps this woman can tell me how to end this." His eyebrows went up as he looked hopefully at Robbie.

"Well, until then, let's keep her out of sight from others."

"Aye."

"I talked to Margaret about it already," Robbie said. "I also mentioned her poor eyesight, which I think she dinna believed me. She said she grabbed the oats bag when it was near the flour sack." He looked at Gavin questioningly.

Gavin smiled and shrugged his shoulders. "It could be that she ken where they were from memory."

***

Alana followed Margaret around all day, doing her bidding. She only saw Gavin occasionally when he stopped in to bring fresh milk or to eat. Seeing him was the highlight of her day.

Alana cleaned up after the evening meal, and Margaret went to the solar to see if the family needed anything else. When she came back, she held a tiny puppy. "This wee puppy here is too small and weak. I dinna think he made it to its mother to feed. She seems nae to care. Milord said to give it to ye to try to nurse it until it is strong enough to survive," Margaret replied.

Alana's heart fluttered. Was Laird Duncan giving it to her? All she could make out was a wee ball of fur in Margaret's hands. She remembered when Thunder was a tiny pup. She instantly felt an emptiness in her gut at the thought, but pushed it aside. She had to help this little one. He needed her.

"Grab a cloth and put it in a basket," she ordered.

Alana straightened and quickly did as she asked, placing the basket on the table.

Margaret placed the newborn puppy in the basket. Alana studied the puppy as Margaret poured some goat milk into a wooden bowl and grabbed a small rag. She moved the bowl beside the basket. "See here," Margaret said. Alana's head snapped to her. "Fold the cloth so it comes to a small tip and dip it into the milk."

Alana drew closer to watch. She squinted her eyes as Margaret demonstrated. She did not want to make a mistake.

"Then just bring it to the puppy's mouth," she instructed while moving it right under the puppy's nose. The puppy immediately opened its mouth and started sucking. "And there ye go," she said, pulling it out of the puppy's mouth though it continued to suck.

Margaret handed the cloth to Alana. She concentrated on dipping the fabric and bringing it over to the puppy. Maragret made her anxious, but her worries about getting yelled at were nothing compared to her wanting to aid the helpless pup. She hoped she was doing it right.

Gavin walked in to see what they were doing.

"Ah, ye got the runt of the litter," he said, smiling.

Alana did not look up but knew it was him and not Leslie because a sense of peace washed over her from his presence. She continued to focus on feeding the puppy. A smile came to her face as the puppy latched on to the cloth. Gavin exchanged looks with Margaret, and he nodded.

"Ach, this will take all night!" Margaret threw her hands up in the air. "I have a lot to do. Let's take it into yer room, and ye can tend to it there."

Margaret grabbed the basket and a candle as Gavin took the bowl, and they made their way down the hallway until they got to Alana's room.

Margaret lit a candle and placed it on a large wooden chest before setting the basket on the floor.

"I'll build ye a fire," Gavin said as he set the bowl on the trunk.

"Well, I still have unfinished work. I'll be back in the morn to wake ye," Margaret said.

Alana nodded and sat beside the basket, trying to make out the puppy in the dim light.

It was not long before Gavin had a fire blazing, and she could see the dark puppy. Gavin fetched the bowl from the trunk and set it on the floor in front of her. He sat cross-legged beside Alana. She concentrated hard as she fed the puppy.

"It's so small. Its eyes arena even opened," Gavin said.

She smiled.

After a few minutes, Gavin said softly "Ye're out of milk. Do ye want to hold it?"

Her head came up to look at him, excited at first, then worried she might drop it. What if she held it too tight? Without being able to see, she might inadvertently hurt it.

"It probably willna move around much since its

siblings are nae squirming about. Perhaps a change in position will do it good, stretch its muscles."

She contemplated for a bit.

"Cup ye hands on yer lap, and I will place the puppy in them," he instructed.

She obediently cupped her hands as he placed the small animal inside them. She smiled, though she did not dare to move her arms. It was so tiny and soft.

***

Gavin's heart lightened as he watched her. Giving the puppy to Alana had been a great idea. He was sure it was Robbie's idea. Taking care of something so helpless was an easy way to get her mind off of her own problems. He didn't feel any tenseness coming from her. She was awkward with it, but Gavin thought it was more because her sight was so bad.

She was like a wee child, so innocent despite her hard life.

"Rub yer thumbs gently to massage it a bit," he suggested.

She slowly moved them back and forth against its side. It squirmed around until it found one of her fingers and started sucking it. She laughed and pulled it out of its mouth. "It's so soft," she whispered.

She had always loved animals from the first lifetime when they were cursed. God, how he loved her. They had to figure out how to end this curse. He was so sure they had succeeded when Alex killed Gregory MacDonald, but the curse still hung over them.

He still had not come across the one holding the curse

in this lifetime. He could not be much older than he was since Gregory died months before Alex. The next time he was in the village, he would see what he could find out about the seer. She was their only hope. Satisfied that he had a plan, he took a deep breath. Alana looked up from her hands.

"I guess we should put the puppy back," Gavin said.

She looked down at her hands as he gently cupped the animal and placed it back in the basket.

He took his neckerchief off and laid it over the puppy, tucking it around the sides of the blanket. "There, now it will stay nice and cozy the whole night," he said as he got up and brushed his hands to get the dirt off them. "Well, I hope ye have a good night, Alana."

"Ye too," she said louder than she usually talked. And then softly, she said, "And thank ye."

He knew she thanked him for more than his well wish for the night. He could feel deep inside that she had started to trust him, if only a little. That was a big step.

He left the room and quietly closed the door as she pulled the blanket off the bed, wrapping it around her. She lay down, putting one arm out to touch the side of the basket, and whispered to the puppy, "Good night, little one."

Chapter 16

A soft knock woke Alana up. The door creaked open a crack, and a small flicker of a candle broke the darkness.

"Alana. Are ye awake? I brought some milk for yer puppy." Gavin whispered.

She sat up. "Aye, come in."

He opened the door more and bent down to grab the bowl he had placed on the ground to open the door. "I thought ye should feed it before ye started yer day." He placed the bowl and candle on the chest. "I'll start a fire for ye."

Once lit, he turned around. Alana wore the same clothes as the day before, and the blanket was scrunched in a pile beside her. He picked up the blanket and shook it out, laying it nicely on the untouched bed.

"Is yer bed nae comfortable?" he asked.

She started to dip the clean cloth Gavin had brought into the milk and answered without hesitation, "I never slept on a bed before."

"Ah, well, that would take some getting used to, I suppose." He said it calmly, but his insides ached over the lifestyle she had. "There are some other clothes in the trunk.

Perhaps there is something more comfortable than a dress for ye to sleep in."

She looked up from feeding. "I dinna want to dig through someone else's things."

"Well, this is yer room now, and everything in it is yers," he explained.

She looked down at the puppy with big eyes. Gavin smiled, knowing she wondered if the puppy was hers since it was in her room. She was so easy to read.

When Alana finished feeding the puppy, Gavin gently handed it to her so he could put some fresh cushioning down in the wicker basket. Then, he took the puppy and placed it back in the basket.

"I have chores to do," he said as he got up. "Look through that trunk. Today is laundry day. Margaret does laundry on Tuesdays and Fridays, and if ye miss it," he shrugged, "Well, yer dress willna get clean."

She looked down at the dress she wore. "Aye."

Gavin opened the door. "Before ye leave for yer duties, perhaps ye should pull back the curtains to let some light in for the puppy. It willna be able to see it with its eyes closed, but the feel of the sun always perks me up."

She looked up at him and smiled at his comment, nodding.

He closed the door and walked down the dark hallway, grinning. He made Alana smile already that morning. His heart felt light all day as he thought of her.

***

Gavin rose from his midday meal when horses approached the keep. Worried someone was looking for Alana, he raced upstairs to find Robbie in the solar with his family. "Milord, someone approaches."

"Aye," Robbie said as he got up. "I'll be in my drawing room."

Gavin quickly made his way down and out the front door. There were three riders. He stayed at the top steps until he recognized the one as Brodie MacKay, Robbie's (and at one time, Alex's) best friend. Relieved, Gavin smiled and quickly descended the stairs to greet them.

"Sir Brodie," he called as the horse stopped at the bottom of the stairs.

"Gavin," Brodie replied with a nod of his head. "Is Laird Duncan at home?"

"Aye, he is," Gavin replied, grabbing the reins while Brodie dismounted.

The stable master, Leslie, appeared and grabbed the horses so Gavin could lead the guests up to the keep.

Gavin did not recognize the other two soldiers. They were much younger than Brodie, so he would not have served with either of them in his previous life.

"Right this way, Sir Brodie," Gavin said as he led him down the hallway.

Brodie gestured for the other two to stay in the entranceway before following behind Gavin. At the study door, Gavin knocked and opened it. "Milord, Sir Brodie is here."

"Brodie!" Robbie stood and walked around the desk, embracing him.

"I will tend to yer men, Sir Brodie," Gavin said with a low bow. "Would ye care for something to eat?"

"Aye. That would be nice," Brodie replied.

Gavin went back to escort the two soldiers into the main

hall. "Please sit, and I will get ye something to eat and drink."

He returned to the kitchen, where Margaret and Alana were still eating. "Sir Brodie is here with two others and requires a bite to eat and drink," he said to Margaret.

He quickly snatched a bite from his unfinished plate across from Alana and, while that close, winked at her. Her eyes grew big, and she looked down at her plate. Her reaction made him laugh.

"Aye," Margaret said as she sprung up. "Let's go, lass, the guests first," she said to Alana.

Margaret took out three mugs and started to pour some mead into them.

"Just two for now. Sir Brodie is in the drawing room, nae doubt sharing Milord's finer whisky."

He brought the glasses to the soldiers, returned to the kitchen, and put another spoonful in his mouth before grabbing a plate for Brodie. The drawing room was empty, so he went to the solar to find Brodie greeting the family.

Mary Ellen was a MacKay as well. Although Mary Ellen grew up on an estate far from where Brodie lived, they became close during her and Robbie's courtship.

Most of the children were familiar with him as well. Brodie made it a point to visit them when she was at her parents' estate.

"Yer meal, Sir Brodie," Gavin said, placing it on a table.

"Gavin," Robbie said. "Go to Willie's house and tell him Sir Brodie is here. We will be feasting tonight." He held up his glass before taking a swig.

"Aye, Milord."

"Bryce," he called to his eldest, "Grab yer bow and get

us a fine doe to roast."

"My men can go with ye," Brodie said.

"Aye," Robbie replied, "Perhaps that will give me time to clash swords with ye before Willie arrives."

***

Gavin returned to find Robbie and Brodie sword-fighting in the courtyard. He carried over a bucket of water for them.

"Ye've gotten sloppy over the years," Brodie said.

"Aye, well, I dinna have anyone as fine as ye to spar against. Ye're one of the finest."

Brodie shrugged. "Naw as fine as Alex was. He was always a great challenge."

"Aye, he was," Robbie said, shooting a quick look toward Gavin, who looked up as he placed the bucket down. Gavin missed Brodie's friendship. The three of them were like brothers when he was Alex. "Stay and watch Gavin. Ye may pick up a few tips," Robbie called as he turned to leave.

Gavin smiled and swung back around. He was so lucky to have Robbie as a confidant.

Robbie and Brodie reminisced about old times as their swords clashed until Robbie called a halt. He walked over to the bucket of water and drank from the ladle, Brodie teasing him the whole time about how out of shape he was.

Robbie laughed. He was as fit as any soldier, only a little rusty in his swordsmanship. Robbie pushed Gavin toward Brodie, saying, "Ye wear him down for me a bit, lad."

Though Gavin had trained under Robbie a while back, Robbie had feared something would happen to him when he started experiencing Alana's pains. Over the last few years, he had only trained with straw targets. Gavin suspected that since Alana was safe, Robbie felt there was no threat.

Robbie and Brodie continued, reminiscing about their soldering days as Gavin and Brodie sparred.

"Remember the time Alex had to empty the cesspits for the week?" Brodie asked Robbie as he countered Gavin's attack.

"Aye," Robbie laughed. "He was on guard duty the night Beatrice couldna get out of the privy because someone wedged a board against the door to keep her in."

Gavin remembered that week. He had taken the punishment because he was on duty that night. Gavin's swings came with more force as the conversation continued. Thinking about it irritated him. He found out later that Cameron did it. He purposely set him up because Alex beat him at a sparring match in front of a woman Cameron was trying to woo. Apparently, the woman was taken with Alex after that, though he had no interest in her.

"Ach. He was so bitter that week. Come to think of it, he was bitter for years after that!" Brodie laughed.

He would not have been as bitter if they had not teased him as much for stealing Cameron's woman. It was so far from the truth. Gavin suspected it would not have been a big deal had he not known he had a soulmate out there. Finding her was his whole objective in Alex's life, as it had been in this one until he found Alana.

Brodie became more passionate with his swings to match Gavin's increased intensity.

"He found out who had done it on the last day of the week," Brodie wailed.

"Aye," Robbie said, nearly in tears from laughing. "But

I dinna ken who it was."

"Aye, me neither," Brodie replied.

Gavin swung wildly out of control. "It was Cameron, and I beat his—" Gavin cut himself off as his sword met Brodie's block with a fierce crash. It seemed like time paused with their swords raised against each other's, Brodie's eyes locked on Gavin's.

They lowered their swords.

Gavin could feel the heat rise to his face like a lad caught with his fingers in a honey jar. He looked at Robbie, but he was no help. He was trying to keep a straight face.

"Well, now," Robbie said quickly. "Shall we all retreat to the drawing room?" He turned and walked back to the house, not waiting for an answer or to see if either followed.

Brodie sheathed his sword as he studied Gavin, who looked at the sky and combed his fingers through his hair as he took a deep breath. It was a common thing Gavin did. A trait he had in every lifetime. *How am I going to explain this to him?*

Gavin did not look again at Brodie but sheathed his sword, sauntered to the water barrel, and picked it up. He kept his eyes cast down, waiting for Brodie to go before him. He could not look him in the eye.

"Sir," he mumbled as he waited and thought of how to explain his blunder. Brodie finally turned and made his way back to the keep.

Robbie was the first person he and his kindred spirit had ever told in all of their lifetimes together. The only reason he told Robbie was because Anna was his sister, and things happened that could not be explained any other way. So, he took the chance and told him.

Robbie, Brodie, and Alex had been inseparable from

the time they had soldiered together, but Brodie was not present when Alex explained the curse. Since Brodie never questioned him about anything, he never told him. Now Gavin felt guilty for telling Robbie and not Brodie.

Would Brodie believe him or just think he was crazy? He could understand how someone would doubt the truth in the matter. *God, how am I going to explain this?*

Gavin dropped the bucket off in the kitchen and slowly continued to the study.

Robbie had poured a drink for Brodie and himself, and both were seated when Gavin entered. He closed the door quietly behind him, then leaned against it. He first looked at Brodie, who seemed more than a little irritated, then at Robbie, who raised his eyebrows, almost curious about how he would get out of this one. *Nae aid there.*

"Well?" Brodie asked, breaking the silence.

Gavin took a deep breath as he looked at the ceiling and combed his fingers through his hair again before taking a step toward Brodie and looking him in the eye.

"I am…" he paused. There was just no way to say it without sounding crazy. "…was… Alex." That was all he said.

Brodie looked at him for more explanation, but it did not come. He snorted and exclaimed, "Are ye serious? Ye expect me to believe ye?" Both Brodie and Gavin looked at Robbie, who seemed to find it humorous. He chuckled, offering no help.

Brodie turned back to Gavin. "Are ye telling me that everyone is walking around as someone else?" his voice raised. "That everything I've been taught as a child from my parents and the church… everything that I believe in what happens after life is bull shit!"

"Nae!" Gavin exclaimed. "I'm saying that…" *God, I should've told him when I was Alex instead of some sixteen-year-old who dinna ken his own arse from a hole in the ground.* He swept his fingers through his hair again. "What I'm saying is…" He took a deep breath before continuing slowly, "is that I… Anna and I… were cursed."

"Cursed?" Brodie spat with raised eyebrows, then stole a look at Robbie, who tipped his head to one side, raised a brow, and shrugged one shoulder. Brodie turned back to Gavin. "By whom?"

"Well…" Gavin began sheepishly, "Gregory MacDonald."

"Gregory MacDonald?" Brodie exclaimed as he shifted in his chair.

Robbie finally became serious and suggested, "Perhaps ye should start at the beginning."

Brodie glanced his way in disbelief, then back to Gavin. "Aye. Start at the beginning."

"The beginning. Aye," Gavin said. He paced the floor several times, contemplating how to say it and wishing he had not blundered. Finally, he stopped, took another deep breath, pulled a chair over to face Brodie, and sat, ignoring protocol. He leaned forward and began. "A very long time ago, a different lifetime ago, I fell in love with a woman who was promised to someone else, a powerful sorcerer. It was an arranged marriage, which she did not want."

Brodie listened with a clenched jaw. At least he was listening.

"The sorcerer found out, and she was asked to choose between the two of us. She chose me. The sorcerer cursed us that we would always long for each other, but our union would forever be unattainable. Then he ran her through with his sword."

Gavin watched as Brodie tried to comprehend all that he said. Brodie shook his head and turned to Robbie, who was trying to suppress a laugh again as he watched Brodie. Gavin could tell it was infuriating him more.

"Did ye put him up to this?" Brodie asked him irritably.

Robbie shook his head and chuckled. "Nae, my friend. He is serious."

Gavin glared at Robbie. His reaction did not help. He was making it worse.

Brodie turned back to Gavin, obviously vexed. "So, if ye really were Alex, tell me something about myself that Robbie doesna ken."

"That Robbie doesna ken?" Gavin exclaimed in a high-pitched voice. "We did everything together!"

He looked between them for a minute as he thought, and then a smile came to his face. He leaned in toward Brodie and said, "So, whenever Robbie came downstairs and placed something on the table that he was going to take with him, ye would put it on the chair and push it under the table as ye leaned on it. When Robbie thought he placed it somewhere else and started to look for it, ye would help him."

Brodie's expression slowly turned somber as Gavin talked.

"As ye search, ye would put it somewhere Robbie already looked and pretended ye found it there, teasing him that he was losing his mind."

Robbie snapped his head to Brodie. "That was ye? All this time, I blamed it on Alex!" He turned to Gavin and said, "Ye always sat there and laughed, never helping me look."

Gavin shrugged. "There wasna any sense in wasting my

energy looking for something that wasna lost."

Brodie's expression turned serious as he glanced between the two of them. "Ye really are serious."

Gavin looked at Brodie and nodded. "Aye, I am."

Brodie moved his hand to his head and massaged his forehead.

Gavin continued his story quietly, "When Anna and I survived, and Gregory did naw, I thought I broke the curse, but that wasna the case."

Brodie turned to Robbie. "And ye kenned this the whole time?"

Robbie nodded. "After Gregory attacked us, I questioned Alex about why he said he hadna met Gregory MacDonald, yet the man recognized him. And Anna recognized him when he came out of the woods. I could tell by the way she tensed. Even the sight of the man who had attacked her did not give her that intense of a reaction."

"I would have told ye as well, but ye werena around when Robbie questioned me. It was the first time I had ever told anyone." Gavin tried to judge what was going through Brodie's mind, but Brodie continued to stare at him with a blank face.

"Both of ye were my best friends," Gavin said as he looked from Brodie to Robbie and back to Brodie. "I'm sorry for nae telling ye."

Brodie nodded and was quiet for another minute. "And how did the two of ye meet this time?" Brodie gestured to Robbie and Gavin.

Robbie filled him in on the details of their meeting and all that had transpired more recently.

"So ye found her?" Brodie asked.

"Aye," Gavin nodded with a big smile.

A knock on the door interrupted them, and Gavin immediately stood and moved the chair back to suit his status. Robbie threw a look at Brodie and shook his head. Brodie nodded, understanding that nobody else knew any of this.

The door opened, and Bryce entered.

"We downed a nice buck!" he said.

"That is great, son. Now, go meet us out in the courtyard. We will be there shortly and ye can cross swords with one of the best swordsmen I ken," Robbie said.

"Aye!" Bryce said, closing the door behind him.

"So, when do I get to meet Alana?" Brodie asked.

"Well, I dinna want yer men to see her. The fewer people who ken she is here, the better," Gavin said. "I will introduce ye later, but she will most likely nae remember ye."

"Aye," Brodie replied as they got up.

"Go help Margaret prepare the meal," Robbie said as he ruffled Gavin's hair from behind like he was a ten-year-old lad.

"Aye," Gavin said as he left the room in much better spirits than he entered. Brodie believed him! What a wonderful feeling it was to be known by Brodie. They had been such good friends.

***

Robbie and Bryce fought with Brodie and his fellow soldiers in the courtyard. As Brodie and Robbie sparred, Brodie asked, "So, when are ye going to take Lord Reay's offer to have Bryce train under him? Ye were younger than him when ye did."

Bryce looked at his father with hopeful eyes. The last time they visited Mary Ellen's family, Robbie brought Bryce to pay a visit to Lord Reay.

Robbie soldiered with the MacKays for several years until his father died, and the lairdship fell to him. The Duncan clan was not as vast as other clans, so his sons needed to train elsewhere. The Duncan clan did not have a formal army. He always intended for him to train with Lord Reay, but he had not yet been ready to let him go. And now, with all that had transpired with The Watch and rumors of another Jacobite rising on the horizon, he wasn't sure he wanted to let him go. But he also knew that delaying his training would not be good either. He had already discussed it with Mary Ellen, and they agreed to let him go when he was sixteen.

"Did Lord Reay ask ye to convince me?" Robbie asked.

"Well, he kenned I'd be stopping, so… aye, he did."

Bryce glanced between his dad and Brodie anxiously. He had expressed his desire to go several times. Robbie saw from the corner of his eyes but did not let on either way what he decided.

Willie arrived. His family went inside to visit Mary Ellen and the kids as Willie made his way to the courtyard.

"Brodie!" he called in greeting. After a quick welcome, he took up swords with him.

Chapter 17

Gavin walked out of the general store in the village the following morning and loaded the last of the supplies he acquired. He had already been to the tavern and purchased enough whisky and ale to restock what the men had downed the night before and what would be needed for the next few days since Brodie and the two soldiers would stay a couple more nights.

He thought about Alana as he rode back. He woke early and brought milk to her room so he could watch her feed the puppy. She seemed more relaxed and smiled again. Gavin was so happy he could not keep from smiling back at her.

It would take him slightly under an hour to get back with a packed cart, but thoughts of Alana and now Brodie made the journey less dull.

He was excited that Brodie knew and believed him. It was comforting to confide in not only Robbie but also Brodie. He would love to sit and talk with both of them about old times, just the three of them, but it was not in his status to do so. It had been hard to listen to them and not join in, so hard that he misspoke. He chuckled at the thought. He had been fortunate nobody else was around when it happened.

He was halfway back to the house when Gavin heard a man yell from behind, snapping him out of his daydream.

"Make way!"

Gavin nudged his horses and cart closer to one side of the path to allow the rider to pass.

The man did not look at him as he passed, but Gavin's heart jolted when he saw the Grant plaid. It was the man who attacked Alana. It had been dark when it happened, but he was sure of it.

His chest tightened, and he clenched his jaw as the man passed. Even if the man looked directly at him, he would not have known Gavin had anything to do with the rescue of Alana.

Another man followed behind the first before catching up to ride alongside him. The men were going much faster than a full cart would allow, but Gavin nudged the horse on to pick up the pace.

***

Leslie knocked on the Laird's study.

"Enter," Robbie called out.

"Excuse me, Milord," he said, then turned to Brodie. "Sir."

He turned back to Robbie. "There is a Henry from clan Grant to see ye."

Robbie flashed Brodie a look. "Did he say why he was here or ask ye anything?"

"Nae, Milord." Leslie shook his head.

"Where is he now?" Robbie asked.

"In the hall, Milord."

"Where are my comrades?" Brodie asked.

"They are in the hall as well, Sir," Leslie answered.

"Stay with Alana, and dinna mention anything about the guests. Keep her in the kitchen."

"Aye, Milord," he said as he bowed.

Brodie got up. "Shall I escort him here?"

"Nae," Robbie said as he got up. "I willna have him any deeper in my house. But, please, join me."

***

Gavin's heart was pounding by the time he reached the castle. He left the cart at the base of the steps and entered through the kitchen door to look for Alana. He burst into the kitchen and startled everyone, but he didn't care. He immediately went over to Alana and gently touched her arm.

"Come with me," he ordered quietly.

She looked from him to Margaret.

Margaret opened her mouth, but Gavin shook his head and said, "She isna here. And ye've never heard of her."

Fortunately, Robbie told him he had already informed Margaret and Leslie that she was to stay out of sight of company. He hoped it was enough to have them not question him.

Alana's face turned white, and she did not move when he tugged her. Gavin poured milk into a mug with his free hand before picking it up.

"Let's go feed the puppy," he said, keeping the panic out of his voice.

She nodded and let him pull her along.

The Gift of the Healing Stones

***

Robbie entered the hall quietly on the other end, observing the man as he looked at the tapestries that lined the wall. He cleared his throat as the man reached his hand to touch the bottom of one with a fair woman dressed in white and gold. Her outstretched arm was ready for a falcon with wings spread to land.

Henry immediately pulled his arm away and snapped around. He looked from Robbie to Brodie and back as Robbie took the Laird's seat by a large hearth at the far end of the hall.

"Ye requested my presence?" Robbie asked.

Henry slowly made his way to the other side of the hall, not bothering to bow.

"I believe ye have something of mine," the man stated.

"Who the hell are ye that ye come to my land, my house, talking to me as if I were a commoner!" Robbie yelled.

"I'm Henry from the Grant clan in Grantown-on-Spey, and I have come for my betrothed."

"Yer betrothed? And who, pray tell, may that be?"

"Ye ken exactly who. Alana Grant. Ye snatched her away from me. I was bringing the wench back to her father. She was promised to whoever killed the wolf that attacked him."

Robbie was boiling inside. He knew exactly what Henry was doing when he "snatched" her away, but he showed no emotion on his face.

Brodie, though, put his hand on the hilt of his sword and took a step closer to Henry.

"And why would I have this lass?" Robbie asked.

"The men in the tavern said ye searched for the wolf. Ye wanted the lass for yerself," he spat. "Ye left in a hurry after she was taken."

"And they saw this lass with me?"

"Nae, but yer man wasna there when ye left."

"My man's horse was lame. However, I see nae reason to explain myself to ye. I dinna have yer lass," he lied, sending up a prayer of forgiveness for the lie.

"Ye ken her brother," he said. "He was a Watch deserter. I'm sure the Redcoats would be interested in learning that ye aided a deserter," Henry said slyly as he raised his eyebrows and sneered at Robbie.

"Ye dare to come into my house and accuse me of treason! The man wasna wearing the Watch uniform. How would I have ken? And, he was severely wounded, more likely from raiding cattle than soldiering. He was just a lad. Nae old enough to be a soldier!"

"Well, he was… and ye did. And I want my wench back."

"Well, ye may leave my hall and search elsewhere because she isna here."

"Perhaps she isna, but ye ken where she is. I would hate for anything to befall someone so important to ye," Henry said in a menacing voice.

Robbie immediately stood, his face beet red. "Ye dare threaten me in my own home! Who the devil do ye think ye are talking to!"

Brodie had unsheathed his sword at the man's comment and stepped closer to him. The two soldiers at the other end of the hall were up and halfway across the hall when Robbie yelled again. "Get this man out of my sight!"

Henry glared at Robbie as the soldiers escorted him out.

Brodie ordered, "Ride him to the border. Ride him hard. Dinna stop until he's off Duncan land."

Robbie sat back down and shook his head. He was fuming. How dare he come in threatening him. And the lie did not sit well with him either, but he did it for Alana's sake. Had it been any other lass, he would not have gotten involved in the first place, never searching for her or the wolf.

Had the roles been reversed, he would have been as mad as Henry, but he would never have been disrespectful. And he certainly would never have treated a lass as Henry had.

Henry left a bad taste in his mouth. He fought the urge to spit.

Brodie put his hand on Robbie's shoulder. "Ye did what ye had to do."

Robbie took a deep breath and got up. "Aye."

They walked to the entrance of the house and opened the door, watching from the top of the steps as the two soldiers escorted Henry at a gallop down the path until they disappeared into the woods.

Robbie went inside, leaving Brodie there, and went to the kitchen.

"Where's Alana," he asked, seeing only Margaret and Leslie.

"Gavin took her to her room, Milord. They are feeding the puppy," Margaret answered.

He nodded and moved toward the servants' hallway before returning to the kitchen.

"Which room is hers?" he asked. He never ventured into the servants' quarters.

"The third door on the right, Milord."

He nodded and made his way down the corridor. He stopped at the third door and knocked.

"Gavin. Alana. It is I. Open the door," he ordered quietly.

Gavin opened the door. After seeing Robbie alone, he looked down the hallway both ways as Robbie peeked in on Alana. She was sitting on the floor with one hand on the basket handle protectively, yet her face was etched with fear.

Robbie looked at Gavin. "He's gone."

"What do ye mean *he's* gone?" Gavin asked.

Robbie frowned. "Henry Grant. The man who came for Alana."

"What about the other man?"

"What other man?"

"There were two Grants that passed me on the way back from the village," Gavin replied anxiously.

Robbie's heart thumped as he recalled Henry's threat. He immediately turned and quickly walked down the corridor.

Gavin chased after him, placing his hand on Robbie's arm. "What happened?" he asked, continually looking down the hallway toward Alana's door.

Robbie turned to face him. "He threatened my family, that's what! Brodie's men took him to the border."

Gavin looked back toward Alana's room, then back to Robbie.

"Bring Alana to the solar with Mary Ellen and see which of my children are with her. Tell her to lock the door, then come find me." With that, Robbie turned back toward the kitchen.

"Aye."

The Gift of the Healing Stones

Robbie suspected his younger two children would be in the solar with their mother, but the older three were most likely still out doing chores before they did their studies.

As he entered the kitchen, he ordered Leslie, "I want Bryce, Alex, and Anna brought to the solar immediately!"

"Aye, Milord!" Leslie bowed and then ran out the kitchen door.

Robbie continued toward the great hall as his mind wandered to his wife, children, and the threat Henry had given. He found Brodie sitting at one of the trestle tables with a mug in his hand.

"Henry traveled with another man," Robbie spat.

Brodie slammed the mug on the table and immediately stood, "How do ye ken?"

"Gavin said they passed him on the way here," he replied, turning toward the door. He slapped his leg. "Come, Orion!"

The dog stood and ran out the door on Robbie's heels. They could see Bryce and Alex returning from the field on Leslie's horse as they approached the barn. His chest tightened when he saw Anna was missing. Leslie headed at a fast pace toward the woods.

"Where's yer sister?" Robbie asked, trying to keep the fear out of his voice so he would not scare them. She was supposed to be helping them.

"She went to take a break," Bryce replied. "She usually goes to the stream."

"How long ago did she go?"

Bryce shrugged. "Perhaps a half hour ago. She should be returning soon. She usually doesna stay that long."

Robbie looked toward the woods, where the path led to the stream. Leslie was halfway to the edge of the woods.

"Did ye see anyone who shouldna be here?"

The lads both shook their heads, concern starting to etch their faces.

"I want ye to take yer brother to the solar where yer mother is and lock the door. I fear there is an intruder."

"Aye," Bryce nodded his acknowledgment.

"Stay there with them and watch over them. Dinna let anyone in unless ye ken them."

"Aye," Bryce said, turning the horse around and taking off for the keep.

Gavin ran down the steps of the keep. He mounted the horse immediately after Bryce and Alex dismounted. He caught up to Robbie and Brodie as they were talking to Leslie.

"Take Leslie back to the house and come back," Robbie ordered Gavin. Turning back to Leslie, he said, "Do a thorough scout of the house, inside and out."

"Aye, Milord," Leslie replied.

Gavin met up with them at the stream. It was a short distance from the edge of the woods. Robbie's daughter, Anna, was not there. It appeared there may have been a struggle. On the bank was a mark from, possibly, a foot being dragged a short distance.

Robbie had always been someone who could stay calm in the face of danger, but he could feel the anger building. He never had anyone threaten his loved ones. He clenched his jaw as he called to his dog, "Orion. Where's Anna? Find Anna."

The dog immediately stopped drinking and started sniffing around at the edge of the water where he was. He followed the scent to the scuffle mark on the bank. Staying there, he sniffed until he turned around and entered the woods.

They remounted their horses and followed the dog with Robbie directly behind. Brodie and Gavin spread out to cover more ground.

About fifteen minutes into their search, the dog barked and took off.

***

"Dinna make a sound," the man ordered Anna when he heard the dog bark. His hand was over her mouth as he sat behind her on his horse, guiding it behind some brush. He reached between the two of them and pulled out his pistol, pointing it toward the direction of the bark.

Anna looked down at the pistol, then out through the dense bushes as she looked for the dog. She could barely see it. The man behind her cocked the gun, and Anna jolted to the right as he pulled the trigger so he would miss the dog.

Gavin yelled in pain.

"Damn!" the man cursed quietly. He quickly replaced the pistol in his belt and started to turn the horse around as the dog darted around the brush, growling.

The horse started. The man let go of Anna to grab the reins as the horse reared, throwing Anna into the brush, screaming.

The horse took off with the dog in pursuit.

Robbie rounded the brush and pulled Anna up onto his horse. "Are ye alright?" he asked, looking her over.

She replied with a tearful nod. He pulled her in close as Brodie took aim and shot.

The man immediately fell off his horse. The dog

attacked him, grabbing his leg as it thrashed its head about. The man yelled in pain. Blood was already spurting out of his wound. He would not survive.

"Gavin!" Brodie called, placing his rifle back into its scabbard on his saddle. He turned his horse toward Gavin.

Gavin sat atop his horse, clenching his arm. Brodie grabbed some material scraps from his saddle pouch and reined in beside Gavin. "Let me see yer arm."

Gavin released his hand to reveal where the bullet had gouged his upper arm, just skimming the edge.

"Ye're lucky, lad. It only brushed ye." He wrapped the bandage around his arm, knotting it tightly. "Any closer in, it would've done severe damage."

By the time he had finished binding it, Robbie stopped beside them. He looked at Gavin, then Brodie.

"He'll be fine. It just braized his arm."

Robbie looked back at Gavin, "Are ye alright?"

"Aye," he replied, then looked at Anna. Her eyes were swollen from crying, but they had slowed to sniffles as she sat across her father's lap, holding him tight. Gavin asked, "And Lady Anna, are ye alright?"

She nodded.

"Let's get back to the house and tend to yer wound properly," Robbie ordered before calling the dog off the man who had already seized his screaming. "Orian! Leave it!"

***

Alana sat on a cushioned seat in the solar, wringing her hands. The normal dull ache in her head started to throb as she fretted over the situation. She glanced around the room, which seemed familiar. The minute she walked in, it gave her a warm, comforting feeling, but that quickly left when Gavin told Mary Ellen what was happening and told her to lock the door behind him.

By the time Mary Ellen got up to bar the door and sat back down, a knock came.

"Mom, it's me and Alex," Bryce said.

She immediately went back and opened the door, letting them in. Bryce had already gotten his sword.

"Dad went to get Anna. She had gone to the stream," he said.

Mary Ellen locked the door and sat beside the younger children, Kyle and Ellie, as Bryce stood in the middle of the room, watching the door with his sword ready. Alana and the younger children watched the door frightfully.

"Oh, for heaven's sake, Bryce, sit down," Mary Ellen said as she picked up Ellie's knitting and handed it back to her before picking up her own. She glanced between the door and the window. "Continue reading, Kyle," she ordered.

For several minutes, Kyle read as he stammered over several words. Mary Ellen would correct him or offer aid to Ellie's knitting. Then a shot rang out, and everyone immediately looked up as Alana cried out as if in pain, clenching her upper arm as she crouched over.

Gavin was shot! She knew it deep down in her soul.

Mary Ellen immediately put her knitting down and went over to Alana. "Are ye alright, dear?"

Alana straightened in her chair, still clutching her arm, and nodded. Tears streamed down her face. Her chest was so tight it was hard to breathe. She remembered when Thunder had bit Gavin and how she had felt the pain as if she had been the one who had been bitten. Why did she feel his pain? She rubbed her arm, and the pain began to recede, but her mind raced. What if Gavin died? It would all be her fault. The more she rubbed her arm, the more the pain eased.

Mary Ellen reached out to touch her arm, but Alana jerked away. Mary Ellen slowly moved away from her. Another shot rang out, and Mary Ellen walked to the window.

After a few minutes, she saw them break out of the woods at a gallop. Once she saw Anna with Robbie, she released her breath.

"Stay here!" she ordered as she unlocked it and ran down the stairs. She opened the door and bolted down the steps. She reached up to grab Anna as Robbie handed her down. She pulled her in for a hug. "Oh God! Yer all right!"

"Gavin's been hurt. He was shot in the arm," Robbie said as they all dismounted.

Mary Ellen froze, looked at Gavin's bandaged arm, and turned to Robbie with wide eyes, the color drained from her face.

"What is it?' Robbie asked.

Mary Ellen shook her head at him. Her expression cleared, and she turned to Gavin, "Let's get ye inside and look at yer arm."

"I'll ride out to find Henry. Nae doubt he will circle back around once my men leave him," Brodie replied.

"Aye," Robbie said. "Bring him to the jailhouse. I'll send Leslie to tell them he's coming."

Chapter 18

Anna burst into the solar, announcing that Gavin had been shot. Alana instinctively raised her hand to her arm, where a slight sting was still present.

The children ran out of the solar and down the stairs. Alana slowly followed. She only got a glimpse of Gavin before Margaret barked orders to heat some water and grab clean rags.

"Does it hurt?" Ellie, the youngest, asked as the kids gathered around Gavin, who was seated by one of the hearths in the hall.

"Aye," he replied, wishing Alana could stop helping and sit with him. She looked so... he did not know... a mixture of concern and confusion. He knew she felt the pain of the shot. She did when the wolf bit him, but they had never talked about it.

"Out with ye all," Margaret shooed the children away as she carried a pot of hot water.

"Go back to the solar so I can talk to yer father," Mary Ellen instructed them.

"Aye," they replied with disappointed faces as they turned and headed up the stairs.

Robbie and Mary Ellen retreated to the study as

Margaret tended to Gavin.

***

They sat on the sofa as Robbie filled Mary Ellen in on all that had transpired with Henry and the other man.

Mary Ellen was deep in thought while Robbie talked.

"I'm sure Brodie and his men will find him tonight," he reassured her as he brushed a stray hair from her face and wrapped it around her ear.

She shook her head and replied, "It isna that."

Robbie put one of her hands in his as he caressed it with the other. "What is it then?"

"It's just that... Alana..."

Robbie waited patiently, but his mind wandered to the possibility that she did not want Alana in their service for fear that harm may come to their family. He could certainly understand that point of view, but he gave Alex his word that he would help. It was the last thing he said to Alex. Besides, they were now already involved. Short of handing her over to her father, they would continue to be involved until Alana was safely wed. His hand stilled as he waited for her to continue.

"She yelled out in pain, clutching her arm when we heard the shot as if it had hit her. And then when I saw Gavin was shot in the same place..." She paused, looking down at her lap.

Oh God. Please let it be that she figured it out, he prayed. He squeezed her hand a tiny bit to urge her on.

She looked up to gaze into his eyes. "I just kept thinking about what ye told me after Alex died, how he had crouched in pain when the avalanche hit Anna."

Robbie could feel his heart speed up. She believed him! *Thank ye, God.*

"Is... Is she... Are they... Gavin and Alana..." she swallowed hard. "Are they Alex and Anna? Gavin's sixteen years old. That's how long ago they died."

Robbie nodded and cupped her face in both hands, "Aye." He smiled. "God, how I love ye." He kissed her and brought her in for a hug. Tears threatened to spill out. Mary Ellen pulled away.

"Did ye ken this the whole time?"

He nodded with apologetic eyes. "Aye."

"With Gavin?"

"Aye."

"And ye never told me?"

"I didna think ye believed me when I told ye about Alex and Anna. I thought perhaps ye might think I believed it because I wanted to believe Gavin was Alex... to keep his memory alive."

Her lips tightened to one side as she thought for a moment. "I suppose ye're right," she placed her hand on his cheek and kissed him. "But I believe ye now."

Robbie let out a long breath. "I canna tell ye how happy that makes me. Nae being able to tell ye was eating me up inside. I ken Alana had a hard life, and to think that Anna..." He could not finish his thought.

"She doesna ken, does she?"

He shook his head. "Nae. I think it is coming to her slowly, though."

"And what of Brodie? Does he ken?"

He chuckled. "He does now. Gavin slipped and said something that he shouldna have kenned when Brodie and I were reminiscing."

She nodded.

"What about the sorcerer ye told me about? Ye said that Gregory MacDonald held the curse over them. Is this Henry Grant the same person?"

"Nae." Robbie shook his head. "He is too old. He canna be much older than Gavin. He'll ken him when he meets him." Robbie brought Mary Ellen in and held her tight for a good minute. "Ah, wife, I am the luckiest man alive to have ye by my side. I couldna ask for anything more."

"I'm so sorry I doubted ye. I feel so bad."

"Well, ye believe me now; that is all that matters." Robbie went on to tell her about Gavin's idea to visit a seer.

They had already agreed to send Bryce to Lord Reay. Mary Ellen came up with the idea that she and the kids would go back with Brodie to take Bryce to Lord Reay, and she would visit her family. That would give Robbie enough time to take Gavin and Alana to the seer.

***

Robbie ordered Gavin to relax for the evening. He played chess with Robbie and Bryce until the evening meal. Gavin ate with the family. He used to eat with them more often when he was younger since he started as a guest. After coming into their service, Margaret always had him running around doing something, and his time at the dinner table with them became rare. Now, Gavin wanted to eat with the servants and Alana. He knew they wanted to keep an eye on him to make sure he did not overdo it, but he did not care. All he thought about was Alana.

She looked bewildered the entire time Margaret tended his arm. A couple of times, Gavin saw her raise her hand to the same spot on her arm where he had been shot, but Margaret kept her busy by ordering and complaining for her to snap out of her stupor. Perhaps this event would jolt her memory.

Alana no longer served any of the meals but stayed in the kitchens, so Gavin did not even get a chance to see her during the meal.

The evening dragged for Gavin. Brodie and his men arrived two hours after the evening meal. The family retired to the solar, but Robbie ordered platters of food brought out for Brodie and his men. Robbie and Gavin sat with them in the great hall as they ate.

"Did ye have a hard time finding the man?" Robbie asked.

"Nae. He hadna gone far. And, aye, he was headed back around, yet stuck to the woods." Brodie took a bite and washed it down with a swig of ale. "We left him off at the jailhouse and said ye would be down on the morrow to set judgment."

Robbie nodded his agreement.

Once the men had their fill, Robbie, Gavin, and Brodie retired to the study.

"I canna tell ye how fortunate I am that ye and yer men were here when this happened. I owe ye." Robbie said.

Brodie raised his hand, cutting him off. He shook his head and said, "Nae, brother. It was nothing that ye wouldna have done in return. I am only sorry that I canna stay longer as my men and I are due back." Brodie rubbed his chin before saying, "I suspect her father may come looking for her when Henry doesna return with her."

"Aye. I fear the same. And I dinna want my family here if trouble arises, but I canna leave Gavin injured."

Brodie nodded, and Robbie continued. "I ken ye came to escort Bryce back. Last year, I vowed to Lord Reay I would send him."

"Aye, my friend," Brodie broke in with a smile, not letting Robbie ask his question. "I will deliver him safely there."

"I thought it would be good if Mary Ellen and the kids visited her parents."

"I will escort them safely to her parent's house," Brodie promised.

"There isna anyone I would trust more with my family than ye. Thank ye."

"I will return once they are safe with yer in-laws and Bryce delivered to Lord Reay. I havena taken time off since…" He did not say it, but Gavin knew it was when his beloved wife, Jamilyn, passed from an illness. Robbie kept him informed of Brodie's life since Alex had been so close to him.

Robbie nodded.

"Three years," Brodie continued. "With the lads in training, I havena wanted to take time off to spend it alone in an empty house. I will stop at Grantown on my way back and see if I hear anything about what Alana's father may be planning."

"Aye," Robbie said. "They wouldna think a MacKay was working with me."

Gavin listened quietly to the whole conversation. A smile broke out on his face. To have both Robbie and Brodie helping him was more than he could have ever hoped. Knowing he had friends he could talk to about the curse was so good. It was lonely to have a secret that most folk would think was crazy. Anna knew Alex told Robbie their secret. Robbie had told Anna when they thought Gregory MacDonald killed Alex. So, when Alana finally remembers, she will feel relief knowing that Robbie understands... now, if only Alana would remember.

If they ever had a chance at breaking the curse, it was now.

Robbie looked at Gavin, then back to Brodie. "If Gavin is recovered by the time ye come back, we will go to my cabin along the coast. Perhaps we can find this seer."

The cabin had been the family vacation spot since Robbie was young. They never brought any servants there but shared the responsibilities of cooking and hunting. They had spent their days swimming, fishing, playing games, and riding horses along the beach. Robbie continued the tradition with his children.

Gavin's eyes lit up, and a smile formed across his face. "Truly?"

Chapter 19

Gavin watched Alana from atop his horse as she stretched and started to sit up in the cart. He watched her the whole ride. *This seer has to be able to help us.*

They had traveled for two days, and the sun sank slightly in the sky. Robbie told him they would make it to the cabin before nightfall.

Gavin smiled as Alana checked on the puppy in the basket. The puppy had been a good idea. Caring for something else always helped him get out of a slum. The puppy had finally opened its eyes a few days ago and started walking. Robbie even brought a goat so the puppy would have milk.

Robbie made Gavin rest after being wounded, which enabled him to spend more time with Alana. With Mary Ellen and the rest of the family gone, there was much less cooking and cleaning. Promising he would not carry anything, Gavin followed Alana around to the chicken coop or out while she hung laundry. She still did not talk much, but Gavin kept up small talk about the weather, the puppy, or his childhood stories. Despite not talking herself, she seemed to enjoy being around him.

At first, she was reluctant to leave the house, but Gavin

assured her that Henry could not hurt her anymore. He had been hung in the village two days after the attack on the Laird's family.

Brodie came back close to two weeks after he left. He stopped at the tavern at Grantown and listened as a group of men talked about the wolf and Alana, but other than foul jokes of how Henry was taking a slow ride back to spend quality time with his soon-to-be wife, they did not seem overly concerned that he was still gone.

Though relieved with the news, Gavin knew Alana feared her father's wrath when he discovered Henry's death. Gavin felt his body tense as he thought of the abuse Alana endured at the hands of her father. He would never lay a hand on her again.

The smell of salt hit Gavin, and he realized they were getting close to the shore. Even Alana sat up straighter and looked around as she inhaled deeply.

***

Alana squinted to get a better look at the two-story house as the men unloaded the cart. The house was familiar and gave her a calming feeling. She wanted to smile but was too bewildered to. Why did it seem like she had been there before?

She turned to take in the view of the ocean. She had never seen so much water. She wished she could get it more in focus.

"Come on in, Alana," Gavin said as he handed her the basket with the puppy and guided her through the door. "Ah, Milord, this is so nice," he exclaimed as they walked into a large room with a kitchen on one side and a dining area on the other. A large hearth was centered along the wall midway. On the far side of the dining side of the room was a door that appeared to be a bedroom. Stairs went up to a loft that looked over the first floor. There were three doors to the bedrooms above.

Gavin's eyes lit up as if he was a young lad. He looked at Alana, whose expression was not as carefree. She watched as Robbie opened all the windows to let some fresh air in. *It was always the first thing they did because it was so musty from being closed up for so long.* The thought made her heart race. She massaged her forehead with her free hand as the usual dull pain began to throb. The basket she carried seemed to weigh more than she could manage. Her arm lowered, and she started to sway.

Gavin grabbed the basket and guided her to the bench at the table. "Are ye well?" he asked, placing the basket on the table.

She said nothing but continued looking around the room, then up at the balcony. Her heart raced. She sat while the men brought in the supplies, cared for the horses and goat, and started a fire. Gavin brought in some milk for the puppy as Robbie and Brodie spread the remaining food from their journey.

Alana had just picked at her food, not eating anything. Shortly after the others finished eating, she started yawning.

"Why dinna ye go upstairs and sleep, lass? Pick out whichever room ye like." Robbie said.

Gavin handed the basket to Alana and grabbed a candle. He guided her to the stairs, lighting the candle in the placeholder on the wall at the bottom and again at the top. Once at the top, Alana looked at all the doors and immediately turned to the one that had been Anna's.

Robbie smiled.

***

Gavin knew Alana recognized the house. It was written all over her face. He was sure if it were not for her blurry vision that she would remember her life as Anna. He wished she would open up to him. They had spent much time together the last two weeks, but she still said nothing about things looking familiar. At least he knew she enjoyed his company. He even made her smile several times.

Gavin returned once she settled into her room.

"There is a village not far from here where we can get some provisions to last a few days," Robbie stated.

"I can take Gavin with me tomorrow, and we can make some inquiries there as well," Brodie said.

They had already discussed that Brodie would take Gavin, so no rumors spread that the Laird sought out a witch.

"Aye," Robbie agreed. "'Tis less than an hour's ride from here. Perhaps ye and I will hunt first thing in the morn, though."

"That sounds like a plan," Brodie agreed.

"Vanora," Gavin said. "That is the woman's name. She is said to have the sight."

"And where did ye come by that information?" Brodie asked.

"One of the servers at the tavern down by the docks told me."

"Dundee is a major port. I'm sure that tavern has just as many sailor stories of witches and warlocks as ye would hear in London," Robbie said.

Slowly, the conversation moved more into older times.

Though Gavin did not remember all the stories they told, the fact that he could join in the conversation with friends from a previous life was more than he could ever hope for.

He often crossed paths with someone from a previous life, a sibling, or a friend. He knew them, but they did not know him.

If felt so good to be recognized.

Chapter 20

Brodie, Gavin, and Alana followed the path through the woods, using the directions given by a man they met in the quaint town while picking up supplies. They left later in the morning after visiting the little village.

They quickly found the path after half an hour, behind a large fallen tree with the roots and ground standing taller than a man. They came to a Y in the path just as they were told. They went to the right, finding a large rock after a bit, confirming they had chosen correctly.

Brodie led the way with Alana seated before him, and Gavin took up the rear. He purposefully placed Alana with himself so Gavin would not be distracted. They could travel the wrong path for hours if they missed one landmark.

Gavin tried to keep his mind on the surroundings and remember landmarks, but his mind kept going back to what this woman might tell him. *What if she said there was nae hope, that the curse couldna be broken?* He shook his head to get it out of his mind.

When they asked about Vanora, the man responded, "Vanora, the healer?"

The healer? Perhaps she could take the curse away herself.

Gavin could not decide if he was excited or dreading hearing what she had to say, but not knowing was worse.

They did not tell Alana exactly why they were visiting this woman, only that they hoped to get some advice from her. For all she knew, it concerned her father.

Gavin wanted to leave Alana and talk to the woman alone, but Robbie and Brodie agreed she should go. Perhaps she needed them both to see how they could break the spell or break it herself.

Gavin felt that neither Robbie nor Brodie were overly confident that this visit would amount to anything, but he had to try. He had been so sure if he killed his assailant, it would end the curse, but when he finally succeeded, they died anyhow just to do it over again. It was disheartening, to say the least. How many lifetimes was his only goal to kill his adversary without one of them dying in the process? Gavin's light brown locks sprung as he shook his head, thinking about it.

***

After an hour, the path led close to the edge of the woods before curving and running parallel to the edge. Every once in a while, they saw the shore below through a break in the trees. The shoreline curved, creating a cove butted up against a cliff on the other side. The fierce waves crashed against the cliffside of the cove.

Right past the wood line, a gentle hillside leading to the beach had an array of wildflowers of every color. For a brief second, Brodie saw a woman coming out of the water, but the branches got in the way the next second. *Was she naked?* He felt tightening in his chest as he nudged his horse with just a bit of pressure from his legs. The horse obeyed immediately.

Brodie continued to look out toward the shore for another break in the trees. His next view was of her in a thin white dress, perhaps her shift. The wind blew the gown, so it formed every curve of her. Her red hair was in the air as if she had flicked her head up from a bent position.

He lost sight of her again.

Was this the woman they sought?

He flicked his reins, and the horse moved into a trot. She was much too young. The man in the village talked about how she healed him as a lad, but this woman looked younger than him. *Unless she was a maid of the sea...* His heart raced. When the trees parted next, he saw her walking up toward the edge of the woods.

Another fifteen minutes passed as the path weaved deeper into the woods until it stopped in front of a small cabin. Smoke billowed out of the chimney, implying someone was home.

Brodie looked back at Gavin, who shrugged his shoulders. Trees surrounded the house except for one side, where a patch of herbs and a few vegetables grew. Brodie looked around cautiously before dismounting and reaching up to help Alana down. He looped the reins on a branch, more to prevent the horse from feasting in the herb garden than running off. The war horse would not take off without him.

Gavin did the same, then grabbed Alana's arm and nudged her toward the door.

***

Gavin was both excited and cautious. He let go of Alana's hand, wiped his sweaty palms on his plaid, and looked nervously at Brodie, who tipped his head toward the door, urging him on.

Gavin knocked and stepped back as they waited.

The door creaked open and the same beautiful woman Brodie had seen answered. Her damp, auburn hair fell to her waist. She wore a white shift with a Duncan plaid draped over her shoulder like a toga, tied with a belt at her waist. The plaid went down to her ankles, but since it lay over one side, one leg showed through her thin white shift.

"Hello," the woman spoke quietly in an angelic voice. She glanced at them all, finally resting on Brodie, and smiled.

"Are ye Vanora?" Gavin asked, pulling her attention to Gavin, then Alana.

Looking back at Gavin, she replied, "Aye, I am."

"My name is Gavin, and this is Alana and Sir Brodie."

She glanced at Alana and Brodie as he introduced them, lingering on Brodie before looking back to Gavin. "I've been waiting for ye."

Gavin's heart jolted. *She was a seer!*

She opened the door to welcome them in. The small one-room house was lit only by a small window and a blazing fire in the fireplace.

Gavin hesitated, stealing another look at Brodie.

"Come, come," she said as she moved by the hearth and turned to watch them enter. They stepped inside, and Alana tripped over the threshold, but Gavin steadied her quickly.

Gavin searched for the words he had gone over in his mind for the entire ride, but they seemed to have disappeared. He felt like a lad, nervously telling his father he did something he should not have.

"I have come to… seek yer wisdom, in matters… not of—" Gavin started but was cut off by the woman.

"Nae." She raised her hand. Gavin's shoulders slumped in disappointment. "First, we will tend to this lass here."

Tend to Alana?

Vanora slid a chair from the table to the fireplace before she guided Alana to the chair. Once Alana was seated, the woman turned and pulled out several small jars that lined the narrow table that stretched the room's length.

She put what appeared to be dirt in a wooden bowl and added a pinch of this and a sprinkle of that. Then, grabbing a bundle of dried herbs hanging from the ceiling, she broke off several leaves and added them to her bowl.

Gavin's heart beat faster. The villagers called her a healer. He was so intent on ending the curse that it had not occurred to him that she could heal Alana's eyesight. At least, that is what he hoped she was doing.

"I hadna anticipated the lass being in this bad of condition," the woman declared as she reached for a bucket next to the fireplace. She looked into the almost empty bucket and pinched her lips together. She poured the water into a wooden cup and handed the bucket to Brodie. "Would ye mind, Sir, going to the stream and getting me some more water?"

***

Brodie could not take his eyes off her. He felt as if he was under the spell of her beauty. Feelings that had been dead in him for years seemed to surface. A pinch of guilt seized him as he thought of his deceased wife.

"The stream?" he asked. He had not seen any stream on his way.

"Aye," she said, "'Tis nae far, straight out the front door a hundred paces or so and to the right."

Her smile was more beautiful than the sunrise. Brodie grabbed the bucket, and their hands brushed each other, making his fingers tingle where they touched. He turned around and left the cottage, wondering if the woman had bewitched him. He did not believe in sorcery until Gavin convinced him that he was, well… had been… Alex. Seeing this woman standing out by the ocean, he could almost imagine her emerging from the sea and shedding her siren skin.

Brodie shook his head as he gathered the water from the stream, a stream which he should have noticed or at least heard when they arrived. He could not believe one glimpse of her distracted him so much that he missed it!

***

Gavin placed his arm on Alana's shoulder as Vanora went about grinding her mixture with an oblong stone. He felt her instantly relax.

Once ground to her satisfaction, she poured the water from the cup into it as Brodie returned. She handed the cup to Brodie to refill and stirred her poultice with a wooden spoon. She continued adding water until the contents of the bowl resembled a thick glob of mud.

With the bowl in her hands, she walked over to Alana and knelt before her. "Close yer eyes, my dear," she instructed soothingly.

Alana glanced at Gavin, who stood beside her.

He nodded. Vanora was going to cure her. *Thank you, God!*

Alana closed her eyes, and Vanora applied the salve she made over them. Vanora rose, placing the empty bowl on the floor. Gavin stepped aside as she walked around the chair to stand behind Alana.

Vanora reached around to place her hands over Alana's eyes. She closed her eyes, and the room instantly became still, as if time stopped. After a minute, Gavin noticed Vanora's chest rise and fall as she took deep breaths. The flames cast a glow on her, making her copper hair redder.

Gavin glanced at Brodie, who shrugged his shoulders and raised his eyebrows.

Soon, Vanora's breathing normalized, but Alana's became rapid and shallow. Her arm began to twitch every once in a while.

Gavin moved around toward the front, looking from Vanora then to Alana. At one point, Alana's head jerked. Was that normal? Vanora twitched herself but held her position behind her with her hands over Alana's eyes.

The brisk twitches made Gavin nervous. Was Alana all right? He knelt and took one of Alana's hands into his in hopes of comforting her, but as he blinked, he seemed to get dizzy, and stars flashed before him. He closed his eyes, hoping to suppress the dizziness. The spots disappeared. All was black, then a blurred vision, until it slowly came into focus.

Alana's father grabbed him and slammed him against the house. Nae… nae him. These were Alana's visions he saw! His head felt as if it split. He felt himself shudder.

Her father picked up a log as a wolf attacked him. Gavin opened his eyes briefly. The vision disappeared. He looked up at Brodie before closing his eyes again.

He was in a room, and a flash of something flew through the air before he felt the sting of it on his cheek. He fought against the pain as Alana twitched. He concentrated on his breathing as he felt the lash of a belt three times on his back. The scene changed, and everything was calm. He was in the woods. A stick glided in the air, and the wolf retrieved it. The second time it brought back the stick, everything turned gray. The stick was out of its mouth, and it growled.

He felt himself in a panic as she backed up against a tree and held out Alex's dagger, waving it frantically as several pairs of eyes slowly crept out of the surrounding woods. "This is it," her thoughts penetrated his. He felt Alana shiver as she was swept up onto a horse so fast the scenery became a blur, which turned into ripples of water. The vision lightened, and a sense of serenity washed over him.

A fish made a trail, surfacing several times before turning into a stone, skipping across the water, and making a final big splash. His heart felt light. Waves came in, and Gavin could feel his body move as if jumping over them with a joyful heart as she went under.

Suddenly, he panicked as she was being held underwater. She tugged on the rope around her waist, and a large stone tied to the end dragged her down. Alana jerked, and her hand almost pulled out of Gavin's grip, but he held tight. He couldn't breathe.

The water turned into dark clouds rolling by, giving way to fluffy white ones. A falcon flew toward her, landing on a windowsill, and once again, peace and serenity washed over him.

The Gift of the Healing Stones

Turning toward a fireplace, he saw the flames as they danced a mesmerizing dance before growing. Smoke filled the room, and he had trouble breathing. The room shook... no, the ground shook. Despair ran through him. He looked up as the hillside shifted and massive amounts of rock, dirt, and snow rolled down. His heart thumped in panic.

She was being dragged at a fast pace around a mountain before she got up to run to keep up. "I have to keep up, so I'm nae dragged." Her thoughts were inside of his head again.

He felt someone running beside him, tugging one hand as they tumbled to the ground laughing. He rolled on his back, trying to catch his breath from laughing so hard. He looked up to a vibrant blue stone spinning on the end of a ribbon. She joyfully reached up to grab it. Suddenly, her hands extended to someone as she descended the steps. He sensed her turmoil about what would become of this person she loved so much if she chose the other.

He felt the piercing of a sword in her back as he looked down to see the tip of it protruding from her front. She collapsed, and everything went blank.

Gavin's head still pounded from the first vision when she was slammed against the house.

A blue swirl broke the blackness for a brief second. Gavin felt as if he was moving and became disarrayed.

Another blue swirl appeared, and he felt his eyes twitch with the swirl.

A couple more times, he felt as if he was moving in the dark, followed by the swirl, until at one point, the pain in his head receded ever so slightly. The movement stopped, but the flashes got longer. With each flash of blue, his headache eased. Several times, the flashes repeated without moving until finally, his head seized, hurting. Then everything was black again.

After the visions stopped, Gavin opened his eyes, tears streaming down his face. He removed his hand from Alana's and wiped his eyes. She had been in pain this whole time, and he did not even know.

Vanora took deep breaths but kept her eyes closed, and Alana's eyes covered with her hands.

Gavin sat back, crossing his legs as he watched and waited.

Alana's twitching eased considerably, and after several minutes, Vanora lowered her hands and opened her eyes.

"She will rest now," Vanora said. She turned to Brodie. "Return in two days. I need some supplies from the village. Ye will fetch them for me and bring them when ye return."

With that, she rambled off her list of supplies.

Chapter 21

Robbie placed his rifle in the corner as he walked into the cabin. Brodie sat by himself, holding a mug. He looked like he was deep in thought.

"Well?" Robbie asked, strolling over, and placing the game he caught in the traps on the table.

Brodie looked at him, gave him a quirky smile, and shrugged before pouring Robbie a drink.

Robbie looked around for Gavin, but he was not there.

"He's watching over Alana."

Robbie accepted the drink and sat down across from Brodie. "Well, did he find what he was looking for?"

Brodie looked at him thoughtfully as Robbie took a swig of ale.

"What?" Robbie asked, putting down his mug.

"Well… before Gavin could get his question out, she told him she had to tend to Alana first."

"Tend to her?"

"Aye. Ye see, the folks in the village referred to Vanora not as a seer but a healer," Brodie replied.

"A healer," Robbie repeated, picking up his cup and taking another drink.

"Aye. So, she sat Alana down and put this muck on her

eyes before laying her hands on her. She stayed like that for at least half an hour while Alana twitched and moaned. Gavin held Alana's hands, and he seemed to drift off in the same way."

"So, this woman healed her eyesight?"

"I dinna ken," Brodie replied. "She's been sleeping ever since."

"And Gavin?" Robbie tensed and began to stand. *If anything happened to him...*

"He's fine." Brodie waved his hand so Robbie could sit back down.

Robbie looked up at the loft and then back to Brodie skeptically. "If anything happens to Gavin..." Gavin was under his care.

"Truly," Brodie assured him. Robbie sat back down, and Brodie continued. "He said he saw visions of her life."

"But she said nothing about the curse?"

Brodie shook his head. "She said to come back in two days."

"Two days? Perhaps she is nae a seer... only a healer and she wants to check up to see if Alana is better," Robbie offered.

Brodie shook his head, but his features were soft as if lost in a daydream.

Robbie chuckled. "Are ye smitten with the old witch?"

Brodie shook his head again. His eyes were as big as saucers. "She isna a witch. Perhaps a..." he paused, then leaned back.

"Perhaps what?"

Brodie leaned in close to look Robbie in the eyes. "Perhaps a *ceasg*," he replied.

Robbie laughed. "A siren? Ye, the last one to believe in

mystical powers," Robbie said as he wiggled his fingers in front of Brodie's face.

Brodie pushed them aside and smiled at Robbie. "Aye, I ken. But ye dinna see her as I did. I saw her by the sea before we arrived." Brodie took a deep breath. "Her auburn hair was like the color of autumn leaves… and… her voice…" He paused.

"I thought she was an older woman," Robbie stated.

"Aye, that's just it! The man said she cured him as a lad; he couldna have been but five years my youth. And she looks younger than me."

"Perhaps it was her mother that cured the man."

"Perhaps… or maybe she is a *ceasg*."

Chapter 22

The first thing Alana noticed was that the pain in her head was gone. She kept her eyes shut tight. The pain always worsened when she opened them and sat up.

Then she noticed she lay on a soft bed, not the floor as she usually slept. Her eyelids were heavy, but she eased them open a slit. Still, no pain. The vision of the ceiling was clear. Her sight was back! Her eyes flew open the rest of the way.

She heard a goat bleating and slowly turned her head toward the sound. The opened window was in perfect focus. She sat up, her heart pounding.

She looked around the room. A fireplace with a stone mantel adorned the wall across from the bed. No fire burned as it was a warm day. In the corner was a stand with a pitcher and water basin. It was simply decorated but appealing, and it looked expensive. She had seen it before.

She glanced over the bed. On the floor beside the stand lay cloths with dried mud. She instinctively put a hand to one eye as she remembered the woman. The woman had cured her sight! She stretched out her arm, wiggling her fingers, and smiled.

A scratching sound and a small whimper caught her

attention. The puppy!

She crawled to the foot of the bed and leaned over to see the cutest little brown and black puppy staring up at her with wide eyes.

"Well, hello! It's nice to see ye, too." She reached down to pick the wee thing up and pulled herself back up to a sitting position. She was half expecting the pain in her head to come back from the movement, but it did not.

She lifted the puppy to eye level to examine it more closely. "Yer more handsome than I imagined," she said as she brought it to her face to feel its soft fur tickle her cheek. She laughed and moved her cheek up and down against its body.

The door opened, and Gavin walked in with a bowl of milk.

"Ah, yer up," his eyes lit up when he smiled at her. Her stomach filled with butterflies. Some of his light brown locks had escaped his leather tie and cradled his round face.

She smiled at him. She felt a kinship with him as if she had known him all his life, but she did not recognize him.

"Gavin," she said quietly, connecting his face with his voice.

"I brought some milk for the puppy," he said, placing the bowl on the ground.

She bent over and placed the puppy on the floor, surprised again that her head did not throb from bending over. She watched as the puppy scuttled over to the bowl.

Gavin held it to prevent the puppy from tipping it over.

Alana studied the puppy and Gavin as her heart grew light. She was happier than she could ever remember. She felt refreshed. Gavin was looking at the puppy.

"Thank ye," she said quietly.

He immediately turned his head and smiled, giving her a strange tingling feeling. She was suddenly bashful. She never initiated their conversations before.

"So, yer sight is better?" he asked, his eyes seemed to twinkle with joy.

"Aye," she replied shyly.

"Do ye…" he began, then looked around the room. "…ken where ye are?"

She looked around quickly and nodded. "Aye. We are at Laird Duncan's vacation house."

Gavin let out a breath as his shoulders slumped a bit. "Aye."

She heard a hint of sadness in Gavin's voice and wondered why her answer saddened him. He said she was correct.

He picked up the puppy once it finished and handed it to her. "Ye slept for almost a whole day. I dare say ye should eat something. The midday meal will be ready shortly." Gavin stood and walked to the door. He turned around before leaving. "I'll see ye downstairs in a few minutes?"

"Aye."

***

Alana walked out of her room and took in the view of the large room below. Her eyes widened, and a warm feeling came over her. It looked so familiar. She walked down the stairs with the puppy in the basket, placing it on the floor at the base of the table.

Gavin lifted a small cauldron off the hook in the hearth and carried it over, placing it on a wood slab in the middle of the table set with wooden bowls.

"Sir Brodie went to the village to get supplies for the healer and hasna yet returned, but Milord said we'll eat without him," Gavin declared.

Alana looked around slowly, taking in the kitchen before turning around to view the rest of the first floor. She stopped as her eyes locked on the door to the master bedroom. The door was opened, displaying a large bed.

A strange sensation overcame her. *My parents' room! Nae, how can that be?* She was frozen in place, unable to pry her eyes away. *Why does she recognize this place?*

"Ah, yer awake," Robbie said as he entered the house with a pitcher of fresh milk.

His voice added to the feeling she was experiencing. Her heart sped up as she turned to look at him. Her eyes grew big. The second she saw him, she recognized him. He was older, but she knew him. She stared at him in silence. How did she know him? She could not believe it.

He stood still with the bucket in hand as she studied him. His name came to her. Her lips seemed to move on their own accord as the word "Robbie" escaped as a bare whisper.

A smile slowly came across Robbie's lips before saying, "I ken ye couldna have forgotten *me*."

She started to sway, and Gavin quickly guided her to a bench at the table where Robbie placed the milk pitcher.

"Ye must eat something," Gavin said, slopping a spoonful of stew in her bowl.

They sat in silence for a bit as Alana studied them. Suddenly, it hit her: He was her brother... well... Anna's brother. She snapped her head at Gavin. She knew who he was. He was hers.

Gavin smiled with a twinkle in his eyes. Oh God, the curse! They thought they had broken it, but they didn't. They were doomed! How could he be smiling?

She looked away.

In this life, she had always been suspicious of others because of her father's abuse, but she always felt comfortable around Gavin. Now, she knew why. He was her soul mate. With him, she felt…safe, but the apprehension was still there. They could not have a life together. The uneasiness would always be there.

It was true. There was no hope for them. She knew it in the pit of her stomach when she remembered that Alex had succeeded in killing Gregory MacDonald, the man who held the curse over them. They planned to marry several months later, but the avalanche…there was no way to end the curse.

Gavin extended his hand across the table and touched her hand. "Ye need to eat, Alana."

Some of her fears subsided. It pulled her. She wanted to believe. It was part of the curse… the feeling that they could overcome it. Oh, there was always a speck of doubt in the back of their minds, but when they touched, hope prevailed. She loved him so much. Love had to conquer. Didn't it?

She picked up her spoon and looked at the bowl. She could see her food! A small smile came to her lips before they wrapped around the spoon.

Robbie took a spoonful of stew before saying, "So, ye remember? Do ye ken where ye are?"

She looked around as she slowly chewed and nodded. Once she swallowed, she looked at him and replied, "We're at our vacation home."

***

After they ate, Gavin took Alana down to the shore. As they walked from the house, he was quiet, giving her time to take everything in. He set the basket with the puppy down and spread a blanket close to the water's edge. He took a deep breath and looked out to sea, then at her.

"It is beautiful here," he said, stretching his legs and crossing his ankles.

She grabbed the puppy that had escaped from the basket and put it on her lap. "Aye."

"It's a lot to take in," Gavin stole a glance at her as she focused on the puppy.

She knew he wanted to talk about the curse. After dinner, her fears returned. Every lifetime, they would be so full of hope, thinking they could outsmart fate, but they truly believed they succeeded last time. There was no way to break the spell. None. She could not go through it another time.

Her life up until then was horrible with her father. She knew he had to have felt her beatings and wanted to save her, but to have him die in her arms one more time when they thought they were so close to ending the curse was too much to take. Her father's beatings were only physical pain. Her soulmate being ripped away from her was worse.

Well, she would not make that mistake again. They thought they had done it. They killed Gregory, and both of them survived. There was no way to break the curse. Eternity in hell would be less painful than living through it time after time.

He looked back at the sea and asked, "Have ye ever

been to the sea?"

Her head snapped to him. Didn't he know?

"Well," he lifted one shoulder and smirked. "this time around."

She let out the breath she was holding. "Nae." She shook her head.

The puppy escaped from her hold, and Gavin grabbed her hand as she reached for it. "Let him explore. He willna go far."

The sensation of his hand on hers surged throughout her body... warmth, love, hope. She did not pull away.

"What do ye remember, Alana?"

Her gaze lifted from their hands and met his. If she doubted whether her memories were real or just a dream, it all vanished when she looked into his eyes. They were the same dark, piercing eyes she remembered. They seemed to see right down to her soul. Her heart raced. He was indeed her kindred spirit... but she could not have him. With his hand on hers, there was hope that there was a way. She took a deep breath and turned to where the puppy was sniffing the water, following it as it receded.

As the next wave came, it pushed the puppy over. It quickly got up and ran back to the shore. She smiled and then looked back at Gavin. She loved him so much.

"I remember..." *The curse and many dashed hopes and deaths*. She pulled her hand out of his. "that there isna any hope for us." She looked away.

"Alana." When she did not look back at him, Gavin called her again. "Alana." She slowly turned her head. "The healer... she is a seer. I... I hoped she could tell us how to end this curse."

She searched his eyes and tears began to build up in her

own. She shook her head. "We were so sure if we killed him, it would be over. Every time we are hopeful, then our hopes are dashed."

She looked back out to the sea. She had loved it here at one time. She did have fond memories, but now even that was tainted with hopelessness.

"Alana, we have to try."

"I want to try. I truly do, but my heart canna take another disappointment. Ye shouldna have—"

"Nae! I considered nae searching for ye, but I kenned ye were in danger. I… I feel yer pains."

She knew it. But this would end much worse for her. Had Henry brought her back to her father, she would be dead now. She would not realize what she was missing for perhaps another twenty years.

"I couldna leave ye in a life like that."

Tears streamed down her face. "A thousand beatings is nothing to the pain of having ye ripped from me. I canna go through it again." God, she wished she were dead!

***

Gavin saw her eyes glance at the dagger at his waist. His heart raced. He would die if she tried to kill herself.

He immediately grabbed her hands in both of his and shifted to kneel before her.

"Dinna say that. Please," he pleaded. He understood. He would rather die than go through it all again, but he had family that loved him. He knew that by starting over, they had a chance to live several years without being bogged down by the reality of it. Of course, there was no guarantee that either would live a happy childhood. Alana sure had not this time.

She tugged at her hands, but Gavin would not let go until she promised to go with him. He knew the minute he let go, the only thing left in her mind would be doubts.

"Let us see what the seer says. Please."

She looked down at their hands. "Aye," she whispered.

Chapter 23

The men secured several sacks of supplies to the horses for Vanora as soon as everyone had broken their fast.

"Do ye ken how to ride?" Gavin asked her as he walked the smallest of the three horses to her.

She shook her head even as she remembered how close she had been to her horse in her previous life.

"We'll go slow for ye," Gavin said as he helped her onto her horse.

Gavin and Alana rode side by side behind Brodie, making no more conversation than to point out a unique tree or an animal.

Once off the wagon path, Gavin fell behind. The path no longer allowed more than one horse at a time. It allowed Alana to think. She had distanced herself for so long from everyone, ever since her father had sent her brother away to join the Watch. Now that she remembered her previous lives, she wanted to be with Gavin more than anything. It explained the sense of peace she had in his presence. Initially, she tried to push him away like everyone else, but her mind kept drifting back to him.

Now she knew why she was not able to. It was not possible. It was their destiny.

She had chosen him when she was betrothed to another. Her brother and betrothed had arranged her marriage to bind the fragile alliance between two families. It was known that her betrothed had several mistresses. He even brought one to their engagement celebration. Not only was her betrothed the science advisor and astrologer to the king, but it was whispered that he was a powerful sorcerer.

She had secretly been in love with another long before the arrangement was made. Thinking of him made her heart race. Her betrothed had found out and brought her before the assembly. She was forced to make a decision.

Her chest tightened as she remembered. Standing before them, she studied them, each so different from the other. The one was all power and self-centered, the other ordinary and selfless. One was dark with sharp features, the other pale with softness. There could be no two more different. It occurred to her that as sure as she was that the one would give her happiness, the other would bring her only fear and pain.

She had intended to choose her betrothed for the sake of her family and people. Still, in that instant of fear of a lifetime of misery, she walked down the three marble steps toward her lover, mindless of the subjects who would benefit from the union her brother arranged. As her hand clasped her lover's, her betrothed unsheathed his sword and cursed them both. She could feel her whole body tense, recalling it. Thinking of it always brought intense fear and anger.

She swore she could feel the blade sliding in as she remembered that day. She clutched the saddle.

Gavin nudged his horse, so he was right beside hers, causing them to stop in the narrow path. He touched her arm. She took a deep breath and eased her grip.

Brodie stopped his horse and looked back with a frown. Gavin nodded to her, and she put her horse back in motion. Gavin followed.

The feelings were always so intense when she thought of that moment, but the touch of her kindred spirit always softened her. The misery she would have had to endure in that one lifetime with a cruel man would have been far less painful than what she had lived with over and over again. She knew her choice was fatal, but the thought of living without the one she loved was too much. She never imagined the outcome. She would have been better off choosing her betrothed and taking her own life.

Her thoughts broke off as the path led toward the edge of the woods, where she could see the ocean in occasional breaks in the trees.

Brodie's pace seemed to slow with each break in the trees until the path curved back through the woods. Soon, the small cottage came into view, and Alana's heart raced. Could Gavin be right? Was there really a way out of this hell hole?

***

They came to a stop. Brodie and Gavin dismounted, but Alana was as stiff as a statue.

"We have to try," Gavin whispered, breaking her daze. She looked from atop her horse to see his outstretched arms reaching up to help her. He pleaded with his eyes. She reached for him, letting him set her down before Brodie thrust a sack into her arms.

Gavin and Brodie each grabbed a sack, and they all

turned toward the door. Gavin wiped his sweaty hands on his britches before knocking. She had to be able to help them. They were out of ideas.

Vanora opened the door. The woman's red hair fell off her shoulders in soft curls, which lay against her tartan, making the red lines of the plaid stand out more than usual. Her intense blue eyes focused on Alana after a glance at the group.

"Ah, so I see yer sight is better," she said.

Alana curtsied, "Aye, ma'am. I thank ye."

"And the pain in yer head? Has it gone away, too?"

Brodie stole a look at Gavin. After Gavin experienced Vanora healing Alana, he suspected as much. He had felt the throbbing in his head up until the blue swirls began. Usually, when they felt each other's pain, it was only the initial onset of the affliction. He had no idea she was in pain the whole time. He could feel the bile rise to his throat. He wished she would have told him.

"Aye. Thank ye," Alana replied.

"Ye are quite welcome, my dear," she said as she cupped Alana's cheek.

Vanora looked at Brodie, who nodded and lifted his sack slightly. "We brought the items ye requested."

"Come in, come in." She backed into the room, opening the door wider. "Just put everything on the bed." She gestured to the bed opposite the kitchen. "Have a seat, my dear, as the men carry the rest of the items in. I will heat some water for tea."

Alana looked around at herbs hanging from pegs on the wall as Vanora busied herself heating water and looking through herbs to steep.

Brodie and Gavin made one more trip to the horses.

After placing the sacks on the bed, Gavin sat across from Alana at the small table.

Vanora poured each of them a cup of herbal tea and sat down at the table, looking at each of them. Upon locking eyes with Gavin, he spoke up.

"We would like to thank ye for what ye have done for Alana," he began.

"It wasna a problem at all. But that wasna why ye came in the first place, was it?" Vanora asked, her voice soothing.

Gavin was so nervous. He suspected she already knew the reason for their visit but did not say so. "That is correct. We have come in hopes that…" Vanora looked at him patiently as he searched for his words. Her attention was so calming, the way she just smiled, like a mother would with a small child. "That ye would… ye see, we were cursed… and…"

"And ye hoped that I could lift yer curse," Vanora finished for him.

"Aye," Gavin said before unconsciously holding his breath while waiting for her answer.

Her eyes saddened as she shook her head. "I canna."

Alana's shoulders slumped, and she bent her head to look at her hands, which grasped each other on the table. It was obvious she was close to tears.

Vanora opened her hand and gently covered Alana's hand. "*I* canna break the curse, but there is always a way to break it." Alana met her gaze. "All hope isna lost, child."

Vanora got up and walked to the small bedside table where several stones lay. Grabbing one, she carried it over, placed a long black pointed crystal in the middle of the table, and sat back down. She took Alana's hand, who sat beside her, and Gavin's on her other side. She merely nodded to Brodie before closing her eyes.

Brodie looked at Gavin and Alana as they closed their eyes, following Vanora's example. He grabbed each of their hands, completing the circle, and closed his eyes.

Vanora's breathing was deep and controlled; eventually, they all breathed in sync as if they were one. Soon, the scene of the curse flashed before their eyes, but not like the visions during the healing process. At that time, Gavin felt the emotions with the visions, the pain, fear, and joy. Every emotion that went through Alana had flowed through him. This time was different, somehow detached. It was as if it was someone else they watched.

A woman descended the steps and reached for her lover. Her betrothed unsheathed his sword. "If I cannot have ye, nae one will! I curse ye both! For eternity, ye shall both long for each other, but yer union will forever be unattainable," he yelled as he drove his sword completely through her from behind.

The sword came out her front, almost piercing her lover. As the sorcerer pulled out his sword, her lifeless body fell into her lover's arms, and her tiara fell to the white marble floor in a pool of blood. The vision of the tiara in the bright red pool of blood against the pure white marble stone stayed for several seconds before fading into a blur of nothing.

After several minutes, Vanora's breathing normalized, and she let go of Alana and Gavin's hands, opening her eyes as they all did. They watched her as she stared at the gemstone in the middle of the table until she finally looked up at them.

Taking a deep breath, she began. "Ye need to return to where the curse was cast."

Gavin and Alana glanced at each other.

"Ye will profess yer love there and have it blessed with the blood of the one who gave it," Vanora added.

Alana's shoulders dropped again as she shook her head. "That will never happen."

Vanora softly placed her hand on Alana's. "Ah, my sweet child. Ye've had so much pain that ye have lost yer faith." Vanora's voice was quiet yet confident, like a siren's song, luring a sailor to the rocky cliffs.

Gavin did not need any more convincing.

Alana jerked her hand away. "It took us centuries to kill him without succumbing to our own injuries from the attempt, and now ye say we need to kill him in the place where he cursed us?"

Vanora shook her head with a smile. "Nae, child, naw kill him. Death will only bring more death. He needs to bless it, swear by his blood."

Alana let out an exasperated breath and turned her head. "He will never agree to that!"

Vanora took a cleansing breath and looked at Gavin, then at Brodie as she thought. As if coming to some resolution, she nodded and stood.

She walked over to her bedside table, pulled a sachet from beneath, and set it on the bed. Sitting on the bed, she searched through her sack, angling it toward the window to see the contents clearly without emptying it all on the bed. Pulling out several items, she returned to the table and sat down.

***

Vanora held out a vibrant green stone with swirled patterns

toward Alana. The stone was smooth as if polished by the sea. She waited for Alana to open her hand before gently placing it in her palm.

The stone was cool in her palm.

"This stone is malachite. It has given me great peace during times when I felt there was little hope. It has helped me to forgive and move on. May it ease yer heart and bring ye tranquility, child."

As Vanora talked, Alana could feel the tension leaving her shoulders, if ever so slightly. She looked down at the stone and slowly closed her hand around it.

Vanora pulled out another green stone, but instead of the green swirls, this one was dull green with traces of light brown and pale yellow. The stone was odd shaped with divots, yet smooth, like the first one. She held the stone in her palm toward Gavin.

"Green Jasper. It drives away evil spirits. Rub it to help ease the negative energy between ye and the one ye seek."

Alana's heart was racing. Hope warmed her insides. Could they truly end all this pain?

"Thank ye," Gavin said, taking the stone from her palm. He cast a hopeful look toward Alana.

Alana smiled back. They could do this.

***

Brodie watched Vanora hand the two stones to Gavin and Alana. He was not sure he believed the stones had power, but he could understand Alana changing her outlook on the situation because she thought they did. It was a mindset, that was all.

"And for ye," Vanora said to Brodie, who sipped his

tea as he looked at the stone that Gavin held. Brodie's eyebrows rose as he looked down at her tiny fist on the table before him. She slowly opened her hand.

Brodie's heart sped up. He recognized the stone. It was said to be a treasure of mermaids. The aquamarine, or seawater stone, was long, thin, and light blue—a translucent crystal. He glanced at her. Her lips formed a soft smile. Her eyes captivated him. They were the same color as the stone in her hand... the color of the sea.

He casually set down his cup and looked back down at her hand. The stone was not smooth like the others but ragged and big enough that it took up half of her tiny palm.

Slowly, he picked it up.

"This stone is very powerful. It will help and protect you in many ways in your travels."

He nodded, studied the crystal between his fingers, and then looked back at Vanora. "Thank ye."

She smiled. "Ye are quite welcome, Sir. Thank ye for the supplies. I dinna get to the village often as I dinna own a horse. The supplies should last me quite some time."

Vanora turned back toward Alana, then to Gavin. "The one ye seek can be found in Inverness," she said, standing up and gathering her and Brodie's empty cup.

Gavin and Alana picked up their cups and finished their tea as Brodie put his stone in his sporran and stood.

Chapter 24

"Inverness," Robbie said after they informed him of the details of their visit. "Well, we will all go to Inverness together, and I will help ye find him. And where is it that this curse was cast?" He glanced between Gavin and Alana, then focused on Brodie's stern expression.

"Brunswick," Brodie replied.

"Brunswick?" Robbie questioned, turning back to Gavin for confirmation.

"Aye," Gavin confirmed with a nod of his head, his loose locks bouncing in front of his face.

"I thought ye said he was Scottish," Robbie said.

"Aye," Gavin and Alana agreed together.

"Scot," Alana added. She looked past Robbie and Brodie, who sat across from her, as she stared at the wall. "Michael Scot," she clarified. "He was born along the Scottish border." Her body tensed, thinking of him. "He was tutor, science advisor, and astrologer to the young Frederick II, King of Sicily."

Alana clenched her jaw, still gazing at the far wall. Gavin took the water pitcher from the table and poured her a glass. She looked down at the glass, and her heart warmed. He was always so thoughtful. She glanced at him, accepted it with a smile, and took a sip before continuing.

"My name was Ingibiorg. I was the daughter of Henry the Lion and Matilda of England. I was an ill child and was cared for in private in the castle with limited visitors. A young servant lad would sneak in and befriended me." She stole a look at Gavin and smiled. "Gabriel," she whispered. Her stomach fluttered as she recalled. "Sometimes he would see me looking out my window, which overlooked the flower garden he maintained."

She looked back at Robbie and Brodie and explained. "I wasna allowed flowers in my room because they made it hard for me to breathe, but when he saw me looking out the window, he would theatrically pick flowers and place them in a vase outside where I could see them." She got butterflies in her stomach as she remembered how she looked forward to seeing him there, watching him for hours as he trimmed the roses.

"My mother died when I was young, and my father when I was ten and five. As the years went by, I was still confined to my solar as ordered by the priest who tended me when I was ill, but Gabriel would sneak in and spend time with me, telling me about the happenings in the castle and village." She smiled as she went on. "Sometimes I would read to him."

Alana took a sip and a deep breath before becoming more serious. "When my brother, Ottis IV, lost favor with Pope Innocent III, he made negotiations to marry me off to Michael Scot."

Whenever she thought of Scot, she could feel the anger all over again, yet as she told the story now, it seemed to lessen the pain. Was it the act of voicing it aloud, or was it the stone? She put her hand in her pocket and curled her hand around the stone as she continued.

"My brother felt my union with an advisor to a king so young would serve him well. The king was in good standing with the church, so the arrangements were made. It was kenned Michael had several mistresses. He brought one of them to the engagement banquet. But when he found out about Gabriel, my brother brought them both before me to choose. All of the council members were present."

She paused to take a deep breath, and her fingers rolled the gemstone around in her pocket. It had to be the stone that quieted her heart. "I kenned my marriage wouldna be a happy one. I would live in fear but was ready to do my duty. At one point, I looked at Gabriel," she glanced at Gavin as she took her hand out of her pocket and placed it on his. "My own archangel," she whispered, then turned to Robbie and Brodie. "I kenned he would be taken away, perhaps placed in the dungeon, and beaten. I could bear my own fate, but I couldna bear to see him suffer."

A tear rolled down her cheek, and she wiped it off. "Michael drew his sword and proclaimed that if he couldna have me, naebuddy would. Then he cursed us, saying we would desire each other forever, but our union would be unattainable."

After a moment of silence, Robbie asked, "How do ye plan on getting this man to bless yer… yer love for each other? Is that what she said? What does that even mean?" He looked toward Gavin and then to Brodie to confirm that he had heard the same thing.

Brodie raised one eyebrow and shrugged his shoulders.

"The stones," Gavin exclaimed, and they all turned to him. "She said it will drive away evil spirits. She specifically said it would help the negativity between us."

"A stone?" Robbie asked skeptically.

"Aye," Gavin replied. He took out his green jasper stone and showed it to Robbie. "Ever since she gave it to me, I feel less anger recalling the curse than when I usually dwell on it... on him."

Robbie stole a look at Brodie. He shrugged again.

"We ken this person they seek cannot be more than ten and six years old, so perhaps he is not so set in his evil ways," Brodie said.

Robbie stared at him in disbelief, and then they both turned to Gavin.

Gavin looked down at the stone. He turned it around between his fingers on the table and whispered, "He isna always an evil person."

He locked eyes with Brodie, then with Robbie.

Alana shook her head. "Nae, he isna."

Robbie's eyes darted from Gavin to Alana and back, but he was quiet as he waited for more.

"It's..." Gavin paused as he thought. "It's just... when he sees me... or Alana... it comes back. Naw like a dream or a distant memory but with all the emotions. Like it just happened."

Alana nodded her agreement. She had never thought about it that way. It had to be the stones. Usually, their hatred for the man overtook either of them the second they thought about their circumstances. The stones seemed to have taken away the emotion of it all, letting them think about it with a better understanding.

They sat there quietly for a moment until Robbie took a deep breath, placed his hands flat on the table, and pushed himself up. "Then Inverness it is. We shall leave in the morn."

Chapter 25

Alana watched the castle get bigger as they crossed the River Ness to Inverness. It stood on top of a hill overlooking the city. She had never seen anything like it before. She looked at it as Robbie pointed out the features of the castle.

Gavin rode on his horse beside her. She sat in the coachman's chair beside Robbie. Gavin was just as impressed, asking Robbie questions, though Brodie was more knowledgeable about the castle than Robbie.

Alana smiled as Robbie talked. When she looked back toward the castle, a man on a horse caught her eye as he passed them, heading in the opposite direction. She did a double-take before her smile left, and she put her head down.

Robbie got quiet and turned to look back at the man in time to see him turn in his saddle, studying Alana intensely. He looked at Robbie and the others, then quickly turned forward, nudging his horse faster. The man wore britches instead of a kilt but was too old to be the one they sought.

"Ye ken him?" Robbie asked.

"Aye, he's the blacksmith."

Robbie nodded and shared a look with Brodie, who

nodded as well.

"The quicker we find this lad, the better," Robbie told Gavin.

***

"Market day," Robbie said as Brodie came out of his tent when he heard the distant sound of merchants moving into the city, setting up, and calling out their wares. They searched from the time they arrived until dusk, then set up camp outside the city. "This would be the best day to find him if he's in the city."

They searched for a person they did not know what he looked like, what his name was, or where he lived. Robbie shook his head at the thought as he looked toward the path to the city and saw another cart heading there. The only way they would find this person was for Gavin or Alana to recognize him.

"Aye," Brodie agreed.

They quickly packed up their camp, hoping they would find him and be on their way. If not, they would camp on the other side of the village and search the outskirts the next day.

***

Brodie and Alana split from Robbie and Gavin, hoping to cover more ground. They met back to share their midday meal. As they approached a merchant selling cheese, Gavin touched Robbie's arm.

"There," he said, nodding toward a cart selling vegetables across the cobblestone path.

Robbie looked at a barefoot lad with worn clothes that were too small for him. He viewed the vegetable display. The lad briefly turned to look their way. Gavin instantly turned his back to him, hiding Alana's view from the boy as Robbie and Brodie averted their looks briefly before casually moving in closer.

The merchant finished with a customer and turned toward the lad just as he pocketed a couple of carrots.

"Hey!" the merchant yelled and grabbed the lad's arm.

The lad swung around and pushed the man, slipping his scrawny wrist out of the man's clasp. Robbie reached into his pocket and tossed the merchant a coin to quell his anger and took chase behind Brodie.

Gavin grabbed Alana's hand, and they raced behind Brodie. Robbie cut between merchants as the lad dodged onlookers and horse-drawn carts, gaining enough advance to elude Brodie.

Gavin tried to keep Brodie in sight as they maneuvered their way hand in hand around the town folk. At one point, someone kicked Gavin's leg from behind, sending him face-first to the ground and Alana's hand slipped through his grip.

Alana gave a quick yell before it was muffled.

Gavin rolled over and picked himself off the ground in time to see the blacksmith tossing Alana onto his horse and jumping on behind her.

"Stop!" Gavin yelled and got up, but they were on their way. He ran after them. "Stop!" His heart was racing, and his chest hurt. He would never catch them on foot. He stopped frantically looking around. Their horses were on the other side of town. He rushed back to where he last saw Brodie.

The Gift of the Healing Stones

Brodie reappeared from a side street, but Gavin did not see him. He anxiously looked between where he last saw Alana and the end of town where their horses were. He knew he had to wait for the others but wanted to get his horse and take leave.

"I lost him," Brodie said, then looked at Gavin's panicked expression as he stared down the street. Brodie looked around. "Where's Alana?" Brodie grabbed Gavin's arm and swung him around to face him.

"He took her!" Gavin jerked his arm out of his grip and spun around toward the other end of the village where their horses were.

"The lad took her?" Brodie exclaimed as he snatched Gavin's arm, spinning him around again to face him.

"Nae! The blacksmith," he yelled. "I have to get her back!"

He turned to go, but Brodie held fast. "We cannot leave without Robbie."

"I'll go by myself," he struggled to get loose, but Brodie tightened his grip.

"Ye cannot go by yerself. Use yer head, or ye'll get yerself killed."

Gavin seized his struggle.

"He'll bring her back to her father. We'll get her back," Brodie said, loosening his grip.

Her father's! It felt like someone stabbed him in the chest. Gavin swallowed. He knew what her father would do to her. He looked to the sky and took a deep breath, raking his fingers through his long locks.

How far was Grantown-on-Spey? As if he had spoken aloud, Brodie said, "It's a half day's ride. We'll get her by day's end."

***

Robbie kept his distance as he followed the lad. The boy was cautious, constantly looking over his shoulder. He wove through different streets, sometimes going around a whole block and ending up in the exact location. Robbie was starting to think the lad was lost when he finally reached the city's edge, where several unmaintained dwellings partially stood.

The boy walked by several of them before entering one.

Robbie made his way to the shack, and placing his hand on the hilt of his sword, entered. The foul odor of waste and decay hit him immediately, and he put the back of his other hand to his nose and looked around. The lad knelt to pick up a malnourished toddler. He held the two carrots out to a woman in a well-worn dress. She sat on a mat for a bed, with her back against the wall, breastfeeding a baby.

"Give it to yer sister to boil so yer brother can eat it," his mother said.

The boy turned to give it to a lass who was a couple of years younger than he but just as ill-fed. As the lass looked up to take the carrots, she saw Robbie standing in the doorway, and she inhaled deeply. The boy turned to see him before looking for a place to escape.

"Nae, dinna run. I mean ye nae harm. The carrots are paid for," Robbie said. Robbie looked at the woman. "I want to help."

The woman stared at him, then looked toward her son and back at Robbie. She blinked, "Ye'll nae bring him to the tolbooth?"

Robbie shook his head. "Nae. I am Laird Duncan from

Dundee. I'd like to hire the lad."

"Hire him?" Her eyes narrowed suspiciously. "For what?"

"Honest work, ma'am," he replied, reaching into his sporran and pulling out some coins. The lad's eyes grew big.

"What is yer name, lad," he asked.

The boy looked to the hand with the coins, then to his mother.

"What is it ye will have him do?" she asked.

"I would like for him to accompany my friends, a soldier, a young man, and a lass on a journey, partly by boat."

"By boat?"

"Aye. They will be gone for about a month, and I will bring him back here when they return."

She glanced at him and then her children, who all looked on the verge of starvation.

"I give ye my word that he will be well cared for," Robbie said, moving the coin closer to her. "I will be back through this way in a week and will bring ye more coin."

She looked at her son, whose eyes lit up. The coin in his hand would feed her and the children for more than a week. She slowly stretched her arm out, reaching for the coins. He slowly walked closer so she could reach them.

"He will be all right. I promise," Robbie said as she took the coins. "What is yer name, lad?" Robbie asked.

"Michael," the lad replied. "Michael Macintosh."

***

Robbie and Michael walked back to the village. Robbie

considered coming back for Michael but did not want to chance him taking off and hiding. Robbie had already inquired about passage to Hamburg. It was the closest port to Brunswick. There was a merchant ship that would set sail in two days.

Robbie purchased food at the first vendor he came to so Michael would not succumb to starvation. He studied the lad. He would have to acquire some clothes and shoes for him as well.

When he did not find the others when they reentered the market, he returned to the cart. As he approached, he noticed the cart was gone, but Gavin stood there with his and Brodie's horse as he anxiously looked around. Robbie immediately noticed the scrape on Gavin's knee as Gavin nervously brushed his fingers through his tousled hair.

"Damn! Come on." he grabbed Michael by the arm as he shoved the last piece of bread in his mouth, allowing Robbie to guide him. As they got closer, Robbie felt Michael stiffen and pull back. Robbie glanced down to see him looking at Gavin.

"No harm will come to ye," Robbie said to him. "Come now," he nudged Michael along.

Robbie looked at Gavin with his eyebrows raised and a tip of his head in a silent question to confirm he had the right lad.

Gavin glanced at Michael, then back to Robbie, and nodded before blurting out, "He took her!"

"Who took her?"

"The blacksmith!"

"He took the cart, too?"

"Nae. Brodie's looking for a place to store it for a night or two. We're wasting time here!" He yelled as he mounted his horse.

Robbie grabbed Gavin's leg. "Calm down. Ye'll only get yerself killed. Ye may not get a chance like this for a thousand years," he said, grabbing Michael's arm and pulling him closer. "Dinna do anything that would jeopardize this."

Gavin clenched his teeth as he looked down at Michael and back at Robbie. Gavin was impulsive, and Robbie knew it would get him into trouble. He looked ready to bolt.

Brodie rode up on Robbie's horse and quickly dismounted. "Let's go," he said.

Gavin sped off.

"Ach!" Brodie yelled, jumped on his horse, and took off behind him.

"Ever ride a horse, Michael?" Robbie asked as he tossed the lad atop before climbing on behind him.

Michael shook his head. Robbie held the lad around his waist, so he was snug against him and put his horse into motion, which blew the lad's stench right into Robbie's nose.

Chapter 26

Alana fought the urge to jump off the horse and run as they entered Grantown-on-Spey, but she had already tried to run when they stopped to water the horse.

Her captor quickly flung himself at her, and both fell to the ground. She tried to crawl away, but he pushed her over and climbed on top of her, pinning her to the ground. His straggly black hair fell from his shoulders, and he narrowed his eyes staring at her over his beaklike nose.

"Yer father has been looking for ye, lass. He's offered quite a reward to get ye back."

As she struggled to get loose, he pulled a dagger out from his belt and pressed it against her neck.

"Now, I wouldna want to hurt ye, but I will if I must," he said.

They were so close to ending the curse, and now this. If her dad killed her, who knew when they would have another chance to end it. Gavin would come for her. She knew it.

She glared at him until he was satisfied she would not run. He picked her up, threw her back on the horse, and continued. She prayed the entire ride that Gavin and the others would find her before they got to her father's house.

They had to know that was where he was taking her.

As the town was upon them, the urge to jump was greater. A month ago, Alana would not have cared if she broke her neck or got trampled by the horse trying. She stuck her hand in her pocket and held tight to her stone.

It was dusk as they made their way through the town. Two men crossed the street, heading toward the tavern. One of them looked up at them.

"Cormac," the man called to the blacksmith. "I see ye found something of value in Inverness this trip, aye? Douglas will be pleased."

Alana scowled at the man. Word that she had been found would spread to the whole town by dark.

"Aye, he will," Cormac said as he reached into his saddle bag.

"Do me a favor and get me a bottle of their finest whisky." Cormac tossed the man a coin. "And get yerself something as well."

"Aye. I'll be right out."

As the man opened the door, he yelled, "Cormac found Douglas's daughter!" This comment was followed by several responses ranging from laughs to disappointed "ahs" that faded as the door closed.

Cormac chuckled as he rubbed his hand on Alana's thigh and leaned closer to her, saying, "Ye are quite a reward, lass. All that property comes with ye. A nice dowry."

Alana jerked her head away from his.

"Yer father said no sense in waiting 'til he's dead to move in, as he's missing ye. And ye're a fine hand on the farm."

The man came out carrying a jug of whisky. "Thank ye,

John," Cormac said as he leaned down to grab the jug and secured it to his saddle.

***

The sun was almost entirely down as they approached her father's house.

"Douglas!" Cormac called out.

The house was dark. Perhaps he was gone or... dead. Alana briefly allowed herself to hope.

"Who's there?" her father called from the broken window.

Terror at the sound of his voice made her instinctively jump, but Cormac sensed this and tightened his thighs around her bottom and grabbed her arms from behind.

"Dinna do it," he commanded her before yelling, "It's Cormac, and I bring yer daughter!"

The door immediately flew open, and her father appeared in the doorway. The last bit of light showed his form, much thinner than the last time she saw him. He slouched as he leaned against the door frame, watching them as they rode up to the door.

"So ye found her," he replied in disgust.

She glared at him but knew he could not make out her expression. He appeared to be shaking. He never shook before. Perhaps it was because he was trying to hold his anger while Cormac was there.

Cormac dug in his saddle bag, pulled out the bottle of whisky, and held it out toward her father, who immediately pushed himself off the door frame and grabbed the bottle.

"Aye, let's celebrate," he said. His tone immediately changed.

Cormac dismounted, keeping a tight grip on Alana before pulling her off the horse. They followed her father inside the house. It was dark inside except for the little light the full moon brought in through the open door and window. The odor of urine and waste hit her immediately. The constant breeze through the broken window did not rid the house of the stench. Bile rose to her throat. She willed herself not to be sick.

"Start a fire so we can see," her father ordered Alana.

She did not want to do his bidding. What would he do if she refused? Dread washed through her. She had to buy her time. Gavin and the others would show up soon.

She shrugged out of Cormac's grip and walked over to the fireplace. She barely made out several large branches that he had dragged in and stacked in the corner. She began to break off the branches. As she worked, she watched her father. He *was* shaking. He pushed the stuff from one side of the table to the other and placed the bottle of whisky down. He fumbled for cups.

Alana collected debris from the floor for kindling. Using the flint and strip of steel on the mantle, she got a small fire going. She blew on the small flame and continued to feed it while keeping a watchful eye on her father. Her father was frantically trying to open the bottle but could not. His body shook too much.

"Let me get that for ye," Cormac grabbed the bottle before it fell over. He opened it up and poured them both a glass. Her father sat down, accepting the glass Cormac offered, and downed most of it in one gulp. He took a deep breath and a long sigh.

Alana's insides tightened as she watched. His shaking visibly lessened, and he took another sip with much of the same reaction as the first.

"So," Cormac began, "Ye said whoever brought yer daughter home would take her as his wife, and the land was her dowry."

Douglas grunted, took another swig, and then replied, "All but the house and a couple of acres surrounding it, which encompasses the chicken coop and coral." Her father stole a look at Alana with an evil grin. A chill ran down her spine. He poured himself another glass of whisky and drank half the glass in one gulp.

Her father got up and walked to the mantel. Alana backed away until her legs hit the side of the bed, but he made no move to grab her. Instead, he grinned at her, took down a scroll, brought it back, and unrolled it on the table.

"Put yer name and sign under me mark, and it will be done."

Panic consumed Alana. She could not believe what she was hearing. She glanced at the door. God! Where was Gavin?

The tremors left him altogether as he poured them each another glass while Cormac read over the document. Alana could feel her insides shaking. She could not believe he had a marriage contract ready. He must have paid someone to write it because he could not read.

Cormac took the quill her father provided, which she knew was for this occasion. They never had one before. Cormac carefully dipped the tip in the ink and signed the document.

Nae! Alana looked again at the door. Oh God, she was betrothed! This could not be happening.

"There," Cormac said as he placed a couple of objects on the ends of the scroll to keep it from rolling in on itself and smearing the ink. He nodded to Alana's father and raised his glass in a toast, clearly ready to replace his wife, who died a little over a year ago. Both drank to the agreement.

Alana was frozen. She wanted to run out, but her feet were glued to the ground.

Alana's father poured another glass, but as he brought it to his mouth, he suddenly pulled it away and said, "Why dinna ye go get the priest now? Ye can marry tonight."

"Now?" Cormac questioned, his cup stopping at his mouth.

Nae! God, nae!

As soon as her father nodded, Cormac set his cup down and got to his feet. "Well, all right then. I will."

Alana's heart raced. She looked to one, then the other. Neither paid her any attention. If Cormac left, she was sure to get a beating.

Cormac walked out the door, and Alana's father picked up the bottle. He chuckled and leaned back in his chair, taking a long gulp.

Alana looked at her father, then the door as the sound of Cormac's horse faded. She snatched one more look at her father, who had closed his eyes as he was taking in the effects of the drink. Alana darted toward the door. Her father's eyes flew open. He bolted in her direction, grabbing her at the waist from behind, spinning her around, and slammed her up against the wall.

"Where do ye think yer going, lass?" he asked.

He was going to kill her. She had to get out of there. She attempted to sprint to the door again, but he punched her in the stomach, and she doubled over, moaning.

"Ye left me here, leaving me to tend to everything! Is

that the thanks I get for bringing ye into this world?"

Oh God, nae! She would not shrink to him. She raised her head from her crouched position and glared at him.

"Both ye and yer damn brother. He deserted like a coward! Now I have nae money. Ye should have been here tending the animals, but ye left!"

He grabbed the empty cup from the table and threw it at her, but she dodged out of the way despite the pain tearing through her stomach.

"He was just a boy when ye sent him away!" she yelled. She had never dared something like that before but could not keep it in anymore. If he was going to kill her, she was going to tell him what she thought.

He grabbed the bottle of whisky off the table. "A damn coward," he repeated, taking another gulp, his eyes never leaving Alana. "He couldna even tell me he deserted. He's that much of a coward. All he wanted was ye."

A jolt went through her chest. He had asked for her?

Her father glowered at her and took a step closer. "Ye're a deserter, too, just like yer damn brother."

Alana straightened up despite the pain.

"Look at ye in yer nice gown and shoes. Are ye Laird Duncan's mistress or just the Duncan clan's whore?"

"Neither!"

Her father shook his head and said, "Andrew would be so disappointed to find out his little sister became a whore."

"I'm nae a whore!"

"Yer a disgrace, that is what ye are." He took another swig of whisky. "He asked about ye. He did not give a bloody damn about me, but he asked about ye... the coward." He took another gulp, quickly pulling it away as the whisky rolled down his chin. He swiped his arm across his mouth to wipe it with his sleeve.

She glanced at the door and back.

"Damn fool. I wanted to shoot him."

Nae!

"Nae son of mine will crawl back a deserter, but that damn Laird Duncan…" He scrunched up his face and took another guzzle. "He grabbed hold of the rifle as it went off, putting a hole in my roof." He pointed randomly to the ceiling, carefully studying his daughter.

"Ye tried to shoot him!" She looked around for a weapon to use and spotted a log at her feet before looking back at him. If he tried to shoot Andrew, he would kill her. She had to kill him first. *Gavin! Please come fast!*

"Ye both disgust me."

As he tipped his head to finish the bottle, she bent down and grabbed the log, swinging it up towards her father, but he saw her and swung the bottle at her head. She saw it coming and instinctively covered her head with her free arm.

She screamed as the bottle hit her forearm. He raised the bottle and swung again, but she dove to the floor out of the way, and the bottle shattered against the wall above her, fragments of glass raining down. Her arm pained her so much she sat up and vomited. She clutched her arm against her stomach protectively with her other arm as she rocked her body and cried.

"Look at ye. Ye're just a weakling." Her father laughed as he stood over her. "Good for nothing."

Angrily, he turned around when she did not respond. "Ah!" he yelled, taking two steps and flipped the table onto its side. Everything on the table clattered to the ground.

Chapter 27

Robbie and Michael stopped just outside of Grantown-on-Spey to make camp. Brodie and Gavin continued to Douglas's house, avoiding the village altogether.

The sun had just gone down, and the narrow path leading to the house had trees on either side that did not let much of the moonlight in. They were halfway to the house on the path when Gavin doubled over.

"Ah!" he bellowed.

"Gavin!" Brodie turned in his saddle.

"Keep going," Gavin groaned as he straightened up, the initial pain easing. They had to make it in time. *Please, God, help us not be too late.*

In a couple more minutes, Brodie slowed as he heard a man whistling. The man was almost upon them when he noticed them. He went quiet and stopped his horse.

"What did ye do with Alana?" Brodie asked, confident that it was the blacksmith despite the darkness.

"Ye!" the man spat. "I brought her back to her father and am on my way to fetch the priest. We are to be wed this night."

"Ye left her there alone!" Gavin yelled. His heart would surely burst from the jolt he had in his chest.

"Nae," the man replied with a half chuckle. "She's with her father."

"Her father! He'll kill her!" Gavin roared.

"Nae. He may teach her a lesson perhaps, but we are marrying as soon as I bring the priest back."

"Go back," Brodie ordered.

"I'll nae go back. I told ye, I'm going to fetch the priest!"

"Ah," Gavin moaned again as he clinched his arm to his stomach with his other arm.

The barely visible image of Brodie holding his pistol was followed by the sound of it being cocked. "Now!" Brodie ordered.

The man swore and turned his horse around.

***

Alana crawled against the wall until she got to the edge of the bed and tried to use it to help herself up. She could not die before they arrived.

Her father pushed the table, now on its side, as he walked to the door and picked up his rifle. He turned around and watched Alana from the door as she struggled to get up.

"Where do ye think yer going?" he asked, taking a step closer, the rifle casually at his side.

She would not make it. He was going to shoot her, and she would miss her opportunity to end the curse. *I'm so sorry, Gavin.* Her whole body shook as she rose, holding tight to her injured arm.

"Did ye think I'd let ye just walk out of here?" he asked, taking a step closer. Alana looked at the door behind him, then back to him.

"Well, do ye!" He shoved the table, pushing her off balance onto the bed and trapping her legs.

"Ah!" she cried. The sudden movement sent a shock through her arm so much that she barely noticed the pain of the table hitting her legs. He raised his rifle and took a step closer.

"Have ye nothing to say?" he asked, taking another step closer.

She curled her head into her chest as her upper body lay on the bed and closed her eyes. He advanced on her, yelling, "Say something, ye worthless wench!"

"Douglas!" came a yell from the door. Her father immediately spun around as the rifle discharged into the door frame next to Cormac.

Brodie's pistol went off immediately after. Alana's father staggered back, dropping his rifle and raised his hand to his bloodied chest. Disbelief crossed Douglas's face as he watched Gavin run to Alana.

"Alana!" Gavin pushed the table away, freeing her trapped legs. The table slid, bumping into her father, who lost his balance and fell.

Cormac stood at the door, mouth wide open, staring at Douglas as he used the last of his fleeting energy to reach for the rifle in front of him.

Brodie walked over and placed his foot on the rifle.

Her father looked up at Brodie and said in a bare whisper, "I'll kill h..." His stretched-out arm relaxed as he drew his last breath.

Cormac turned, walked out the door, and retched outside.

Oh my God, they made it! Alana wanted to reach for Gavin, but her gaze went to her father, half expecting him to get back up and come at her. Is he really dead? She wanted to believe so. She couldn't pull her eyes away despite the agony in her arm. Her body was trembling so much that it worsened the pain.

Gavin brushed her hair away from her face, whispering soothing words to her.

"Let me look at yer arm, Alana," Brodie said quietly, as he knelt before her.

She ripped her gaze from her father to Brodie, then Gavin, who nodded. Slowly, she removed her hand, holding the injured arm against her body, and swallowed her moan. She knew it was broken when Brodie probed around her arm, trying to feel if anything was out of place. She cried out in pain.

"It's a clean break," he said before looking the rest of her over. "I need to find something to use to keep her arm from moving," he said to Gavin, looking around the filthy room before removing his neckerchief.

"We're going to get ye out of here, lass," Brodie said as he wrapped his neckerchief around her, securing her arm against her body.

She moaned when he picked her up, cradling her body against his. He skirted around her father's lifeless body. Cormac stood half in the doorway.

"Where do ye think yer going?" Cormac asked.

Gavin shoved him out the door as he walked through. Cormac staggered back, slipping on his own vomit and falling to the ground.

"She's me betrothed!" he yelled as he got up.

Oh God, she was!

Gavin gave Cormac's horse a swat, and it took off.

"Me horse, damn it!" Cormac yelled as he started

running after it, then stopped and turned toward Brodie and Gavin. He caught up as they finished mounting and took off.

Alana curled into Brodie's chest. She was safe.

Chapter 28

Robbie left camp a couple of hours earlier than the others to gain passage for them, but when he said one of them was a woman, no amount of money would change the captain's mind.

"They're bad luck," one captain said as he spit on the ground.

Robbie spent the next couple of hours acquiring clothing for both Michael and Alana. He purchased a new hat for Alana and traded his extra shirt with a peasant lad who was wearing one that was too small to fit him comfortably. He purchased some trousers, a shirt, and shoes from a woman with several children close to Michael's size. By the time Brodie and the others met up with Robbie just outside town, he had all but boots for Alana.

"I canna. It hurts too much," Alana whispered when presented with the clothes. She looked down at her arm, still tied in place.

"One of us will help ye," Robbie replied, looking at Gavin, who adamantly shook his head, his curls bouncing.

"I canna," he said, turned, and walked away.

Robbie glanced in disbelief. Brodie took the clothes from Robbie and led Alana deeper into the woods to help her.

"It's the curse, ye see." Alana followed with her head cast down. She was terribly embarrassed.

He glanced at her briefly before removing the bandage securing her arm.

"We had thought, early on ye ken, that if we... well... had relations... that it would end the curse," she explained, her cheeks suddenly hot. He loosened the bandage, and her arm dropped. "Ah," she moaned.

Brodie walked behind her. "And it dinna?"

Alana was grateful for the distraction.

He untied her skirt and let it drop to the ground.

"Nae."

Brodie came around front, holding the trousers open and bent down low enough that her shift would not get in the way. She placed her good arm on his shoulder and lifted her leg as he fitted the first leg into the pants, then the other.

"We were picnicking in the woods. Everything seemed so peaceful," she said as he slid the pants up, leaving them unbuttoned. "We kissed for a while..." She knew her face was beet red, but he was not looking at it. Thank God! "which was nothing new." Brodie quickly released her simple *casaquin* and stays. He untied her shift and immediately walked behind her to help her out of it from there.

"What happened?" He took the shift and cut a wide strip from the bottom with a knife.

"Well, as soon as he began to... well... undress me," she continued shyly as Brodie brought his hand with the strip of cloth around her waist on one side and grabbed it with the other hand.

Alana raised one arm and the other one out as far as she

could bear as Brodie placed the wide strip over her breasts from behind. "And?" he asked.

"We heard a loud crack... Ah!" she exclaimed as Brodie tightened the wrap, causing her to jerk as he secured the wrap. The sudden motion pained her broken arm.

"Sorry, lass."

She took a deep breath and continued. "A large branch from above fell on him."

"Mm... hmm," Brodie said as he picked up the shirt Robbie had acquired and walked around to the front of her, holding it open so she could slip it over her head. She groaned, holding back the tears as he helped her feed her injured arm through the loose sleeve.

He finished buttoning up the pants under the lengthy shirt. "Let me secure that arm for ye again,"

As soon as Brodie finished tying her arm against her body with the neckerchief he had used before, she called out. "The stone!"

She needed it. She could not believe how much peace a rock could give her.

Brodie fished through her skirt pocket until he found the stone and handed it to her. "I'll get ye a proper sporran," he said. He gathered her clothes, and they walked back to join the others.

Gavin smiled as she approached them. She blushed.

"I think we need to shorten her hair a bit," Brodie said as he gently held out a long lock for consideration.

"Aye," Robbie agreed.

Not her hair!

Robbie reached for his dagger and walked around her. "I'll just cut it to the shoulder."

Alana stuffed her hand in her pocket and fisted the

gemstone.

Gavin caressed her arm. "It will grow back."

She did not know if it was the stone or Gavin's touch, but one or both had a calming effect on her.

She focused on Gavin to keep from crying as Robbie cut her hair. At one point, though, her eyes drifted to Brodie and Michael. Michael smirked while he watched. She quickly focused back on Gavin. Michael's reaction annoyed her, but she knew that it would be much more than a slight annoyance if she did not have the stone.

"Everything is going to work out. Ye'll see," Gavin whispered.

She gave him a small smile and nodded. He was always hopeful, but she had to agree they had the best chance of ending this curse once and for all. The fact that Michael was so young made it possible he did not even know why he did not like them. And both had stones, which lessened their ill feelings toward him.

"Okay, let's see ye now," Robbie said as he walked around, pulling out a woolen bonnet and placing it on her head. "There ye go," he said, smiling as he admired the transformation. "I would talk as little as possible," he suggested.

Gavin removed his sheathed knife from his belt.

"Here, take this. Ye'll never be defenseless again," he said as he secured it to her waist so that she could access it with her uninjured hand. Once secured, she pulled out the simple knife and looked at it. She remembered another much more ornate knife that Alex had gifted her with, which had aided her in a near-hopeless situation.

"Thank ye, but now ye have no knife."

"I'll pick one up in the village before we sail."

She smiled at Gavin and placed the knife back in its sheath. She felt better now having it there as security and the fact that it was Gavin's made her warm inside.

Robbie did a double take at Gavin, who looked at her fondly. "Ye ken that ye cannot look at her like that."

Gavin looked at him, becoming serious. "Aye, I'll remember,"

Robbie nodded. "Now, let us get ye some boots while Brodie obtains passage for all of ye."

Chapter 29

Brodie stood on the ship's deck with Michael at his side, watching as they made their way through the bay. Michael was so excited. His attention bounced between the shore and the sailors as they called out orders while climbing the Jacob's ladder and adjusting the sails. He breathed a little easier now that they were on their way.

Gavin and Alana, now Alan after her transformation, watched from the other side of the ship. After spending the day with everyone together, Brodie could tell there was some animosity between Michael, Gavin, and Alana.

Gavin and Alana seemed to be able to ignore the lad mostly. Brodie thought of the stones Gavin and Alana had. Perhaps it helped with the bitterness Gavin bore the lad.

His thoughts drifted back to the stone tucked away in his sporran. The aquamarine was a good luck charm, especially for sailors. It was the color of Vanora's eyes. A rush of warmth washed over him. He thought of the first vision he had of Vanora. The brief image of her at the shore as she tossed her wet hair in the air made his heart beat fast and put a smile on his face.

She stirred feelings in him that had been dead for three years. Thoughts of his late wife, Jamelyn, pierced through him. He missed her. She was never far from this mind. Everything reminded him of her. How could he have forgotten about Jamelyn these last few days? Was it the stone? He could not deny that Gavin and Alana's stones eased them… but a stone?

Perhaps it was a purpose. That was it! This quest took his mind off his emptiness and gave him reason. It was a distraction. And while his mind was preoccupied with Gavin and Alana, Vanora appeared. That was it.

"Can we see the rest of the ship?" Michael asked, bringing Brodie back to the present.

"Aye," he replied.

***

"Looking at ye, I thought ye were made of tougher stuff than ye sounded last night," said a sailor standing in front of Alana in the line to break their fast as he looked at her.

She glared at him, piercing her lips, which only magnified the scars that were beside both her eyes and mouth.

"Aye," another man said as he walked behind the line with his full bowl and shoved her. "Ye cried all night like a wee lass." The shove jolted her broken arm, and she swallowed hard to keep from crying out in pain.

Brodie softly whacked Michael's head from behind as he openly snickered over Alana's embarrassment.

There had been no extra hammocks, which they knew before boarding. They brought their camp bedding but had to sleep against the wall, half under the men in the hammocks. Every time Alana shifted, her arm hurt. She tried to keep quiet, but during the men's shift change, one of the men bumped her, sending excruciating pain through her arm. She could not help but cry out.

On top of it all, the stench from all those bodies was nauseating. Amazingly, though, her father's house had been much worse.

All night long, someone would cough or fart. At one point, the man above her coughed up and spewed on the floor. It landed so close to her face that some splattered onto her cheek. She gagged, willing herself not to be sick.

Gavin gave her a nudge and she stepped up to the cook and held her wooden bowl out. He slopped a spoonful of sticky porridge into her bowl with a good whack, which caused her almost to drop it. The cook grumbled and flicked his head, indicating her to continue.

She slowly turned around to walk behind the line. As soon as Gavin had his porridge, he caught up to her, and they found a spot on the ship's deck to eat.

***

Brodie and Michael joined them. Michael's attention was mostly on his meager clump of porridge as he ate, but occasionally, he would raise his eyes, darting them from Gavin to Alana as if he feared they would snatch his bowl.

Brodie pulled out strips of smoked meat, handing one to Gavin, who broke it and handed half to Alana. Brodie then split the other, giving Michael the other half. Michael immediately plucked it from his hand and ripped a piece off with his teeth.

Brodie looked at him disapprovingly for his rudeness,

though he realized that the lad had eaten more in these last three days than he probably had in a month.

Michael was only ten years old but looked much younger than his age. His skinny arms were almost down to the bone, and his eyes sunk in, giving him a wicked appearance. Brodie realized that malnutrition caused him to look wicked despite the suspicious looks he gave Gavin and Alana. When away from them, Michael was a carefree, curious lad.

They spent hours the day before walking the ship and watching the sailors. Michael's endless questions about the vessel and the seamen's work showed a keen mind.

But when Gavin or Alana were around, his animosity toward them seemed to permeate from him. It was best to keep their distance. Michael's bitterness toward Gavin and Alana was as obvious to Brodie as Gavin and Alana's love for each other. Brodie was certain that an onlooker would detect it as well.

Robbie and Brodie warned them about holding hands and Gavin doing things for her that she could do for herself. It was evident to Brodie that Gavin had heeded their warning, but Gavin's affection for her was written all over his face.

The seamen were a rough lot. Despite her becoming comfortable around Gavin, Robbie, and himself, over the last week, Brodie knew she was not around strangers. She would walk with her head down to avoid making eye contact with them.

She looks submissive. The thought made Brodie frown. Even passing as a submissive lad was not good on a ship with all men. She could not be left anywhere by herself.

It was good that they would be at their destination in

two days. If it had been a longer journey, she would most likely catch the fancy of one of the seamen. A discovery that she was indeed a lass would not be good.

***

A steady rain fell all day. Gavin and Alana spent most of the day below deck, taking turns tossing a button they had found into each other's wooden bowl.

One grate on the floor was left uncovered, allowing some fresh air and a little bit of light below. A barrel was under the grate, catching most of the falling rain.

A few lanterns hung from the ceiling as they swayed with the boat's motion. One sailor sat on a chest below one of the lanterns as he carved a whale figurine. He would hold it up to the light, turning it at different angles before whittling more. He had been there for close to an hour when he cursed and dropped his knife along with the figurine, drawing everyone's attention from below.

"Ye cut yerself, Charlie?" one man questioned.

"Aye," Charlie grumbled, wrapping his thumb to stop the bleeding.

"In all the years ye've been whittling, that's the first time I've ever seen ye do that," the man commented.

Charlie looked at the man, then Gavin and Alana, then at Brodie and Michael on the other side of the room as he pocketed his carving and put his knife away. Getting up, he mumbled something as he climbed the ladder to the deck.

Gavin and Alana went back to tossing the button into their bowls.

***

They stood in line on one side of the butcher table in the galley while waiting for their dinner.

"What ye got there, Cook?" asked one of the crewmen in the middle of the line.

"Stew," the cook replied as he took a spoonful out of the cauldron, which sat on the butcher's table, and poured it into a man's bowl.

"I hope it is better than the last time ye made stew," called a man at the back of the line who gained a few snickers and agreements.

The cook held up his empty ladle and shook it toward the back of the line. "It'll warm yer insides and fill yer belly well enough!" With his eye still on the man at the end of the line snickering, he went to get another spoonful but missed the pot, bumping the outside of the cauldron. The spoon fell out of his hand.

He immediately bent down to catch it before it hit the floor but unconsciously grabbed the rim of the hot cauldron. "Ah!" He pulled his hand away and ran to a bucket of water, where he dunked his hand. "Damn it!"

"John, are ye alright?" the man who made the snide remark earlier asked as he ran to the other side of the table where the cook was.

"Get out of me kitchen and back in line!" the cook yelled.

The man hurried back in line as the cook grabbed a rag and put it in the bucket. Grunting, he wrapped his hand in the wet cloth, picked the spoon up from the floor, stuck it back in the cauldron, and continued to serve the stew as he glared at each person.

Once served, Brodie and Michael walked past the men,

with Gavin and Alana following. The last man in line observed Michael as they approached. He leaned into the sailor in front of him and said something.

Brodie heard a few words… Charlie, cook, cut, and luck. Sailors were a superstitious lot. The fact that they were relating the two incidents with luck did not sit well with Brodie. He boldly met the man's eyes.

As they crossed the deck to go back below, an order was called out to secure a loosened sail, which started to flap.

One boatmate scurried up the ratlines toward the particular sail. He stepped on the boom and slipped as he reached for the shroud. The sailor fell, and his foot got caught in the lines he climbed up, and he dangled as a commotion below began.

Sailors called out as he swung himself, grabbing onto the lines. He pulled himself up hand over hand. Another seaman rushed up and untangled the man's foot, allowing him to right himself. Once safely upright, the sailor hurried to tighten the loose line binding the sail.

Brodie saw several eyes turn their way as Michael looked up in awe as the man recovered and continued about his work.

A couple whispered to others, who turned to look their way. The hair on Brodie's neck rose. He nudged Michael along to continue below deck as he looked at Gavin with a flick of his head. Gavin nodded and gave Alana a shove to put her back in motion.

Michael climbed down the ladder first, jumping from the third rung, surprisingly not spilling his stew. "Wow! Did ye see that man hanging from his foot? He got right back up and kept going."

"Gavin," Brodie said as he descended, ignoring Michael.

Gavin looked down to see Brodie jerk his head.

Gavin handed Alana's bowl down to Brodie and quickly made his way to the bottom. Alana slowly descended the ladder, carefully holding on to the side with her good arm.

Robbie looked around. Everyone went on deck when the uproar began. Michael was over at the side of the room, watching through the grate as he ate his stew.

"We are about to have a big problem," Brodie whispered. The men above were getting louder. Brodie looked at their belongings. Their bedrolls were rolled up but not tied so they could carry them easily. "I want ye to make ready to leave without making it obvious. Roll up what ye can in yer bedding and tie it so ye can carry it on yer back."

"What's yer plan?"

"If we make it 'til dark, we'll put a few things in the ship's boat and try to get out during the shift change."

"And if we dinna make it until dark?" Gavin asked.

Brodie did not answer but checked to ensure his pistol was ready before placing it back in his belt.

Gavin and Brodie quickly unrolled their bedrolls, filling them with a few belongings before rerolling them. The roar of the seaman above grew louder as accusations of which one of the four was the source of bad luck. They finished securing the rolls so they could carry them on their back as the crew seemed to come to a decision.

"Aye!" they agreed.

"Bring him up!" one ordered.

"Can we make a plea with the captain?" Alana asked Brodie.

Brodie shook his head as a man began to descend the ladder. "Nae. It'd be better for him to give them a scapegoat to avoid a mutiny."

"What will they do?" she asked as the man's feet hit the ground and another man began his descent.

The seaman looked around until he spotted Michael. "Come here, laddie," the man said as he gestured for him to come.

Michael paled, shook his head, and stepped back until his back was against the wall.

"Come on!" the man yelled and dashed for him, grabbing him by the arm and dragging him to the ladder.

Michael yelled out, his arms flaying.

Gavin tried to go for the man, but Brodie put his arm out and shook his head. He shifted his eyes to his bedroll, then back to Gavin, who nodded.

"Now, wait a minute," Brodie called out to the man as he hoisted Michael up to a man at the top. "What are ye planning on doing with him?" Brodie asked, feigning ignorance as he swiftly followed up the ladder.

Gavin picked up his and Brodie's bed rolls and slung them over his shoulder. Then he grabbed Alana's hand, pulling her to the ladder. When he got to the top of the ladder, the men were preoccupied with shoving a terrified Michael toward the ship's edge.

"Throw him over!" they yelled. "He's a Jonah!"

Michael frantically looked around, screaming. "Nae! Nae!" He tried to run between the men, but they kept pushing him back.

Gavin ran to the stern, threw the two bed rolls into the ship's boat, and returned to help Alana.

Brodie was yelling but could be not heard over the

seamen taunting Michael. He shot his pistol up in the air, and everyone went silent except for Michael, whose voice rang out.

"She's a lass! She's the Jonah!" he pointed to Alana as she stepped on deck with Gavin's hand under her elbow as he assisted her.

***

Gavin's heart jolted as all eyes turned to them. He pulled on her, but Alana stood frozen in place.

With the attention off of Michael, Brodie grabbed him, carried him to the ship's boat with their bedrolls, and tossed him in it.

Gavin knocked out the first man who tried to grab Alana. Another man punched Gavin in the stomach. A third man grabbed Alana between the legs and yelled, "Aye, she's the Jonah!"

She screamed as the man shoved her to the next man. The mob pushed her from man to man toward the ship's edge as she cried out.

"Nae!" God no! This could not be happening. Gavin yelled as he worked his way to the edge, shoving the men out of the way to get to her.

Once she reached the edge, two seamen picked her up horizontally and threw her overboard.

"Nae!" Gavin climbed up the back of one man bent over, watching her fall, and propelled himself overboard after her.

Brodie hoisted the ship's boat up and over the edge just as some crew members saw him and advanced in his direction. He jumped in the boat and let go of the lines, quickly lowering the boat with a jolt in the ship's wake. Brodie grabbed the oars and immediately paddled hard away from the vessel.

Gavin entered the water not far from Alana, who had sunk as she struggled to free her arm secured to her body. *God, don't let her die,* he prayed.

Once he spotted her, Gavin dove deeper, grabbed her, and swam back up.

The ship sped along, passing the small boat as the crew cursed at Brodie with fists in the air. Gavin and Alana broke the surface and spotted Brodie, who turned his boat toward them, fighting the waves the ship created. Gavin struggled to keep them both afloat in the wake. They were not going to make it. The waves pulled him down, and Alana slipped from his grip. He dove back under, grabbing her by her shirt and yanking her back up. With one arm still secured to her chest and her other arm flailing, it was hard to keep hold of her. He wrapped one arm around her waist and pulled her toward Brodie.

Brodie paddled hard straight through the wake, miraculously reaching them without tipping over. Gavin grabbed the side of the boat, pushing Alana against it. She instantly gripped the side with her free hand. Gavin lifted her, and Brodie pulled her in as she cried in pain. The boat threatened to tip over with the shifting of weight.

Michael sat at the front of the boat, glowering at them with arms crossed until the boat rocked. He grabbed the sides to keep him from being tossed about.

Brodie helped Gavin into the boat, and finally, the craft seized its threat of capsizing as if the sea immediately calmed from a storm. The wake eased to a gentle fall and rise.

"Are ye alright?" Brodie asked Alana as he began to unwrap her bandage to check her. The knot was tight due to it being wet. The steady rain made it hard to focus as the droplets rolled down his head into his eyes as he worked.

"I'm fine," Alana said, turning slightly out of Brodie's reach. "Please, let it be!"

Brodie sat back. "Aye. Let's be on our way then." He set his oars back up and began to row in the same direction as the ship, which was still in view.

Gavin was exhausted, but he set up a second set of oars and began to row. He could not believe they escaped, all of them! Every time Gavin looked back, the ship was further away. He kept his eyes on the horizon where the sun was setting until it was dark. How long would it take to make it to shore?

"How will ye ken we are going in the right direction?" Michael asked.

Brodie looked up at the overcast sky. "Well, on a clear night, ye can follow the stars. There is one that doesna move in the sky," he explained.

"But ye canna see it. We'll be lost at sea!" Michael exclaimed.

"Nae," Brodie said. "We were supposed to reach our destination by tomorrow, which was in a bay, much like when we left Inverness. We will hit land tomorrow, though it willna be where we planned to land," he replied as he continued to row. "Now, I want ye to close yer eyes and rest, all of ye."

Gavin was not going to sleep. He wanted to be done with this trip. The quicker they got to shore, the better. It was as if the curse knew what they were up to. He had to stay alert. "I'll help ye row."

"Nae. Rest now."

Gavin continued rowing.

"Gavin, I said to stop! I'll wake ye in a few hours so I can rest."

It took everything he had to stop rowing and place the oars inside the boat. Then he heard Alana's whimpering. His heart melted. He had been so bent on getting them to safety that he ignored her need to be comforted. He felt awful. He moved beside her and pulled her close.

She was shivering. Gavin whispered reassurances in her ear. He knew when she calmed and eventually fell asleep with her head on his shoulder.

Gavin's mind kept churning over the near-death experience. It was the curse, but they made it. This was the best chance they would ever have of ending it. *God, please get us there in one piece.*

Chapter 30

Brodie rowed for a few hours. The rain eased to a soft drizzle, more like a mist. They moved across the water with more ease than Brodie expected.

His thoughts turned to the aquamarine stone in his sporran. It was a common talisman among sailors, believed to give safe passage to the one who possessed it. Maybe that was why the rowing was easier than it should be. Hopefully, he had not turned around and was going in the wrong direction. Certainly, this was not the case since he had the stone with him.

The stone. Brodie had never put any faith in a good luck charm before. Why now?

He could not deny that Alana appeared less disheartened about their dilemma than before she was given her stone, especially considering the challenge of getting someone who despised her and Gavin to bless their marriage. And how easy was that going to be? The longer they were all together, the more obvious it was that Michael disliked them. Or perhaps his hatred was growing stronger each day.

Now, Gavin seemed to have his emotions under control despite his history with Michael. Maybe the stones were more powerful than Brodie had given them credit.

His thought drifted from the stones to Vanora. Where had she come by all these stones and her knowledge of them while being nestled away in her small cabin in the woods? Though she was in the woods, it was near the shore. He remembered seeing her at the shore as if emerging from the water. She looked… magical.

He shook his head and tried to focus back on the present, nudging Gavin. "Get up. It's yer turn to row for a bit."

"Aye," Gavin replied as he stirred.

Alana groaned as Gavin eased her head down on the seat and got up. "Shh, my love," he whispered in her ear. "I have to take my turn rowing."

Gavin carefully took his position and grabbed the oars from Brodie.

"Row for a couple of hours and then wake me. I just need a little rest."

***

Brodie stirred where he slept on the wooden slat before Gavin could wake him. The night sky had cleared a bit, and a few stars dotted the sky.

"How are ye doing?" he asked Gavin.

"This is hard work."

Brodie sat up immediately. He glanced at Michael's sleeping form, leaned toward Gavin, and whispered, "When we get to shore, I want ye to give me yer green jasper stone."

Gavin tensed. Give him the stone? He immediately seized rowing. "Why?'

"I'm afraid Michael will be disagreeable when we get

to our destination. I'm going to give it to him."

Give it to Michael! Gavin did not want to give up the stone, especially to Michael. He knew the only reason he did not want to kill him was because of it. The stone comforted him, but he understood why Brodie wanted to give it to him. Ah! Gavin handed the oars back to Brodie.

"The expression on his face when he sees ye isna a good one. It seems to get worse the longer ye are together."

"Aye. He does look at me with a little disdain," Gavin grumbled.

"Distain? It looks like he wants to run ye through with a sword." Brodie set the oars in place before continuing, "I think ye dinna realize the extent of his feelings because ye hold the stone. Perhaps he would be more willing to help if he had it."

Gavin settled onto the bottom of the boat with his arms resting on the seat he was sitting on.

"The reward of ending all this will keep ye from doing anything to him," Brodie added.

He did not want to give the stone to Michael. Hadn't he given him enough? Gavin sneered at Brodie, but he knew Brodie could not see him. He could barely make out Brodie's silhouette.

"He still doesna ken where we are going. If he did, I am sure he will take a knife to one or both of ye the minute I let him out of my sight."

Gavin took a deep breath. "Aye. Ye're right. He can have it."

***

Brodie stopped rowing once the sky in the distance began

to glow a soft orange. A few clouds were scattered across the sky, but nothing like the day before. He watched as the glow grew until the tip of the sun peeked behind a cloud.

He heard Alana's deep intake of breath and glanced her way, giving her a brief smile when she turned from the sunrise to look at him. They both turned back to the horizon and watched as the sun crept up, creating a light streak across the water from it to them. The streak on the water grew until the sky became bright blue.

Brodie took a deep breath and began to row again.

Michael stirred behind him on the boat floor and sat up.

"Are ye hungry?" Brodie called back to Michael, then raised his eyebrows to Alana.

"Aye," Michael replied. Alana nodded.

"Unroll my bedding. I have two strips of jerky left."

Michael scrambled and grabbed the bed roll.

"Take one yerself and give one to Alana."

Michael immediately froze and glared at Alana.

Brodie half turned where he sat and gave Michael a disapproving glance. "Ye heard what I told ye."

Gavin sat up and raised himself onto the seat as Michael looked at each of them before unrolling the bedroll the rest of the way.

"There, wrapped in that hide," Brodie gestured with his head.

Michael took out the small hide and opened it, immediately taking a bite out of one of the strips of meat.

"Give the other one to Alana!" Brodie ordered.

Michael darted a look at Brodie, then grabbed the meat and thrust it toward Alana.

She thanked him, taking the meat. Michael glared in return before he turned away from them.

Alana handed the jerky to Gavin, who split it in two and offered one half to Alana and the other to Brodie.

"Nae, ye eat it," Brodie said.

Gavin ate his piece and set up the other oars to help row.

"Look," Alana called out as a pod of dolphins jumped out of the water.

"Wow!" Michael exclaimed, catching sight of them.

"What are they?" Alana asked.

"They're dolphins," Brodie replied. He stopped rowing to watch them.

"Ye dinna ken what a dolphin is?" Michael snickered. "Even I ken that, and I'm only ten years old."

Alana's smile faded, and she looked back to watch them.

"Alana grew up inland," Brodie explained. "Naturally, she wouldna have seen a dolphin."

Michael snorted, turning back toward the pod.

Watching the dolphins made Brodie think of Vanora. He could imagine her as a maid of the sea, swimming carefree among them.

"Can I row?" Michael asked after a few minutes, jarring Brodie out of his thoughts.

"Nae." Brodie began to row again. "Ye need to be the lookout since I'm facing backwards. Whoever sees land first calls out "Land Ahoy!" and gets something special when we get on shore. Aye?" Brodie said as he inconspicuously nudged Gavin in the back with his knee.

Gavin nodded and mouthed to Alana, who faced him, "Let Michael win."

"Aye!" Michael said enthusiastically and turned around quickly.

Alana nodded and turned to look back to watch the dolphins.

***

"I see land!" Michael called out by midmorning as he pointed.

"Land Ahoy," Brodie whispered back to him.

"Land Ahoy!" Michael called out.

Brodie and Gavin stopped rowing to turn and look.

"Aye, that's land alright," Brodie confirmed.

Michael grinned at Brodie. After Brodie and Gavin turned back to continue rowing, Michael stuck his tongue out at Alana.

Alana spotted land ten minutes earlier but let him claim the honor of finding it. She shook her head but gave him no more thought.

***

There were no ports on the shore, so they picked a location. Brodie and Gavin dragged the boat onto the rocky shore.

"Ye said I get something special for spotting land first," Michael reminded Brodie.

"Aye, ye do." Brodie lifted Michael from the boat, setting him on dry land. "First, I need to make sure there are no hostiles around." Brodie tossed Gavin's bed roll onto shore, then his own. "Now roll up my bedding while Gavin and I hide the boat. We may need it to escape."

Michael looked cautiously around the shore, then to where the tree line was not far from where they landed.

"Aye." Michael quickly folded the bedding in two,

placing Brodie's few items on it. He opened the folded animal hide to see if he missed any pieces of meat before putting it on the bedding and rolling it up.

Gavin and Brodie carried the boat to the woods and found a downed tree to lay it against.

"I dinna ken where we are, but if trouble arises, take the others to the boat and sail out of here," Brodie ordered as he laid a dead branch on the boat. "Now, give me yer stone."

Gavin dug into his sporran and pulled it out. He looked at the green jasper, rubbing it between his fingers and thumb. He did not want to part with it but knew he needed to. The lad annoyed him even with the stone. He was sure it would be twice as bad without it. He took a deep breath and placed it in Brodie's hand. He immediately turned, picked up another dead branch and placed it on the boat.

They walked back as Michael finished tying up the bed roll, which was twice the size it should be.

"Let me show ye," Brodie said as he knelt and unrolled it. "It needs to be tight from the beginning." He curled the very bottom, using his knee to hold it down when making adjustments. He rolled it up the whole way, then put his knee on the roll to grab the rope, feeding it under the roll and secured it.

Gavin watched, irritated by how much Michael looked up to Brodie. Brodie was Alex's best friend, and he had just befriended Gavin. He did not want Brodie to be nice to his enemy. At the same time, he knew Brodie saw Michael only as a ten-year-old boy. It would be hard for someone else to see a child as someone who had caused centuries of pain.

Once done, Brodie and Michael stood up. Brodie reached into his pocket and pulled out the gemstone, holding it between his forefinger and thumb.

Michael and Alana's eyes grew when they saw it. Alana glanced at Gavin as Michael continued to eye the stone with a smile.

Gavin's heart sank. Michael did not deserve the stone. It was his. Gavin met Alana's gaze and shook his head so she would not ask questions. Just the thought of dealing with Michael without it made him tense. The feelings they had for their mortal enemy were strong.

Alana moved closer to Gavin, grabbed his hand, and placed her head on his shoulder. He gave a heavy sigh and kissed her head. *She understands.*

Michael went to take the stone when Brodie pulled it back, gaining his attention.

"Now, this is a verra valuable stone. If I give it to ye, ye need to promise me that ye willna lose it."

Michael's eyes went to the stone and then back to Brodie. "I willna lose it."

He better naw!

"Do yer pockets have holes in them?"

Michael put his hands in his pockets and felt around for any holes. He shook his head. "Nae. There arena holes in me pockets."

Brodie brought the stone closer so Michael could reach it.

Michael smiled from ear to ear as he looked at it. He raised his hand to grab it and looked at Brodie, who nodded. He gently plucked the green jasper from Brodie's fingers and turned it different ways as he studied it. "It's so beautiful."

"Aye. Now put it in yer pocket. Ye can look at it later. Right now, let's eat." Brodie said as he knelt by a big rock and used his knife to dislodge an oyster.

Michael immediately put the stone in his pocket and went to another large rock. "Here's one," he said.

"Yer going to eat a rock?" Alana asked as she walked over to Brodie.

Michael's head tipped back and exaggeratedly laughed.

Gavin wanted to wring his scrawny neck.

Brodie frowned. "Remember, Michael, she grew up inland."

Michael became serious with Brodie's tone.

Brodie met Alana's gaze. "Nae, lass. It's called an oyster." He used his blade and pried it open.

"A what?" she asked.

"An oyster." Brodie used the tip of his knife to loosen the oyster from the shell and held it out to Alana. She looked down at it, wrinkled her nose and glanced at Brodie.

"It'll fill yer belly," Gavin said, taking the shell that Brodie moved toward him. He brought it to his lips, winked at her, and tipped his head back, swallowing the oyster whole. "See, ye slurp it down."

"Or ye can chew it," Michael said. He opened the shell by bashing it with a rock and used his teeth to scrape it off of the shell before chewing it. He smiled when Alana made a face.

"Here, have one. It isna so bad, and ye need to eat," Brodie said, holding out another oyster he loosened.

She slowly grabbed the shell, looking at the mussel with disgust as it slid. She looked at Gavin, who smiled, and he nodded.

It looked disgusting. She didn't want to try it, but who knew when she would get another chance to eat. She closed her eyes, bringing the shell to her mouth, and tipped it, swallowing the slimy oyster without chewing.

Gavin rubbed her arm as she grimaced. *God, how he loved her.* He thought they lost their chance to end the curse when the men threw her overboard, and now they were so close. In a few days, the curse would be broken. His heart jumped in anticipation.

Michael slapped his knee and laughed at the face Alana made as she swallowed. Gavin's chest tightened, and he shot Michael a look. The lad was already starting to get on his nerves.

After eating several oysters, Brodie grabbed his bedroll and swung it over his back. "Let's be on our way."

Chapter 31

For four days they traveled after they reached the shore. They camped after walking inland for three hours. Traveling on foot for half the next day, they finally came to a village where they acquired two old but sturdy horses for more than they were worth. Unfortunately, language made negotiating a price difficult.

The closer they got to their destination, the more anxious Gavin got. They were so close to Brunswick that Alana even talked to Gavin as if it was a sure thing. Gavin's heart raced every time they spoke of their future together. She even mentioned having children. This was the life that they would finally end it all.

In previous lives, they had given up talking about a future together. Their only goal was to kill their adversary, at least until Alex killed Gregory MacDonald. They did then. They even started planning the wedding.

Thinking about Gregory made Gavin study Michael. He had to admit Michael was more relaxed in Gavin and Alana's company, cheerful as any well-fed ten-year-old lad out in a new world. Unfortunately, Gavin did not share in Michael's good humor toward him. Being in Michael's presence ripped his insides apart. He knew the stone had eased his resentment toward the lad during their overseas voyage, but now he did not have it, and his old feeling of revenge crept up.

He knew he would not kill the lad in his sleep because he was the key to ending it all, but he had to work hard at not wanting to torture the hell out of him.

Gavin was not sure Michael had comprehended anything yet. When Gavin was his age, he did not remember the curse, even though he recognized Robbie. His entire situation did not come to him clearly in one instance. It came gradually. Something would spark a memory, perhaps a scent, object, place, or even a sound.

Until he remembered the curse, whatever would jog his memory only gave him a familiar feeling. Sometimes, figuring out why things were familiar took days or months. He understood Michael's first reaction to him and Alana was hatred and distrust, but Gavin was pretty sure the lad had no idea why.

At one point during Brodie's attempt to get directions to Brunswick, something flickered across Michael's face.

"Brunswick?" Michael said, turning to Gavin. "Is that where we are going?"

"Aye," Gavin replied gruffly. "Do ye ken of it?"

Michael thought briefly before shaking his head, quickly disregarding his recollection. "Nae."

Gavin was glad he did not remember yet. It was best that way.

Alana and Gavin rode behind Brodie most of the uncharted way. Sometimes, they were a reasonable distance away, allowing them to converse quietly without the others hearing.

As they descended on the city of Celle, they were

amazed by the enormous castle. It was the grandest building Gavin, Alana, or Michael had ever seen. Watching it as they got closer and closer eased the tension of their long days.

***

The city was prosperous, with many business establishments. They walked the main street, passing taverns, a bakery, and even an apothecary. They all dismounted in front of the bakery, but only Brodie entered. Gavin tethered the horses as Alana and Michael walked to the window of the next shop. The wall behind the window was full of cuckoo clocks, each one different, most carved with branches and leaves around the face of the clock and a tiny door at the top. A couple had birds and woodland animals carved in the leaves.

Alana had her eye on one that was a half-timbered house, much like the houses in the town. This clock, however, was painted unlike the others. A man was chopping wood below the window. A lass sat on a swing under a tree, and a woman inside the house was rolling dough in the kitchen. A warmth washed over her. That was what she wanted her home to be like. Her heart began to race. They were a couple of days away from breaking the curse. They would have their family, Gavin and her.

Gavin came to stand behind her and put a hand on her shoulder. Placing her hand on his, she turned with sparkling eyes and a radiant smile.

"I've never seen anything like this. They are so beautiful," she said.

"Aye, but nae as beautiful as ye," Gavin kissed her on her forehead.

Alana blushed, looking around. She still wore lad's clothing, but she had unbound her breast. Her curves made it obvious she was not a boy. She turned back to the clocks just as one of them struck on the hour. Its door flew open to reveal a small bird that cooed several times.

Alana laughed in delight as Gavin wrapped his arms around her from behind and whispered, "Someday, I will buy ye one of those, and ye and our wee ones can enjoy it every hour."

Alana turned her head toward him, wrapping her good arm over his. It was going to happen! She could not believe everything that happened over the last several months. She went from living in a cave to finding her soulmate, and soon, they would break the curse that had torn them apart for centuries. Her heart swelled thinking about it.

Brodie came out of the bakery and walked over to them. "What are ye looking at?"

"Clocks," Alana said. "They are beautiful."

"A bird popped out of one!" Michael declared.

Alana smiled and looked down at the boy. When she glanced at Gavin, she saw his frown. She felt terrible for Gavin. Without his stone, he was having a hard time. Michael irritated her a bit, but not to the point that she knew it would without the stone. She squeezed Gavin's hand, and he looked at her and smiled.

"What kind of bread is that?" Michael pointed to the two golden brown twists Brodie held.

Gavin and Alana turned to see.

"She called it a *pretzel*," Brodie said, trying to pronounce it like the baker had as he handed one to Alana. He held out the other to Michael but did not let go, and it ripped right apart. Michael slapped his knee and laughed.

"Good news," Brodie told Gavin and Alana as they ripped their pretzel in two. "I believe Brunswick is a day's ride from here.

Alana met Gavin's gaze. She could not believe it.

"Well, let's be on our way," Gavin said, taking a bite of his pretzel.

"Aye. We still have a good four hours left today," Brodie agreed.

Chapter 32

Gavin could not remember the last time he was so excited. He woke before the sun was up and prayed that this would be the day.

Several feet away, Alana slept on her back. He wanted nothing more than to crawl over to her, pull her up against him, and lay there with her in his arms. He knew Brodie would hear his movement and order him back. It was not as if he would do anything other than hold her. He knew better than to tempt fate, no matter how bad he wanted her.

He listened to her breathing. *God, let this be the day.*

The birds began to chirp as the sky brightened through the trees. Alana yawned and rolled over, so she faced him. Her eyes cracked open, and he smiled at her.

"Today's the day," he whispered.

Her mouth curved into a smile, and her eyes widened.

Gavin stretched noisily, waking up Brodie. He watched Brodie get up and walk to the stream. He then scooted over to Alana, took her hand, and brought it to his mouth to ravish it with kisses.

"Make a fire," Brodie ordered, pulling his sword from its sheath.

Gavin looked up to see Brodie holding his sword, blade

down, as he eyed a few large fish swimming around. Gavin let go of Alana's hand, frowned and let out a heavy sigh. He did not want to eat. He wanted to go. They could eat after. He grudgingly collected dead branches and kindling.

After a couple of tries, Brodie stabbed a trout and flung it toward the camp, where it landed not far from Michael. He jumped up from a dead sleep, yelling.

When Michael saw the fish, he laughed. "Yes, fish!" He was always enthusiastic at the sight of food.

Gavin snarled at him. Every time he looked at Michael, an ire rose from the pit of his stomach. Michael better not give them a hard time when they got to Brunswick. It was apparent he did not realize their mission, but he would. There was not a doubt in Gavin's mind that he would when they reached their destination.

Gavin turned his focus to Alana, who watched him, and his spirits rose. God, how he loved her. Today was the day they would end their godforsaken curse.

***

They traveled the road all morning. It was mid-afternoon, and the city was in sight. Gavin could not contain his excitement. He nudged the horse a bit faster.

"Slow it down before the horse dies of exhaustion," Brodie ordered. The horse had carried them both all morning with minimal stops.

Gavin slowed the horse even though the anticipation was killing him. They still had not told Michael why they were going. It was best that way. A thousand questions went through Gavin's mind. *Will Michael do it? Will we be able to get into the castle? Will it be obvious the curse is broken?* He held Alana a little tighter. *God, please let this happen. Please,* he prayed.

The sky had been mostly cloudy all day, but as they got closer to the city, a darker cloud seemed to roll in from the other side of Brunswick.

"I didna think we are going to make it to the city before the storm," Brodie said.

"We can make it," Gavin said, kicking his horse to a trot.

"Gavin, nae!" Brodie yelled. Gavin did not stop. Brodie swore and kicked his horse to catch up. When Brodie caught up to them, he yelled at Gavin, "Stop! Now!"

Gavin brought his horse to a stop, and Brodie grabbed the reins. "Get off the horse!"

"We can make it!" Gavin argued. *Damit! Why will he nae believe me?*

"Now!" Brodie demanded.

Gavin was mad as a hornet but dismounted anyway. A faint rumble sounded in the distance.

Brodie dismounted and reached for Michael. He turned back to Gavin and said, "Get Alana off."

Gavin snorted and helped Alana off the horse. Just as her feet hit the ground, lighting flashed close by, and thunder crashed loudly. Both horses reared, and Brodie tugged on their reins, but Gavin's horse jumped sideways out of control. Brodie lost his grip, and the horse took off. He shook his head and calmed the mare down.

Damn, his horse! Gavin began to run after it.

"Nae!" Brodie yelled.

Gavin stopped. He knew there was no chance of catching it. At that moment, the clouds opened up, and a sheet of rain came down on them. The wind blew hard, making the rain appear to be coming in waves.

"Go!" Brodie shouted above the rain, pointing to what looked like a big house in the distance off the road, but not nearly as far as the city.

They headed in that direction, Michael running ahead.

"Ye almost got the two of ye killed," Brodie scolded Gavin.

Gavin looked to the ground. "I ken."

"Ye would have blamed it on that damn curse instead of ye naw using yer head." Brodie poked Gavin on the forehead.

It *was* the curse. It was trying to stop them. Granted, he did not use his head when he ran full speed into a brewing storm, but deep in his heart, he knew Michael had conjured up the storm, even if unconsciously doing so.

Gavin pulled Alana along as he held her hand. He took a deep breath, combing his fingers through his wet locks, and tried to bore holes in the back of Michael.

"It's a barn!" Michael called back from a distance ahead.

Gavin glanced at the city longingly. A flash of lightning touched down on the road where they would have been if they had kept going. Gavin snapped his head forward.

"Come on." Gavin sped up, pulling Alana along, leaving Brodie with the skittish horse.

After a couple of minutes, they made it to the barn. Gavin threw open the door to find a horse, sheep, chickens, geese, and ducks. The geese honked and flapped about with the new presence in the barn.

A door on the other side of the barn opened, and a burly woman appeared. She yelled frantically in German to someone, her hands flying to and fro.

A man appeared at the door with a rifle as he shouted at them.

Michael was halfway in the barn when Brodie grabbed his shoulder from behind with his free hand and pulled him back. He raised his hand, which still held the horse's reins.

"We mean ye nae harm," Brodie said. "We're just looking to get out of the storm." As if to emphasize his meaning, thunder crashed, causing several barn animals to spook.

Brodie's horse reared, and he grabbed his horse's reins with both hands and pulled on it to calm it down.

The man and woman started talking back and forth before the man lowered his rifle and turned to Brodie. "*Hier.*" He motioned for Brodie to enter.

"Thank ye," Brodie bowed his head before pulling the horse to allow Gavin and Alana to enter the barn.

Gavin closed the door, and they all began to pull at their soaked clothing, wringing them out where they could. Alana's shirt clung to her breasts. She pulled at it with the arm not in a sling, but as soon as she let go, it reformed against the contour of her body.

The man and woman exchanged more words until the woman turned and went back into the other room.

"*Komnen Sie rein. Komnen Sie rein*," the man motioned for them to come.

They followed the man through the door, which opened to their living quarters. The smell of fresh bread filled the large room, which served as their kitchen, dining area, and bedroom.

"Their house is connected to the barn!" Michael exclaimed.

Gavin frowned at Michael, but Michael paid him no

heed. It did not matter that Gavin knew Michael was oblivious to his part in the delay. Gavin despised him.

"*Kommt rein. Kommt rein. Sezt euch,*" the man said as he gestured to the table.

The woman pulled a worn dress from a chest and brought it to Alana. She pointed to the dress, Alana, and the door.

Alana looked at Brodie, who nodded.

The woman pulled Alana along to help her, and the man took a jug and filled wooden cups with sharp ale. They thanked him, accepting the drink. Michael gulped half of his down, then went into a coughing fit.

Gavin silently chuckled. *Dolt!* He took a small sip so he would not do the same.

The man laughed, slapping Michael on the back. "*Bier,*" he said.

Alana returned wearing the dress. She smiled at the others before her gaze fell on Gavin. Her smile made him forget Michael.

The woman set out some brown bread, a cheese chuck, and a knife.

"*Esst,*" the man said, pointing to the food and touching his mouth.

The couple tried to converse as they ate, but besides the introductions and Brunswick as their destination, not much else was comprehended.

At the mention of Brunswick, the man nodded and rambled on about something, mentioning *Braunschweig* several times.

Brodie nodded. "Aye. *Braunschweig.*"

The couple offered them blankets, which they laid in the barn after making a soft nest of hay to lay on.

Tomorrow's the day! Gavin thought.

Chapter 33

Gavin heard the animals begin to stir. He wanted to wake everyone. Instead, he glanced at Alana's sleeping form. *It ends today!* His heart pounded.

It sounded like the rain had stopped entirely. It was not long before the man opened the barn door, letting in the morning light and waking the animals and everyone. The man greeted them in his own language as he tended to his animals.

Gavin and Brodie began to shake the straw from the blankets and fold them up.

The woman opened the door that led to their living quarters and beckoned them in. They followed her to the table, where she had brown bread with slices of meat and marmalade out for them.

The man returned with a bucket of milk. The woman seemed to rush them along. When the man entered a second time and said something to her, she indicated for them to put some bread in their pockets and leave.

Gavin noticed they were in their best clothes and thought perhaps it was Sunday, and they were going to church. He did not care. The faster they left, the sooner they would get there. They followed them outside to see the man had hooked his horses to a cart. He pointed to Gavin, Alana, and Michael, then to the cart, then pointed toward the city and said, *"Brawnschewig."*

Yes! They were going to give them a ride. Gavin was relieved they did not have to walk. He glanced at Alana and smiled, receiving one back. *It won't be long, now.*

Brodie went to his readied horse.

The woman brought out Alana's dry trousers, shirt, and sling. She placed them on the cart. Gavin immediately began to help Alana with the sling.

"Today's the day," he said quietly to Alana as he secured her arm.

***

Her heart pounded at his words. She could not believe they were finally going to end the curse. She smiled and nodded.

As they made their way slowly through the soggy ground toward the road, they could see other families heading to the city. Once on the road, they were able to move faster.

Alana's focus bounced between Gavin and the city. Whenever Gavin caught her eye, he would smile, and her heart sped up more. She was sure her heart would burst in anticipation. It was pounding so hard she thought everyone could hear it over the sound of the wheels. The day had finally come.

She saw Gavin studying Michael with a frown, so she looked at him as well. Michael was oblivious to their quest. Would he bless them? What if he refused?

As if sensing their stare, Michael turned to look at them. Both looked away. Alana placed her hand on Gavin's arm, and he turned to face her. She smiled, and his face softened.

She let go of Gavin's hand when Brodie informed them they were to act as siblings, the three of them, and he, their father. He did not want to draw unneeded attention to them. It also made it easier to acquire sleeping arrangements if people thought they were a family. No doubt, a young woman traveling with two men and a lad would raise some questions.

"There it is—the castle. We're almost there." Gavin pointed. The excitement in his words set her heart ablaze. She could not believe they were almost there.

She snapped her head to look at him and nodded. The horses' hooves began clapping as they reached the cobblestone streets.

Michael stood up to get a better view. The cart bounced around between the row of houses outside the city. A call came out from one of the houses as the shutters of one window flew open, and someone dumped the contents of a chamber pot below. Brodie moved out of the way just in time.

A soldier stopped them and talked to the couple. He gestured to a side street, and the cart began to move in that direction. The couple stopped the cart in a field next to several more and climbed down. Brodie tethered his horse to their cart. There was a line of people heading into the city.

***

A river surrounded the city, seeming more like a moat. The town was a bustle as people trickled out of their homes, heading toward the town center. Gavin, who walked in front with Alana, turned to Brodie with a silent question only to receive a raise of his eyebrows and a shrug of his shoulders. Something big was going on for that many people to be heading in the same direction.

Another call came from above as shutters flew open and a chamber pot emptied. As the worn shutter flung open, it flew off its hinge and hurled down. Oblivious to the shutter falling, Gavin had pulled Alana in from the edge of the street to avoid the waste dumping on her.

Brodie saw the shutter, put his arm out for Michael to stop, and shoved Alana forward, causing her to trip. She did not fall since Gavin held her arm, but the shutter crashed to the ground where Alana would have been.

Gavin spun around to see what the noise was. His heart jolted as he realized the near miss. Had he not pulled Alana in, the shutter would have hit where he would have been. His excitement at being so close distracted him from being cautious. It was the curse. He had to be on guard. They were so close.

Gavin gave Michael a harsh look as if he had somehow arranged the accident, then turned to Brodie, panicking.

"It's a big city, and accidents are frequent in cities as large as this with so many people about. Stay alert," Brodie said to Gavin as he picked up the broken shutter and threw it to the side of the street.

Gavin knew Brodie thought it was only a coincidence, but it wasn't. It was the curse. There was not a doubt in Gavin's mind.

The closer they got to the castle, the more people there were. It was loud as people excitedly talked in a language they did not understand. Gavin did not hear a horse and cart coming quickly from a side street. Brodie immediately pulled Gavin and Alana back as a carriage entered the intersection, and people darted out of the way as it turned the corner, heading in the same direction as everyone else. The driver yelled at the people as they scattered.

Gavin's gaze met Alana's fearful look. His heart was pounding so hard. *God, we're so close. It canna end this way. Nae, God. Please get us there,* he prayed.

They were a block away from the castle, and people assembled in front of the cathedral. There were so many people they could not see what was going on. Gavin grabbed Alana's hand and veered around the crowd toward the castle. He spared only a brief look to make sure Brodie followed. Whatever was going on, it would not be long before the crowd was large enough that it would make it to the castle.

Brodie grabbed Michael's hand and was tugging him along when Michael stopped and yelled, "What are we doing here!"

The three of them turned and looked at him. Michael glanced back at them.

"Ye ken what we're here for!" Gavin exclaimed sharply.

"Michael," Alana said calmly, moving closer to him. "It'll be all right. Please, I beg ye."

Brodie tugged his hand, and the lad began to walk cautiously.

Gavin and Alana turned back around, weaving through the people going the other way. They stopped in front of the castle, where two guards stood.

They all turned around to face the cathedral like the crowd. "We'll never get inside today," Brodie said. A procession of soldiers escorting a carriage turned onto the street. "Someone important. Perhaps that is what the man was saying last night."

"We have to get inside," Gavin said as he looked around.

As the procession approached the courtyard, the townsfolk cleared a path, pushing others toward the castle. Brodie casually shoved Gavin further away from the entrance toward the far end of the castle. The procession was slow, but finally, the carriage stopped. The crowd turned around to face it.

A nobleman rode beside the coachman.

The soldiers split off, half forming a path to the keep, pushing Brodie and the others further to the side of the castle. The carriage door opened, and a footman placed a step on the cobblestone road. By then, the duke was there, assisting the duchess. Their young son followed with his sister, who helped the youngest. They walked down the guarded path to the palace.

The town folk continued to gather, their gaze bouncing between the castle balcony and the cathedral. As the crowd grew, Gavin gave Alana a shove, using it to their advantage to make it to the castle's edge. Alana looked around the corner. She quickly turned around. "It's gone!" she exclaimed.

"What's gone?" Gavin asked as he looked around the corner to find most of the castle demolished.

"The castle. It's all gone except for the *palas*. It did not happen in the *palas*."

"The *palas*?" Brodie asked as he quickly looked around the corner to see the remnants of the rest of the castle.

"Aye. The part of the castle with the great hall," she replied.

The crowd got larger, and the group moved around the corner. Gavin looked back to see Michael suspiciously looking around, trying to figure out what was happening. Brodie pulled him along, breaking Michael out of his daze, but his focus bounced between the castle and the cathedral.

"So, we dinna have to go inside after all," Brodie said.

Alana looked at what remained of the castle. "There was a large solar over by that wall, there." She pointed.

"Then that is where we need to go." Gavin tugged her.

"Gavin," Brodie called.

Gavin tensed at his tone. He stopped and turned around. He clenched his jaws to keep from saying anything.

"Ye canna just stomp off there. Use yer head and stick with the crowd. The place is undoubtedly well guarded in the back, and we dinna want to draw any attention to ourselves."

Someone bumped into Brodie. "*Entschuldigurg,*" the man said.

"Pardon me," Brodie said to the man as he briefly bowed his head and nudged Michael and the others to move further back. "We'll get there. Have some patience."

Patience!

***

Alana rested her hand on Gavin's arm. She could feel the rubble from the stone wall pulling at her. The closer they got to it, the more the memory flashed before her, but it was distant. She let go, reached into her pocket, and curled her fingers around the stone. Feeling the stone against her skin seemed to calm her anxiety and keep the feelings at bay.

Alana knew Gavin had no barrier between the anxiety

and his feelings. She knew what he was going through. They were so close to where the curse transpired, and that dreadful day continually appeared before her eyes. She rubbed the stone, trying to shake the visions as she chanced to look at Michael.

Michael continuously glanced between the remaining part of the castle, Alana, and Gavin. At one point, he looked to where the curse had taken place. His mouth dropped, and he just stared.

"Ye ken now why ye are here?" Brodie quietly asked when he saw Michael's stupor. They edged a bit closer to the spot as the crowd grew.

"I...I...ken what...happened here," he stuttered.

Gavin opened his mouth to say something, but Alana let go of the stone and touched his arm.

***

Gavin looked at her longingly, but his loathing for Michael boiled within him. He wanted to shake the damn blessing from him. The vision of Ingibiorg falling into his arms as she looked up to him with remorseful eyes gave him a lump in his throat, and he felt the panic he had all of those centuries ago.

A stab of despair washed over him as the scene became vivid. He had slowly sat and cradled Ingibiorg, rocking her as he called out to her. A pool of blood turned the white marble floor crimson. Any thread of happiness had been yanked out of him.

Someone dislodged her from Gabriel's arms, and he looked to see Michael Scot leaving the room. Nobody dared stop him for fear he would turn his sorcery on them. Gabriel rose, yelling in agony as he started toward him, but he was grabbed by two men who pulled him back. Michael Scot grunted a slight chuckle, which was not loud but echoed in Gabriel's head louder and louder.

Gavin heard it now, the laughing in his own head. The feelings were as if it was happening right then: the anguish of losing Ingibiorg and his hatred of Michael Scot. It was hard for him to move. He could feel his arms shaking by the time they made it to the spot. The marble floor was gone, leaving only matted dirt and some stones that had tumbled off the partial wall.

They no longer moved when the crowd widened. The people went around them. It had happened there, right where they were standing. Gavin looked at the ground. He could see the pool of blood. He wanted to cry out in desperation.

"Ye ken what ye need to do?" Brodie asked Michael.

Michael looked at Brodie and then at Alana and Gavin.

"Ye need to break the curse, Michael," Alana said as she rubbed the stone in her pocket.

"Do ye ken what ye need to do?" Brodie asked again calmly.

Michael focused on Alana, who matched his stare but with pleading eyes.

He slowly nodded.

Gavin forced the lump from his throat and snarled, "Good." He immediately reached for the dagger in his belt, and Michael's eyes widened, and he stepped back, bumping into Brodie.

"Nae," Brodie barked, shaking his head at Gavin's rash behavior. "Ye canna pull that out in a crowd during a royal procession." Brodie bent down and pulled out a *sgian-dubh* from his boot. He handed the small knife to Michael, saying, "A blessing is needed. A blessing sworn by yer own blood."

Michael slowly grabbed the knife with fear in his eyes. "W-w-where should I c-cut m-m-meself?"

"Yer finger or thumb. A cut on yer thumb bleeds a lot," Brodie replied.

"I… I dinna think I can do it," he said, gazing up at Brodie.

Rage washed through Gavin. "Just do it, or I'll do it for ye!" Gavin said.

Brodie narrowed his eyes on Gavin while Michael looked at him in terror. Gavin looked at Alana. Empathy showed on her face. *She understood.*

"Michael," Alana said softly as she knelt at eye level with him. Michael looked at her as she tried to soothe him. "Ye can do this."

He looked down at the small knife and then back to her as his eyes welled with tears.

She pulled her stone out of her pocket and placed it in her hand, hanging out of the sling. "I'll give this to ye if ye do it. I'm sure ye can sell it and buy food for ye and yer family to last months."

His eyes lit up as he looked at the beautiful stone with its green swirls. He then glanced at the blade and his lips quivered. "Please. Just a small slit on the end of yer thumb," she begged.

"What do I say?" Michael asked her.

"Just swear by yer blood! I'll slit ye myself and choke the words out of ye. Now do it," Gavin ordered. He was in agony. The desperation between her dying in his arms and the laugh went through his head. He could not take it anymore.

Alana stood and looked disapprovingly at Gavin. Brodie gave Gavin a slight shove. Gavin took a deep breath, looked at the sky, and raked his fingers through his hair with a shaky arm. He knew it was not Michael's fault. He was only a ten-year-old boy, but no amount of reasoning could rid him of his loathing for the lad.

"It'll be all right," Alana said as she nodded to Michael.

Michael looked again at the stone in her hand and slowly brought the knife to his other hand.

Alana grabbed Gavin's hand and squeezed it as they watched him.

The tip of the blade shook as Michael moved it closer to his thumb.

Do it, damit!

Michael fought tears as he punctured the skin making a small slit before dropping the knife. Gavin shoved his and Alana's joined hands toward him. Time stood still as Michael grabbed the meaty part of his hand as if to force it over theirs. Drops of blood dripped down onto their meshed hands. The noise from the crowd seemed to fade away until all Gavin could hear was Michael's quiet words.

"I… I… b-b-bless yer… yer…"

Michael glanced at Brodie. "Union," Brodie whispered in Michael's ear.

"Union… and… b-b-by me bl-bl-blood… I r-release… me… c-curse… over ye."

At that point, the tension eased out of Gavin, and he breathed a cleansing breath as if he had stepped out of a cave he had been in all night, and the fresh air replaced the stale air in his lungs. His knees buckled at the same time Alana dropped the stone. Michael fell back, but Brodie caught him.

Just then, the royal party stepped onto the balcony on the other side of the castle, and the crowd hushed. The soft sound of a violin rose in an angelic song.

Michael immediately righted himself and wrapped his hand around his thumb, squeezing it. He looked at the stone and stepped on it so nobody else would pick it up. Brodie picked up the small blade, cut a cloth strip from his handkerchief, and dressed Michael's wound.

Gavin rose from his knees and froze. It was as if he breathed freely for the first time in his life. He glanced at Alana. Her lips parted, and her eyes widened. She turned to where the music came from. Gavin smiled and turned as well, but they could not see anything. Other string instruments joined in. It was a concert for the royal family, but it was as if the music was playing for them.

Michael was oblivious to the music. He bent down and picked up the stone. He studied it briefly before putting it with the other one in his pocket.

"Can we go home now?" he asked, snapping Alana and Gavin out of their senses.

They looked at each other and laughed, then turned to Michael and Brodie. "Aye. Let's leave this place," Gavin said happily.

Chapter 34

Gavin and Alana led the way hand in hand, swinging their arms.

"We should handfast immediately," Gavin said. Handfasting was a legal and binding marriage in Scotland for a year and a day. All they had to do was declare that they were married. If by a year and a day, no child was conceived, the marriage could be broken.

"Nae," Brodie said. "Ye willna under my care. I had sworn to take ye to break the curse, and I have. Ye dinna need to rush anything anymore."

Gavin snorted as he looked at Brodie.

"Give me yer word," Brodie said as he stopped walking and turned to face Gavin. The last thing he wanted was for Gavin to consummate the marriage at the camp fifteen feet from him and Michael. They would be sneaking off every chance they could. He would have none of that.

"Aye, we'll wait," Gavin promised.

***

They traveled all day, taking turns riding. At first, the adrenaline of breaking the curse kept Gavin and Alana smiling and giggling, but as the day wore on, they got tired, and the excitement of it seemed to wear off.

Michael chattered nonstop about his stones, how much he might get for them, how long it would take to get home, and how he missed his mother. Gavin and Alana's animosity toward Michael diminished, even without the stones.

Gavin talked to Alana, but the conversation became distant as the day went on. During the trip there, the conversations constantly sparked memories and feelings of yearning. Even when they were not talking, Gavin could only think about the need to be with her continually.

By late afternoon, he realized his constant yearning for her was no longer there. He felt different. It was as if the curse had constricted him, and he was now noticing things beyond her: the scenery, the sky, and thoughts other than her.

It was not that he had never noticed or appreciated a beautiful sunrise before, but he always thought of *her* when he saw one. He even did before he had ever met her in this lifetime. Gavin watched in awe as a hawk circled in the distance. The feeling had no connection with Alana.

As he considered that, he connected the hawk with a falcon and his formal life as Alex. *Ah, the falcon.* Before breaking the curse, when he thought of the falcon, it was vividly. Now, the memory was with little feeling behind it. The thought of the falcon still put a smile on his face at the knowing, but it was without passion. Gavin sighed and turned back to Alana, who was talking to Michael.

Gavin was no longer annoyed with Michael but could see Alana was taken with the boy. She pointed out tracks to him and told him how to tell the difference between a wild cat and a wolf track. Michael listened intently, caught up as she talked about living in a cave with a wolf and having to hunt for her food.

She had not talked so freely to Gavin about her time living in the cave. He tried hard to get her to open up about her present life, but she shared little. Even after remembering the curse, Alana did not talk about her childhood. They reminisced about previous lives on occasion and their hopes of ending the curse and raising a family, but she did not share any of her current life with him.

As they made camp, Gavin watched Alana help Michael build the fire, talking him through what was better for kindling and how he was using sticks too big to start the fire. Michael hung on her every word. Why was she spending so much time with Michael?

They all sat around the fire while Brodie cooked. Michael asked how old Brodie was when he started soldiering. As Brodie talked about his early days with his best friends Robbie and Alex, they listened attentively, laughing at his tails.

Gavin enjoyed the stories, laughing with everyone else, but he felt something was missing. Some of the stories he remembered, and some he did not. But even the ones he recalled felt distant. It reminded him of his mother's story about him when he was four and had reached for something on a shelf in the general store. A sack of flour fell off the top shelf but got caught on a nail, and a small waterfall of flour poured out of it. He stuck his head under it and danced around laughing.

He heard the story so often from his mother and customers present at the time that it was familiar to him. He knew it was him and could envision it, but he did not remember it.

His memories of his life as Alex seemed to be slipping. He tried to think back. He recalled them, but only the ones he had discussed with Robbie before or those he had already remembered in this life. The stories Brodie relayed that he did not know had no images with them.

Gavin studied Alana as she said something, laughing. She had a hard life and the scars to prove it. The scars on her face were visible in the firelight. They took away from her looks. He had seen them before but had not really noticed them. It would not have mattered what she looked like with the curse. He would not have noticed.

He felt her pain when she received every mark. Was that connection gone, too? He concentrated, trying to feel what she was feeling as she looked amazed at whatever Brodie said. It was gone, and he was not sure how he felt about that. His whole purpose in life was to break the spell so he could finally be with her.

He had been ready to make her his wife as soon as the curse was broken but had given Brodie his word to wait. Now that the excitement had diminished, it did not seem as essential.

It was like he was a new person… his own person… as if the curse had been physical ropes that tied them together. The ropes would make it so they would always go in one direction, not caring if one may want to go elsewhere. They were content going in the same direction. All that mattered was that they were together. Now, the chains of bondage were broken, and they each had a choice. They had the option to go in different directions if they wanted.

***

The Gift of the Healing Stones

Alana lay on the ground, trying to fall asleep. What a day of emotions. First, she was so excited that they were so close. Then, she was sure they would not make it once the shutter fell and the horse and carriage almost ran them over. The curse had been all she thought of day and night. Would they succeed? What would happen when they did? Would they be able to tell? What if it did not work? The need to be with Gavin was so strong. She could not bear living without him.

Then they were there, and the excitement that the curse was gone overtook her. It was such a relief. She could not keep from laughing. It reminded her of when she first woke after Vanora had cured her eyesight. She had constant appreciation instead of taking for granted being able to see. Just as her sight had been restored and the awe of seeing everything with clarity seemed to lessen, so did her obsession with Gavin. She felt... different.

Before, she was constantly aware of his presence, even without him being near. He was always present in her mind. Thinking back, before she had met him, she had always been aware of something missing within her but had never realized it was him. She had often thought there was more to her life than there was but figured it was because of the abuse she had received at her father's hand. She was sure anyone in a relationship like that would dream of a better life for themselves.

As she lay there, she was aware of the breathing of the others. Gavin shifted in his sleep, and Brodie was softly snoring. Before, all she would have been aware of was that Gavin was there. Now, she was mindful of the others.

She could hear the sounds of the woods as well. The

leaves wrestled when the wind kicked up, making the hot embers glow brighter. An owl hooted not far from them, and she could hear the sound of the small creek by which they had camped. She took a deep breath as the wonder of it all settled. It was a new clarity, a different perception of life.

But what of Gavin and her? They would marry, no doubt. At least, that was what was supposed to happen.

But the passion she felt for him was gone. Did he feel the same way? Maybe he did not want her. She saw him look at her while listening to Brodie's stories. He smiled at her, but it was not the same. Or perhaps his smile was because the story was funny and had nothing to do with how he felt about her.

What if he did not want her anymore? The thought did not disappoint her until she thought of what would become of her. She could not return to her father's house, though as the last remaining relative of her father, it belonged to her. There were too many bad memories in Grantown and the circumstances of how they left. That was not an option.

Perhaps Robbie would keep her as a servant. She knew he had taken her on for Gavin's sake, but part of it was because she had been his sister in her past life… but it was his present life.

His sister. She knew it was true, but as she tried to recall her life as Anna, it faded, just bits and pieces. She tried to think back at her previous lives… her original life. It had been so vivid to her before… even the curse itself. She could see it, but it was without depth. Her feelings were gone as she remembered it. Thank God!

But she did have a lot of good memories, too. Images of Alex and Robbie came to mind since they discussed it several weeks ago. She could see them in her head, but they were detached, much like having her stone with her while in Brunswick. A chill went through her. She did not know how she would have managed that without the stone. The visions kept flashing before her. No doubt Gavin relived every moment. That was how it was when she thought of that night before she had the stone.

Alana took a deep breath. It was over.

Chapter 35

Amsterdam. The bustling port was full of fishermen coming in from their day's catch. Gavin took the horse to see who would give them a reasonable price while Brodie took the others to the dock to find a passenger ship headed for Scotland.

Gavin wandered the city streets, stopping at the blacksmith, the general store, and taverns. He noticed every lass he passed and smiled at them. When they smiled back, he felt warm all over. He never noticed so many lasses before. Sure, there were a couple of lasses that had caught his eye, but he never felt the desire to pursue them.

There was Susan back home. His mother always commented that she asked about him whenever she stopped at the general store. He suspected his mother hoped they would get together. She was the baker's daughter and often came to the store to purchase flour and sugar.

Susan was a year older than him and was quite bonny now that he recalled her. When he returned home, she would always seek him out, bringing him sweet tarts several times during his stay. He knew she was hoping to spark his interest. He would thank her and ask after her family, but never much more than that.

But now that he thought about her and her big blue eyes, it sparked something in him. He smiled as he thought of her. How could he not have felt anything for her before? She was beautiful with her long dark hair that fell just above her waist. He thought of her all the way back to the docks to meet up with Brodie and the others.

***

Gavin sold the horse, enough for boat fare for the four of them to make it to Edinburgh. They did not have enough to get a room in the tavern for two nights, but they did have enough to eat at one.

The serving lass smiled sweetly at Gavin as she placed the mugs on the table for them. He smiled back and watched her walk away, noticing the swing of her hips as she did so. When she returned with plates for all, she stood across the table from Gavin, placing one in front of each person. As she put his down, she leaned forward so he could see down her neckline.

Gavin's eyes grew big, and his heart began to race until Brodie stepped on his foot under the table. Gavin looked up to see Brodie giving him a disapproving look. Brodie immediately started talking about their plan to camp outside the city.

***

After they broke their fast the following day, Brodie and Gavin relaxed at the camp while Alana and Michael wandered off. They could hear Anna talking and Michael's occasional laugh. Gavin could not believe Alana preferred

Michael's company over his. He grabbed a stick and absentmindedly stripped the bark with his knife for something to do. He could feel Brodie's eyes on him but ignored it.

"I thought I'd have a hard time getting ye to keep yer hands off of Alana," Brodie finally said to Gavin quietly.

Gavin shrugged, not bothering to look up. He continued slicing at the stick, making long, thin strips of the bark.

"Does she nae interest ye anymore?"

Did she interest him anymore? It was obvious to Gavin that Alana was not interested in *him*. He sighed and put the blade and stick on his lap before raking his fingers through his hair. "She is in a tree," he said irritably as he pointed in the distance.

"So?"

"She just took her sling off a week ago."

Brodie turned from where he sat to look. Both Alana and Michael were in a tree. Alana pointed, showing something to Michael. A bird's nest. They were in another tree and higher up so they could look down on it. Babies were in the nest. The mother bird flew over to it with a worm. Alana and Michael were far enough away that the mother bird did not seem threatened by them.

Brodie smiled and turned back to Gavin. "Have ye never climbed a tree before?"

"Nae at her age. And she's in a dress." Gavin picked up his stick and knife and began whittling again with more forceful strokes.

"She lived in the woods," Brodie reminded him.

"Aye," Gavin mumbled. "But she seems more interested in Michael than me."

"Ye havena seemed verra interested in anything she

talked about. She's teaching Michael. Certainly, ye have knowledge and experiences, Ye could have joined in on their conversations."

Gavin huffed. He did not want to talk to her *and* Michael.

After a minute of silence, Brodie asked, "What is really wrong then?"

Gavin stopped whittling again but continued to hold the wood and knife, gazing into the distant woods. "I dinna ken how to explain it. It is as if all my life I was inside looking out a window because that was all I could do. I was content with it because I had nae choice. Then, all of a sudden, I could go outside," Gavin knew it did not make sense. He met Brodie's gaze. "I dinna ken any other way to describe it."

Brodie nodded, falling silent for a minute. "Are ye nae happier now that ye are outside?"

"I dinna ken. It's just… different. I want to discover everything that I could see from the window."

"Do ye nae have feelings for her anymore?"

"Aye. I do. But it isna the same. She completed me before. It isna like that anymore." Gavin gazed out to where Alana was in the tree. "I still love her, and I ken she is the one for me, but she doesna seem interested in me anymore." *Nae. She prefers Michael's company!* Gavin clenched his teeth and looked at Brodie. "The curse exaggerated my love for her. Love like that doesna exist in the real world."

Gavin started whittling again. He would think about it no more. He concentrated on shaving the wood the entire length of the stick. When his first stroke ended halfway down, he rotated it and slowly did it again on the next side, but it broke off into a smaller piece. He frowned and rotated it again.

"My wife's mother died in childbirth," Brodie said.

Gavin looked up at him.

Brodie smiled. "We always talked of a family before we were wed, but after the wedding, I was scared she would die in childbirth. I told her I didna want any children."

Gavin met Brodie's sons several times, and he knew Brodie's wife had died three years earlier.

"Love is irrational, Gavin. Had I nae listened to reason, I would have missed out."

Gavin nodded. "I'm sorry about yer wife."

Brodie sobered instantly. "When Jamelyn died... I couldna breathe. I... I dinna ken how I would make it through, yet I ken I had to for my sons' sake."

Gavin's heart ached for Brodie's loss.

"Every day, I went through the motions of living, but I wasna whole. A piece of me was missing... is still missing."

Gavin felt like an ass. He knew the struggle Brodie had after his wife died. Robbie kept him informed of Brodie. Of all the people in the world to tell true love did not exist, he chose Brodie!

"Ye're fairy tale love does exist, Gavin. If ye truly believe Alana is the one for ye, ye need to let her ken ye are interested in her."

Gavin felt as if a heavy weight had been lifted off his shoulders. He inhaled deeply, smiled at Brodie, and nodded.

Michael ran over, pointing, "There's a nest of baby birds in that tree over there."

"Really?" Brodie asked, turning his head to see where he pointed.

"Aye, there are three of them in there," Michael replied.

Gavin watched as Alana picked something up. She studied it absentmindedly as she walked toward them. Gavin's chest swelled. He was going to make her his again.

"What do ye have there?" Gavin asked her.

Alana looked up at him and smiled. Gavin's heart fluttered. The feeling wasn't gone. Maybe Brodie was right, and he had distanced himself because he felt he was competing with Michael for her attention.

"An eggshell," she replied, sitting beside him. She held it out for Gavin to see as Michael scooted closer to see as well. "I've never seen one this color before."

Gavin caught Brodie's nod from across the clearing. *I can do this!* Gavin held out his hand. Alana placed the broken shell in his hand and put her arms around her bent knees while her head rested on the top. She watched Gavin as he studied the egg. "Nae have I. What type of bird do ye think it is from?"

Alana leaned in close to Gavin so he could follow her line of sight when she pointed to the mother bird. "See that bird there? That's the mother bird."

His body heated as their shoulders touched. The flame inside him that burned for her was still there!

***

Brodie rose to secure a meal.

"Can you show me how to hunt? I can go with ye." Michael jumped up.

"Nae. Stay here. I have a limited amount of powder," Brodie replied.

Michael huffed as he sat back down.

"I hunt with a bow and arrow. That way, ye can retrieve the arrow," Alana said.

"I wish ye had yer bow and arrow with ye," Michael replied.

"Ye can also throw a knife to hunt. It's a bit trickier because ye have to judge yer distance, and the motion of the throw startles the prey," she said.

Gavin smiled. "I canna say I've ever hunted by throwing a knife, but I'm pretty good at throwing knives."

Alana pushed herself off the ground and wiped the dirt from her hands. With a sparkle in her eyes, she said, "Well, let's see how good ye are."

Gavin smirked at the challenge. He got up, and they decided on a target. Gavin carefully judged his distance and concentrated. He wanted to impress her. He aimed and released, successfully hitting the tree, though much lower than the target and not as securely into the wood. Not bad for not doing it in a long while. He smiled and turned to look at her. She nodded at him and smiled, but as they turned back to the tree, the weight of the handle pulled the knife out of the tree, and it dropped to the ground.

Gavin frowned.

Alana quickly unsheathed the knife that Gavin had given her and, with no hesitation, threw it, sinking it perfectly in the target.

"Woa!" Michael exclaimed.

Gavin looked at her. She looked so smug that he just shook his head and laughed. They were toe to toe, and his heart was racing. Everything seemed to fade around them. Her eyes grew as he slowly moved in to kiss her, but before he could, Michael called out as he retrieved the knives, "Can ye show me how to do that?"

They stepped apart and faced Michael as he ran to them.

"Dinna run with the knives," Alana called.

Michael slowed, walking them back.

Gavin could tell Alana was just as affected by the moment. She glanced at him, blushed, and then looked down, brushing a stray lock around her ear. He could not hold his smile. She wanted him, too.

Michael held out each of their knives.

"Can ye show me?"

"Aye," she replied, accepting the blade.

Chapter 36

They woke at the break of dawn to make their way to the port. The ship would not set sail until late morning. It would take them no more than an hour to walk, but they decided to start out immediately and break their fast at port.

Needing to relieve herself, Alana walked deeper into the woods behind some brush for privacy. She just started back when she heard rustling a little beyond where she was. She turned briefly to look but saw nothing. Whatever made the sound was larger than a squirrel or mouse. Maybe a deer or wildcat. She sped up. A loud snort and grunting came behind her as she approached the camp. Her heart jolted. It was a boar! She looked up at Gavin as terror tore through her.

At the sound, Brodie immediately drew his pistol and aimed, waiting for the beast to come out. Alana ran toward Gavin.

The boar broke into their campsite as Brodie's pistol shot out, breaking the peaceful sounds of the morning.

Alana flew into Gavin's arms as he sidestepped, swinging her out of the way as the boar thumped onto the ground, grunting in pain.

Brodie drew his sword, finishing off the animal swiftly.

Alana's heart was racing, and her body shook. She was sure the boar would get her with its mighty tusks. She pressed her head into Gavin's chest. His firm hug felt so good. She tightened her grip on him.

Gavin kissed her on the top of her head and rested his head on hers. She suddenly became overheated. She wanted to stay in his arms forever. She felt safe there. She never felt safe growing up, not even before her mother died. Gavin's arms around her made her feel like nothing could harm her. Her racing heart had nothing to do with the near miss. She loved him.

He pulled her away and brushed the wisps of hair away from her face. "Are ye alright?"

Their eyes locked. The concern Alana saw gave her butterflies in her stomach. She had begun to think that he did not want her anymore, but what she saw in his eyes at that moment told her otherwise. It was not the same obsession they had always had, but a deep, sincere concern.

"Aye." She smiled at him. She did not need anything else than his love to be all right.

He immediately pulled her in again and softly kissed her lips. Her heart started beating fast again as he pulled back to see her reaction. She swayed. Her smile broadened, and she gently rested her hands on his hip to steady herself. He laughed and pulled her in for another kiss.

Michael exclaimed in disgust.

Alana stepped away, and her face turned bright red. She looked down at her feet, not daring a look at Brodie.

Gavin laughed.

"Let's be on our way," Brodie said.

Chapter 37

As they boarded the ship, Michael started pointing out all the names of the ship's parts to Alana. Several people boarded, and the deck began filling up as Brodie and Gavin listened to the instructions from the ship's mate.

A family waited their turn to talk to the seaman. Two lasses started whispering as they looked over Gavin. One batted her eyes at him and smiled. Gavin fought the urge to put his arm around Alana and pull her in to show that he was uninterested, but they were supposed to be traveling as a family.

Once finished with Brodie, the ship's mate turned to address the next family. Gavin quickly put his arm around Alana and pulled her in as he smiled gravely at the lasses.

"Gavin," Brodie called as he turned to lead them to their cabin. Gavin immediately released Alana.

***

Alana saw the lasses looking at him and silently laughed to herself when Gavin pulled her in, but then the one who had batted her eyes at him earlier looked disgusted. She looked at Alana's face before looking down at the soiled and well-worn gown that Alana had gotten from the farmer's wife.

The lass leaned in and whispered to her sister as she flung her golden hair over her shoulder. The sister snickered, looking Alana over as well. Alana briefly looked at her soiled dress, and her heart sank. She grabbed Michael's hand and followed behind Gavin.

She should not have climbed the tree in her dress. The well-worn material had torn in several places from snagging on the branches.

She looked at Gavin as she walked behind him. He was a handsome man and could have any lass he wanted. Would people always turn their noses up to him because of her? She knew she was not much to look at with all the scars that scattered her face, not to mention her back and arms. And now, even her hair was short, she realized, as it kept escaping from behind her ears. She looked more like a lad than a lass.

How could he even be interested in someone so damaged? She had nothing to give him.

***

The weather on their journey was pleasant, allowing them to spend most of their time on deck.

Alana was conscientious of how she looked ever since the lookover she received from the lasses. She could not help but feel embarrassed, but Gavin did not seem to mind her looks. They often found a spot on deck out of the way where they could sit and flip a button into the cup.

A few times, the lasses passed by and snickered at them. Alana tried to ignore them, but the feeling that people would always look down at her kept creeping up. She will forever be an embarrassment to Gavin if they married.

She thought he had lost interest in her after the curse was broken, but that changed when they had the knife-throwing match. Then, when he pulled her in from the boar's path and he kissed her, she knew for sure he wanted her. The thought of the kiss made her insides melt, and she yearned to kiss him again.

Now, though, with others around, she could see how being with her may make him regret it later, even if he felt the same for her as she did for him.

***

"Just ignore them," Gavin said as he flipped the button. It hit the rim of her glass and fell onto the deck.

He wanted to pull her in and kiss the frown off her face, but he swore to Brodie that he would treat her as a sister while on board. He could not wait to be back at Dundee and finally marry her.

"There she blows off the starboard!" The call stopped their game. A couple strolling by stopped and looked out, pointing, and talking.

Gavin quickly pocketed the button and grabbed his cup with one hand and Alana's with the other, tugging her up. She promptly grabbed her cup and allowed Gavin to lead her to the side of the boat.

Before they reached the edge, they could see the water spray blowing up in the air. Alana let go of Gavin's hand as she gripped the railing. Another spray shot out, and an enormous fluke splashed down, then another. Alana's eyes were wide as saucers when she looked at Gavin.

"What are they?"

Gavin smiled. Her childlike wonder made his heart flutter. He looked out to the pod. "Whales." He had only seen a whale once, and that was from a distance, but he did not want to watch. The sight of the whales was nothing compared to the joy he saw in Alana's eyes. He turned back to watch her as she marveled over them.

"They are so big!" she exclaimed.

Gavin smiled, watching her scan the water.

"There's nine I count. Nae ten... eleven!" she exclaimed. All of a sudden, she got serious and turned to Gavin. "Do ye think they will tip over the boat?"

Gavin looked around at the sailors and passengers as they watched the whales. No one seemed concerned. He shook his head. "Nae."

Her serious face gave way to her smile again as she turned back to watch them. Gavin busted with pride that all he had to do was say she had nothing to worry about, and she trusted in that.

She continued to watch until they were out of sight. Gavin could watch her all day.

***

They finally docked in Edinburgh. The ship would stay there for the night before setting sail in the morning for Dundee. It would be quicker by sea than by land.

They spent the day ashore, happy to be back in Scotland. Brodie had acquaintances he met up with for most of the afternoon. He took Michael, leaving Gavin and Alana to explore Edinburgh Port.

Alana felt like she was on a cloud as they discussed the future. She wanted to grab his hand as they wandered the streets, but they honored their promise to Brodie to appear as brother and sister.

As they returned to the ship for the eve, they approached an intersection where they could hear a boisterous lot of men on the side street. "Aye. From the look of her face, it looks like she likes it rough," one man said.

"Well, ye better just keep to the brothel. I dinna think her brother will let her slip through his fingers. He watches her like a hawk," another chimed in.

"Oh, aye, the brother. I think he's so protective because he's claimed his sister himself. Most likely gave her those scars," another snickered.

"Naw. I think he just feels sorry for her."

"I think…" The talking faded as they approached the intersection to see the last seamen entering a tavern and the door closing.

Alana's shoulder slumped. She looked to the ground, speeding up as she crossed the street.

"Alana," Gavin said softly. She ignored him and walked faster. "Alana." His voice grew louder. He grabbed her hand and spun her around. She looked down the street to where the sailors had been, but the tavern was too far around the corner to see.

"Dinna listen to them," Gavin said as he raised his free hand to cup her face.

She jerked her face away. "It's true. It's just pity ye feel for me. I ken it. Ye can have anyone ye want. I'd just be an embarrassment to ye. I ken I'm not much to look at." She tried to pull her hand out of his, but he held tight.

"How can ye say that? I dinna care about yer scars, Alana. I've spent every waking hour of my life looking for ye. Hell, I've felt every one of those scars."

She continued to tug at her arm. She did not doubt he suffered from her pain. She felt it when Thunder bit him and when he was shot. It had not been a dull pain but as if it had happened to her. Granted, it faded away after the initial onset. She knew he felt every lash of her father's belt, but that did not change the fact that she would be an embarrassment to him.

He pulled her in, letting go of her hand, and put his arms around her. She stood stiff in his arms, wanting to believe he did not care but afraid his indifference would change.

"Ye say ye dinna mind now, but what about five years from now? Will ye still, then? The tie that bound us together is broken," she whispered.

He gently stepped back with horror in his eyes. "Ye dinna want me anymore!"

She looked into his desolate eyes and realized he had misjudged her comment. She wanted him more than anything. She did not mean to hurt him and could see in his eyes how much he cared and how upset he would be if she rejected him. She loved him so much.

"I do." Alana grabbed his hand, looking down at them. "It's just..." She wanted to put her hand in her pocket to touch her stone but knew it was not there. She had done that several times over the last few days. She wished she still had the stone. It gave her a sense of security. Courage. She was a coward.

"It's just what, Alana?"

She shrugged her shoulder. "I dinna want to disappoint ye. I'm... damaged."

He immediately pulled her in and held her tightly. "I dinna care about yer scars. I love ye." He caressed her back with one hand without easing his hug.

"Gavin!" Brodie called him from behind, startling Alana.

Gavin let go and smiled at her. All Alana's doubts vanished as she looked into the depths of his eyes.

They turned back toward the dock and continued. She could not wait to return to Duncan Castle and begin her new life with him. They would be married, and she would have a better life than she could have ever imagined.

Chapter 38

*D*undee. *They made it!*

Gavin frequented the city doing business for Robbie, so it was easy to procure a couple of horses to travel back to the castle.

The keep was a grand sight. The large manor house had a set of steps up to the front door. Alana's vision was blurry the last time she was there, but she could see it clearly now. She rode in front of Gavin, who squeezed her as the main house appeared. "We're home," he whispered in her ear.

"Aye," she replied with a smile and a touch of excitement washed through her. *Home.*

Two dogs ran toward them, their tails wagging.

"Hello, Orian, Angel," Gavin called to them as they circled the horses. "Where's the pups?"

As soon as he asked, Leslie, the stable master, came into view on his way to meet them at the steps. The pack chased after him, with one smaller puppy trailing behind the others, unable to keep up. As they reined in at the keep, Alana slid off the horse, careful not to step on any puppies that had now reached the horses. She walked over to the wee puppy, still making its way to the others, and scooped it up to cuddle it against her face.

She laughed, holding it close. "My wee Hercules, ye've grown so much."

Michael's eyes were huge as he looked at the keep, which was nothing compared to what they had seen in Celle and Brunswick, but a castle, nonetheless. "We're going in there?" he asked as Brodie lifted him off the horse and placed him on the ground.

"Aye," Brodie answered. "We'll spend the night here and head back to Inverness tomorrow."

"We're staying the night?"

"Aye."

"Alana," Gavin called, holding out his hand. She turned toward him and the house, taking a deep breath. This was the beginning of her new life. She placed the puppy on the ground. Smiling, she put her hand in Gavin's.

"Sir Brodie," Margaret greeted with a curtsy. "Come in, come in." She ushered them all into the hall.

"Wow!" Michael exclaimed, matching Alana's reaction of a quick intake of breath as they entered the grand room. The room was huge, with high ceilings and tapestries along one wall. She felt a sense of belonging. *Home,* she thought again.

She looked at Gavin, who was studying her. She smiled and gave his hand a quick squeeze. He smiled back, warming her insides. She could never have imagined this life. Before, she was content in the woods in a cave, happy to be away from her father. Now, she could not imagine being without Gavin.

"I'll let Laird Duncan ken ye're here," Margaret said, leaving them in the hall.

"This is the biggest room I've ever seen!" Michael exclaimed, drawing a laugh from the others. "Look at how high the ceiling is!" They all looked up to appease the lad.

"Sir Brodie," Margaret said as she reentered the room. "Laird Duncan will see ye in his study."

"Thank ye, Margaret," he replied, leaving the great hall.

"Have a seat, and I will get ye some cider and something to eat," Margaret said to the others.

Gavin and Michael took a seat at one of the tables, but Alana stopped as she went to sit. She studied a beautiful tapestry of a woman holding out her arm as a falcon made ready to land on it.

Michael stood back up and moved beside her as he looked at the work of art. "She's beautiful," he said.

Alana was mesmerized by the tapestry. When she had seen it before, the woman and falcon were blurs blended into the background. Now, she could even see the gold threads woven into the woman's white dress.

"That's Milord's sister, Anna. She died a while back," Gavin said.

So that was why it intrigued her more than the other tapestries that lined the wall, which were just as beautiful. This one was of her in her previous life, yet she recalled little of it.

Margaret came out with cider, cheese, biscuits, and jam, returning their focus to the table.

***

They were just about finished with their refreshments when Robbie requested their presence.

"Milord," Gavin said as he bowed to Robbie while entering the room.

Alana entered with a smile and curtsied low. "Laird Duncan."

Michael, on the other hand, entered in awe of Robbie's wooden desk and shelves of books. Robbie could instantly see how much healthier the lad looked after weeks of eating regularly.

"Welcome back," Robbie said as he smiled at Gavin and Alana. Both were all smiles. Alana held herself up with a sureness she did not have before. He was happy to see the change.

"Ye accomplished what ye set out to do?" Robbie asked.

"Aye, milord," Gavin and Alana replied in unison before turning to each other and grinning.

Robbie turned to Michael, saying, "So, I hear ye rose to the occasion."

Michael straightened up at the compliment and nodded. "Aye, sir."

"I stopped to see yer mother on my way home. She was missing ye, but I made sure she and yer siblings had everything they needed.

Michael's eyes lit up, obviously happy to hear the news.

"I hear ye have some stones ye wish to sell. Can I see them?" Robbie asked.

Michael nodded as he reached into his pocket.

Robbie stole a look at Gavin, who gave a quick nod and smiled in appreciation. Robbie knew Gavin and Alana would want them back. Gavin squeezed Alana's hand as he gave her a wink.

"Here they are, sir," Michael said, setting them on the desk.

Robbie picked them up individually and studied each one. "Well, I'd like to purchase these from ye if ye are still interested in selling them," Robbie offered as he placed them back on the desk.

"Aye," Michael nodded happily.

"Good. For safekeeping, I will give Brodie that and the amount I agreed to give yer mother for yer aid. He will give it to ye when ye get to Inverness. Is that agreeable to ye?" he asked.

"Aye." Michael nodded enthusiastically.

Chapter 39

Gavin smiled at the thought of Alana as he finished loading the cart with the items he bought at the general store. Gavin and Alana wanted to marry immediately, but Robbie convinced him to send word to his family about his decision first. Since then, he had spent every free second he could in the past week with her, discussing their plans for the future and where they would stay.

They discussed with Robbie and Mary Ellen their decision to stay on in their service once they were married. Gavin did not care where he lived so long as he was with her. They considered moving closer to his family, but Alana liked it at the Duncan house. She felt comfortable there, which pleased him.

He was so excited he could not think of anything else.

Gavin remembered something he forgot as he climbed up to the coachman's chair. He went back into the store. As he paid the woman at the counter, her husband entered the store from behind the counter. "Gavin, ye're back. I havena seen ye in a while."

"Good morning, Bernard," Gavin greeted him. "I arrived back last week."

"Did ye bring the lass with ye?" he asked.

"The lass?" Gavin tensed. "How did ye ken I had a lass with me?"

"A man came here several times asking if I'd seen ye. The first time he asked after a lass that was with ye."

Gavin's heart nearly jumped out of his chest. *Cormac?* "What was the man's name?"

Bernard thought for a minute before replying. "Andrew. Aye, that's it, Andrew."

Andrew. Alana's brother? Nae, he's dead. I was there when he died. Or had he just passed out and escaped while his father was passed out? Nae, that canna be, can it?

"I told him to go up to the keep, but he said he dinna what to bother the Laird."

"Where is he now?"

"I dinna ken. Ye may try Gordon's place. I saw him in the tavern a time or two."

"Aye, thank ye."

Gordon's tavern was a place where he often went on his errands. It was on his list that day. He quickly finished his other business and made his way to Gordon's tavern.

"Nae, he left last week when Keith said he saw ye and the lass on the way to the castle," Gordon informed him, helping Gavin load barrels of ale into the cart.

A week ago!

The description of the man did not fit Cormac or Andrew, who was dead, he reminded himself again. Gavin remembered seeing Keith on his way to the village as they were heading to the keep after arriving in Dundee. Keith returned with the household supplies when they were talking to Robbie, but he had not returned since.

"Thank ye," Gavin said as they loaded the last barrel.

"I'll see ye next week," Gordon replied.

***

Alana placed another egg in her basket. Every time she gathered eggs, she thought of her first day there when she asked Gavin if they were in the land of the fairies. She chuckled now, embarrassed at her childish thoughts.

The door opened, and Alana's heart fluttered, thinking Gavin was seeking a kiss between chores. He did that often, but before Alana turned to see who had entered, someone covered her mouth with his hand. Panic washed through her. She tried to struggle. She felt a sharp pain on the back of her head, and everything instantly went black. When she woke, it was to find herself draped over a horse.

She moaned as she stirred. The back of her head hurt, and she seemed to be bouncing around upside down. She forced her eyes open to find she was face down on a horse.

The horse stopped as a knife pricked her back.

"Dinna yell."

Oh God, it was Cormac! She immediately stilled.

"Ye may sit up properly now, *wife*."

Her heart jolted. *Wife?* Did he somehow manage to marry her without her consent?

He grabbed her upper arm, yanking her. "Did ye hear me? Sit up!"

She reached up with one hand and grabbed the saddle to pry herself up to sit sideways on the horse. Her head instantly throbbed with the change of position.

The sun was full in the sky, so she knew a few hours had passed. He could not have married her. Could he? No. This could not be happening. She was to marry Gavin. They broke the curse. They were finally able to be together. How could she be married to another? No. She wasn't. A priest would not have married someone unresponsive.

"I canna be yer wife. Nae priest or minister would marry an unconscious woman."

He grabbed her arm hard. "Ye are mine under contract. Yer father signed ye over to me."

In a panic, she slid off the horse and ran, weaving in and out of the trees. Wife or not, she would not go back there.

"Damn it!" Cormac kicked the horse to put it in motion, trying to maneuver around the dense woods, but he was losing distance. He swore again. Stopping his horse, he dismounted and made chase.

He quickly caught up to her, grabbed the back of her dress, and jerked her to a stop as she screamed. He immediately covered her mouth and barked out, "Ye scream again, and I'll cut yer tongue out. Do ye understand?"

Alana nodded as she held back her tears. She was doomed. She had finally found a life of peace and happiness, and now he would yank it away from her. No. It would not be this way. She would bide her time. Gavin would come for her. She knew it.

She reached down to grab the knife Gavin gave her, which she wore at her waist and found the sheath empty.

"Do ye think I'm such a fool to leave ye with a weapon?" Cormac yanked her up roughly and guided her back to the horse. She put up her hand to push aside a low-hanging branch, but Cormac jerked her to the side, and the branch swung back into her face, scratching it.

He tossed her onto the horse and mounted behind her.

"Sit astride." He gripped her arm, digging his fingers in deep to keep her in place.

She pulled her skirt up to swing her leg over before pulling the skirt down in front as much as possible.

Alana forgot about the contract. Her father signed her over to Cormac with the property. Had Gavin and Brodie not made it to her father's when they did, she would already be married to Cormac. A wave of nausea went through her as she thought about that night. No. She would not have been married. She would be dead.

She considered telling him but did not want to anger him more. She would wait for Gavin and Robbie. They would come.

***

Gavin was anxious to return but had to take it slow with a fully loaded cart. Nobody had stopped by the castle looking for Alana or him. Only the regular tenants and the Laird's brother, Willie, stopped by. Was someone scouting her out, or had the man left to bring word of her arriving to Cormac? A week was plenty of time to make it to Grantown-on-Spey and back. Gavin looked at the woods surrounding the wagon path in case someone lurked in the trees.

As he pulled up to the front steps of the keep, Leslie approached to help him unload.

"I'll be back in a minute," Gavin said.

He went to the kitchen to find Alana. "Where is she?" Gavin asked frantically when he did not see her.

"Ack. I dinna ken! I sent her out to do her usual chores. She returned with the milk and left to get the eggs, but dinna returned. She's probably playing with that puppy again."

"The eggs! She should have done that this morning," Gavin spat, turning to the kitchen door.

"Aye, and she still hasna…" Margaret continued, but Gavin was out the door running to the chicken coop. His heart hammered. He swung the coop door open, startling the chickens. They fluttered around, a couple escaping through the opened door.

Gavin's heart nearly stopped when he saw a nest, the basket, and broken eggs on the ground.

Someone took her.

Gavin ran out the door, quickly closing and barring it, not bothering to collect the chickens that escaped. He tried hard to connect with Alana like he used to, but it was useless. It was gone. He had no idea if she was injured or not.

"Milord!" Gavin yelled as he burst into the solar where Robbie was with his family. They all looked at him, startled. "She's gone!"

Anna ran into her mother's arms, still frightened from being abducted. Robbie got up and ushered him into the hallway, ordering his family to stay put. He closed the door behind him quietly.

"Alana?" he asked calmly.

"Cormac has her."

"How do ye ken that?"

Gavin frantically explained as they made their way to the chicken coop.

"Do ye ken if she's hurt?" Robbie asked as he looked at the evidence of the struggle.

"I dinna ken!" Gavin answered in a panic, raking his fingers through his hair. Oh God. He had to find her. After finally breaking the curse, it could not end this way.

"Ye need to calm down, Gavin. Ye said he wanted to marry her. He willna kill her. We'll get her back."

Marry her! He knew he should have married her immediately. Robbie whistled to get Leslie's attention, gesturing for him to come as they made their way to the stables.

"Aye, milord?"

"Tell Bryce to go to his uncle's house and have a search party sent out for Alana. She's been abducted. They need to search north of here."

"Aye, milord," Leslie replied, bowing quickly, and running back to the keep. Robbie and Gavin saddled their horses and took off toward the field's perimeter closest to the coop where the woods started.

"There," Robbie pointed to horse droppings.

"They have a three or four hour head start on us!" Gavin spat. They would never find her. Was she all right? How could it come to this after all they did to be together? Alana told him Cormac signed a contract. Oh God, he lost her forever!

"I ken. The others will take the road before cutting into the woods. Ye need to calm yerself down. Dinna make any rash moves that will jeopardize Alana or yerself."

***

The sun was low in the sky. Alana began to worry that Gavin and Robbie would not find her before nightfall. Will Cormac continue on during the night, or will they camp? If they set up camp, will he force himself on her? Her mind began thinking of all the possible scenarios and how to escape him.

"Yo!" a man called out to Cormac, who immediately tightened his hand, holding the reins around her waist and put his other hand on the dagger.

"Say a word, and I'll kill ye right here," Cormac whispered in her ear. A shiver ran down Alana's back.

"Who goes there?" the man asked as he approached them. It was Willie, Robbie's brother. He had stopped by the keep several times over the last week, but Cormac would not know him. Her heart raced. They found her.

"Ye nearly got mistaken for a stag," he added casually as he came into sight, holding his rifle to the side, then lowered it.

Cormac's upper body seemed to relax, but his fingers at her waist dug in, giving her a silent message to keep quiet.

"Me name is Grant. Me wife and I are just passing through."

Willie approached them, briefly looking at Alana. She widened her eyes, hoping he could see her despair.

"Ye coming from the port? There's a road that would be faster… and safer," he said, lifting his rifle to emphasize that he almost shot Cormac as game.

"We were on the road for quite some time but pulled off for a rest. We seemed to have gotten disoriented," Cormac replied.

Willie stopped beside them, pulled out a canteen, and took a swig.

Alana's heart was beating so hard she was sure they could hear it. Willie was talking so casually to Cormac. Was he unaware that she had been taken against her will, or was he waiting for others to show up? Maybe he did not recognize her. They were never formally introduced.

"Yer a long way off from the road. I can lead ye there," Willie proposed as he held out the flask to Cormac.

Alana could feel Cormac tense, but he accepted the

canteen, sniffed it before taking a guzzle, and handed it back.

"I wouldna want to keep ye from yer hunt," Cormac replied.

"Oh, it isna any trouble at all," Willie said, holding the canteen out to Alana. "Ma'am."

As she reached for it, Willie let it go prematurely, and Alana leaned over to catch it just as Willie lifted his rifle and hit Cormac with the butt of it.

Cormac fell back, and Alana toppled forward, but Willie grabbed her arm and righted her.

"Are ye alright?" he asked, looking her over.

Her heart was racing, but she was unharmed, other than a scratch on her face and several on her arms where the blood had already dried. She let out the breath she held, "Aye. Thank ye."

Willie gave an ear-piercing whistle before dismounting and walking over to Cormac.

Two men made their way over toward them. Alana looked around, hoping Gavin was coming, but she did not see him. She desperately wanted to be in his arms.

Willie turned to one man and said, "Call off the search."

"Aye," the man said as he turned his horse around.

"Help me get this man on my horse, and we'll take him up to the keep."

A series of "Call off the search!" calls echoed, each getting fainter and fainter.

***

By the time they made it to the road, several men were

already there. Willie ordered them all home. He and another man escorted her and Cormac to the keep. Alana could not believe how many folk were out looking to find her and not to drag her back to her father's house but to keep her safe.

Soon, they could hear riders approaching at a gallop. Alana tensed until she saw Gavin and Robbie. She spurred her horse to Gavin's. The horse barely stopped beside his when she flung herself into his arms. He caught her, pulled her onto his horse, and held her tight.

"Oh my God. I thought I lost ye," he said as he kissed her.

Chapter 40

"What the devil!" Cormac yelled as he came to while they approached the keep.

"Stay where ye are, or I'll run ye through," Willie said from behind.

Once at the entrance, Robbie helped Cormac off Willie's horse. When Cormac's feet hit the ground, he started to shake himself out of Robbie's grip.

Willie jumped down and drew his sword, placing its tip on Cormac's chest.

"I wouldna do that if I were ye," Willie suggested.

The man glared at Willie. Robbie let go of his arm and began climbing the stairs. Willie grabbed Cormac's arm and led him up the stairs and into the keep. Nobody said anything until they were inside the hall.

Robbie sat in the Laird's chair, where he did business with tenants and people he was not familiar with. Willie left Cormac facing Robbie before taking his place standing to the right of his brother.

Gavin grabbed Alana's hand and followed them, standing off to the side.

"Ye trespassed on my land and abducted my servant. What do ye have to say in yer defense?" Robbie asked.

It was a different side of Robbie than Alana had seen so far. He was always casual around her and Gavin, but at that moment, his demeanor displayed the power of his title.

"Yer *servant* is me wife," Cormac spat.

Alana felt the bile rise from her stomach. No. It could not be. He could not have married her while she was unconscious.

Robbie raised his eyebrows. "Yer wife? Really? That isna my understanding."

Cormac snatched a glare at Alana. She wanted to hide. Gavin put his arm around her. Cormac glowered at Gavin before turning back to Robbie. "Her father signed her contract to marry me. I was on my way to get the priest when yer man ordered me back and killed her father."

Gavin let go of Alana and stepped closer. "Sir," he bowed to Robbie, who looked at him and nodded for him to speak.

"When we arrived, her father had his rifle pointed at Alana. He was caught off guard, and when he turned, it went off, barely missing this man," Gavin gestured to Cormac with a flick of his head. Gavin turned to Cormac and said in a harsh voice, "He was going to kill her!"

"That's nae how it happened! He wouldna have killed his own daughter. He had just sent me to get the priest."

Gavin moved closer to his laird and opened his mouth to speak, but Cormac cut him off. "Yer man is just after her land. It has been in her family for generations. It's more land than her father could manage, but the greedy bastard wouldna sell a damn acre of it!"

Cormac gave Alana a look that felt as sharp as a blade and then turned back to Robbie. "He signed the contract!" Cormac reached inside his tunic, but the tip of Willie's sword was immediately on his chest again. Cormac froze with his hand half in the tunic. "I brought the contract with me."

Nae! This could not be happening. She was going to be forced back to her father's house. She would rather die than go back with him.

Robbie nodded to Willie, who removed the blade but stood ready.

Cormac slowly removed the scroll. Willie grabbed it and walked backward until he stood by Robbie again. He handed the scroll over.

Alana held her breath as Robbie unrolled it. At one point, she thought she was going to be sick. Robbie took his time reading the contract and nodded.

Alana's heart sank. She was doomed. She frantically looked at Gavin. She knew the contract was legit. Her father would have made sure of it. Gavin had moved back beside her and ran his hand up and down her back.

Finally, Robbie looked up and said, "There are nae any witness signatures on this."

Alana snapped her head back to Robbie at the comment. Is it possible that she did not have to marry him?

"The priest was going to be the damn witness!" Cormac yelled at the top of his lungs.

"But he wasna there," Robbie said matter-of-factly.

Cormac gestured to Gavin as he yelled again. "Yer man just wants the damn land, like fifty other people. Several folks have offered Douglas good money for it, *including* meself. The bloody bastard wouldna sell, not even when he was starving with nae money to his name!"

"So really, ye just want the land and naw the lass," Robbie concluded.

"Damn right, I want the land. But the land comes with her!" He pointed at Alana without looking at her.

"Well, for one, the contract isna good without a witness. It willna hold up in any court of law, naw in Scotland or England."

Alana breathed a sigh of relief. She looked at Gavin and smiled.

Cormac opened his mouth to say something, but Robbie held up his hand.

"So, the land belongs to Alana. But, perhaps, she is willing to sell it to ye," Robbie suggested as he turned to look at Alana.

She stood there frozen for a minute as everyone looked at her. She never wanted to go back there again. The thought made her sick to her stomach.

"Alana?" Robbie questioned her gently.

She looked at Gavin, who smiled and gave her a reassuring nod.

She turned back to Robbie and nodded. "Aye. I'll sell it to him," she answered as she snuck a look at Cormac, whose eyes grew big at her words.

"Then it is settled," Robbie said. I will have my man draw up the papers. He will accompany ye in Alana's stead to ensure a fair price is set and collect yer payment."

Epilogue

Alana laid her baby on the bed and went over to stir the stew cooking over the fire. The one-room cottage had been completed only one week ago, which was good since the cold weather would have made it burdensome to finish.

They considered purchasing a small house in the village, either in Dundee or near Gavin's parents' house, but Alana preferred the tranquility of the woods. There were too many people in the town, and she liked it near the Dundee manor house. It was the first place she ever felt safe. It was home to her.

Robbie had let them purchase a few acres from him with the money she received from her father's property. There was enough money to build a house three times as big as they did, but the single room was fine for now. The house was close enough to the main keep to make it there in a short amount of time.

Hercules's ears perked up as he lay on the floor by the bed.

"Who's here, Hercules?" Alana asked.

The door opened, and Hercules ran up to Gavin, carrying a large object wrapped in a tartan.

"What do ye have there?" Alana asked as she set the

wooden spoon down on the table.

"It's a present for ye." He kissed her before setting it on the table.

She had never been presented with a random gift before. She excitedly looked at it, then back to Gavin.

"Go on, open it."

She walked to the table and unwrapped the object. The last fold of the tartan fell away, revealing a beautifully carved cuckoo clock. She couldn't believe it. Tears filled her eyes as she remembered his promise to buy her one.

"Do ye like it?" Gavin asked.

She nodded, running her finger up the beautiful wooden branches alongside the house. On top of the roof sat a falcon with its wings partway opened.

She looked at the little door beneath the falcon and asked, "Is there a bird in there?"

Gavin nodded, making the locks that had escaped his ribbon bounce.

"Let's set it up," Gavin said.

Once hung on the wall, they sat at the table side by side, facing the clock as they ate their stew, waiting for the bird to coo.

The End

Keep reading for a preview of

THE HEALER'S LOST TOUCH

Chapter 1

Scotland January 1746
God, please dinna let him die, Brodie MacKay prayed as he leaned forward in his chair, elbows on the bed and his head resting on his entwined fingers. It was the same prayer he'd said for the past two weeks since James had turned for the worse.

He leaned back into his chair and watched James's chest move up and down.

Sir Brodie, yer son has been wounded. The words echoed in his mind as he relived the shock that had gone through him as he heard the words for the first time. He was in Carlisle then, meaning the message had taken two or three days to arrive. He arrived in Sterling two days later.

The wound to James's side had been cleaned and stitched immediately after the battle. It seemed to be healing properly by the time Brodie arrived. James was alert and in good spirits, but became fevered two days later.

He sometimes thrashed in his sleep as he babbled nonsense, causing Brodie to hold him down several times until the healer arrived. Then, they would force something down to make him sleep.

Brodie became hopeful when James slept peacefully the

past day and night, but he was wrong. The morning light brought with it the start of James wailing in pain. When it finally seized, he called out to his mother, Jamelyn, who had died five years earlier.

That was what really concerned Brodie. The possibility of losing his son was just too much to bear. It was not supposed to work that way. It had not been easy to watch his wife die either. Her illness dragged on for months until she withered away to nothing. They did not even know what had ailed her.

Now, James seemed to be conversing with Jamelyn, but Brodie could not make out the mumblings.

God, please dinna take him, too, Brodie prayed over and over again.

"Mom," James mumbled.

Brodie sighed and looked at the frosted window as a chill went through him. He knew he needed to draft a letter to his parents and his other son. He had been holding off doing so, hoping James would pull through, but the conversation with his late wife quickly dashed his hopes.

Begrudgingly, Brodie got up, put some more logs on the fire, and grabbed his leather bag. He stared at it for a moment. A knot formed in his stomach at the thought of writing the letters. Doing so signified he had given up hope.

As he pulled out a sheet of parchment, the contents of a small sachet spilled out into the leather bag. Brodie grumbled as he began to dig at the bottom of his bag to find the small objects and put them back into the sachet.

He tilted the bag one way so the smaller items would fall into the corner. Then, reaching in, he grabbed the objects, pulled them out, and looked at them. His heart skipped a beat when he saw the light blue translucent stone in contrast to the coins he held in his hand. The stone was an aquamarine, often called the *treasure of mermaids*. It was given to him three years ago by a seer, Vanora, whose beauty surpassed anyone he had ever seen. She was more than just a seer, though. She was a healer.

Brodie had seen her heal Alana's eyesight by laying hands on her. He would not have believed it if he had not been there himself. His heart began to race as hope washed over him.

Brodie looked at James. She could heal him if he could get him there. That was the hard part. James was in no condition to travel. Brodie tossed around in his mind what traveling would do to James. The more he thought about it, the more he realized that lying in bed did not seem to be helping him all that much.

"Mom," James murmured again.

If James lingered on for another week and died, Brodie would regret not trying to get to Vanora. James was not coherent. He would not notice being jostled around for five days, even if he died. There was nothing the physician in Sterling could do but give him something to help him sleep.

The problem was the Jacobite rebellion going on. He did not know who he could trust.

Vanora lived in Duncan territory. Brodie could trust Robbie Duncan. Robbie, Alex Boswell, and Brodie had been best friends since they soldiered under the MacKays. But Robbie left the MacKays years ago when he became laird. It was the same year Alex died.

Brodie knew Robbie tried to stay neutral in the rebellion. Robbie's mother and wife were MacKays, like Brodie. The Mackays fought for the crown, but Robbie's sister-in-law was a Robertson, who sided with the Jacobites.

Robbie would not care where Brodie's allegiance lay. Their bond went deeper than politics. He could trust him.

Brodie looked down at the beautiful blue stone. Aye, he would bring James to Vanora, he resolved. All of a sudden, his helplessness seemed to dissipate a bit.

ABOUT THE AUTHOR

Denise Marie Lupinacci is the recipient of two Bookfest awards. She has been fascinated with the Scottish Highlands since she first heard bagpipes and Celtic music.

Denise hopes to transport her readers to a place of beauty, magic, and dreams, if only for a few hours.

Follow her on Facebook.com/DeniseMarieLupinacci.

Made in United States
Cleveland, OH
27 January 2025